LIES HIDDEN

A HARO

A catalogue record for this work is available from the National Library of Australia

In memory of the six million plus men, women and children who were systematically murdered by a state sponsored killing machine.

Of all the things you choose in life, you don't get to choose what your nightmares are. You don't pick them; they pick you . . .
John Irving

LIES HIDDEN

PROLOGUE

Freezing, fetid air crawled over her face as a solitary tear slid down her cheek into her ear. She was acutely aware of its heat as it tracked into the inner depths.

Oh, dear God, help me.

Hardly daring to breathe, Mia eased her eyelids open a fraction. It was difficult to see much, but she sensed she was being watched. Stiff and aching with the all-pervading cold, she was almost overwhelmed by the temptation to stretch and bring some feeling back into her lifeless limbs. But the fear of her silent watchers kept her still. Now she could hear and feel the breath of one of them as they moved closer. Warm, stinking breath bathed her face.

A hissed exchange made her heart thud against her chest. Female voices.

"She won't make it." Stated as a fact and devoid of emotion.

That's me they're talking about. Am I going to die? But why? — are they going to kill me?

A shaft of light fell across her face from what she assumed was the opening of a door. With it came a slight breeze carrying other smells — none of them pleasant. It also brought the sound of voices. Male this time and further away. Movement. Her watchers were leaving. They sounded sick and weary, mumbling and sighing as they left. Someone cried out, and others wept until an urgent plea for silence was obeyed.

The door closed, and she was alone. Mia wondered where they had gone. But then, where was she? Her memory gave her no clues. She only remembered this dark, stuffy place where she lay. Instinctively, she kept quiet.

From outside, a man issued orders, his aggression frightening, his language foreign. Mia's heart raced with the familiarity of his voice. A general commotion followed, with both men and women calling out. Some were angry, others distressed. Then the sound of running feet and heavy boots came towards her. Something or someone crashed against the outside of the building where she lay. She tensed and held her breath.

A woman shrieked and pleaded, followed by a struggle, and then a child screamed. A resounding slap and the thud of a hefty punch on flesh silenced the woman's voice, followed by a soft collapsing noise. The child whimpered before it too was slapped with a ferocity that surely knocked it off its feet. Mia could hear the heavier of the now silent victims being dragged away. She listened hard, desperate to know the fate of the child.

There's been an assault. Someone needs to help them.

A strange noise followed a short period of silence. Many feet moving in unison — not marching, but walking or shuffling on the spot. This was accompanied by a low, guttural humming, implying a threat. It sent shivers down her spine. A shout ended the sound, again in the same foreign tongue. It wasn't the language of the females who had watched her earlier, but inexplicably, she understood both. A gunshot rang out. Silence.

She curled into a protective ball and wrapped her arms defensively around her head. With a racing heart and a powerful urge to escape, her eyes flicked open. They felt sore and gritty. She panicked when she saw she was virtually encased in a roughly hewn wooden construction, like a coffin, but with higher sides and the top only partially enclosed.

"What the hell?" Her voice rasped. Her throat was raw.

Frantically, she searched for other clues to establish her whereabouts. She attempted to lift her head to reach a gap in the wood, but was too feeble. Why, she wondered. *What's happened to me?* The commotion continued in the distance, but she felt safe inside her strange box-bed. Her rapidly beating heart slowed. With tremendous effort, she stretched. The cold had permeated right through to her bones, and she ached unbearably from lying on a hard surface. Despite the cold, her head felt hot and leaden. A pain throbbed across her forehead and eyes. Her mouth was parched, and her swollen tongue made swallowing difficult and extremely painful. As she stretched again, her joints cracked, and her muscles threatened to spasm.

PART ONE

Apparitions are often confused with hauntings. The difference is that apparitions are 'live' (intelligent consciousness) and hauntings are 'recordings'.
Loyd Auerbach, *Psychic Dreaming*

Denial, perhaps, is a necessary human mechanism to cope with the heartaches of life.
Richard Paul Evans, *The Christmas Box*

CHAPTER 1

Mia rubbed her head. "Those bloody dreams again." She groaned and rolled over as if turning would leave the awfulness of the dream on the other side of the pillow. Staring at the wall, she tried to clear her mind and focus on reality. But she couldn't shake off the fear and helplessness she had experienced in the dream world.

It was a world where she was repeatedly dragged into, and it was becoming more realistic and tangible. Initially, it was a muddle of vague, grey images that floated silently in and out of her field of vision — nothing she could quite make out. But now, the indistinct images had coalesced to form solid objects, real people, sounds, and smells.

Screwing her fists into her eyes, she wished she hadn't tried so hard to understand earlier dreams. Her attention to them seemed to have turned them into dark, threatening nightmares that were far too realistic.

Mia had read somewhere that you could make a conscious decision to stay in control of your dreams before sleeping. It didn't work for her. Once she was asleep, the dream had complete control, and she would be carried along until it released her. She thought it possible that she wasn't trying hard enough.

Falling against her pillows, exhausted and disorientated, Mia was stiff and cold, just as in the dream. It's tension, she reasoned. Who wouldn't be tense after such a depressing and menacing dream? The doona had migrated to the bottom of the bed, too. Surely that explained why she was so cold.

Like so many times in the last few weeks, she was determined to dismiss the dreams as a distorted re-run of a film befuddled by her sleep-sedated brain. The trouble was: she couldn't recall any film like it.

Try as she might, she could not shake-off the fear and unpleasant atmosphere that still seemed to linger in her room and in her head. Her friend Lisa wasn't much help. She said the dreams were probably a prediction, which was hardly reassuring, given how awful they were and that she found herself sick and very near death in them. No, thinking about it as a prophecy was not an option for Mia — far too frightening.

"Mia, love, are you awake? You're very late this morning. Mia, can you hear me?"

"Yes, Dad, I'm up," she lied as she dropped her legs over the side of the bed. The action made her nauseous. She ran to her ensuite and retched into the toilet. Nothing came up. She slumped down on a chair and gasped for breath.

"Mia, what's wrong?" Oscar called through the bedroom door. "Mia, answer me."

Mia took a deep breath. "I'm fine, Dad."

Oscar hesitated outside the door. She didn't sound right to him.

"I'll be down soon."

Oscar waited a few more seconds. "Your mum has your coffee on the go. Don't be too long."

"Okay."

Once she was sure Oscar had gone from her door, she threw herself back onto the bed and buried her head in the pillow. She knew she would be late, but she had no energy. With reluctance, she forced her uncooperative body from the bed and went to shower.

Refreshed and wrapped in her fluffy, pink housecoat, she looked at her reflection in her dressing-table mirror. Her eyes were puffy and red, and her face blotchy.

"Oh shit! I can't go to work like this."

Looking good was paramount to Mia. She enjoyed admiring glances from men and relished the envy of other girls. Those green-eyed looks from wannabe babes, who would do almost anything to look like the gorgeous Mia, fed her ego daily. Ignoring the time, she soaked her eye pads with soothing eye lotion and lay back on the bed, trying to relax. In the dark again, her mind drifted back to her dream. The atmosphere and smells returned. Images appeared, slowly creeping into her peripheral vision. Mia snatched the pads from her eyes and sat up, gasping.

For God's sake, Mia, get a grip. What's wrong with you? They're just dreams.

She returned to her dressing mirror, sat down with a thump, and took a few deep breaths. "Right," she told the mirror. "Now for the war paint."

As she applied her make-up, she noted with relief that her eyes had benefited from the quick eye-pad treatment. She grabbed her neatly pressed uniform from the wardrobe door and slipped into the tight-fitting outfit. Gazing at herself, she agreed with the reflection that she looked good. The make-up had done its job nicely, with no sign of the tired face that had mocked her in the bathroom mirror earlier.

Mia checked her appearance several times, twisting and turning to see herself from every angle. She was a beauty by any measure, with her long, dark, lustrous hair and flawless olive skin. But she considered her long, elegant legs to be her best feature. She was ready for her public — her envious public.

Pushing the dream firmly to the back of her mind, she went downstairs for her habitual daily coffee, her essential morning boost. And, just as they did every day, her parents tried to get her to eat, but Mia was determined to keep her much envied size-eight figure. Eating anything at all was carefully considered. She was confident she looked perfect as she slid onto the high stool where her mother had her coffee waiting on the kitchen counter.

Her abandoned bedroom was the opposite of perfection: towels littered the floor, as did her dirty clothing. Not that she liked an untidy room. But she knew her mother would pick up behind her. Mia would return from work to find her room neat and clean. Her discarded clothing would be washed and ironed, and her ensuite put back into pristine order. She convinced herself her mum loved to do it, and Mia was more than happy with the arrangement. After all, she reasoned, her mum was a full-time housewife and wanted to keep busy. It suited them both. Esme loved to fuss, and Mia didn't have time to worry about such mundane things.

"Your father mentioned you seemed upset earlier."

"No, I'm fine. Just the aftermath of a horrible dream."

"Do you want to tell us about it?" Esme probed further.

"Not really, Mum. I'm okay. Honestly." She held her hand up to block her mother, who was approaching with a box of low-calorie cereal. "Mum, I can't eat anything. My stomach's not open yet."

Esme sighed and put the offending box back in the larder. Mia scooped the foam from the top of her coffee and sucked the creamy mixture with such relish that anyone watching her would think she was enjoying something far more substantial. A cup of coffee was all that would pass her lips until lunchtime, apart from a few sugar-free mints. Esme was relieved she was having milky coffee, even if it was only skimmed milk. Nevertheless, she continued to encourage Mia to eat something. It was a daily ritual. Esme offered, cajoled and coaxed, and Mia refused.

"Mia, you talk such rubbish," Oscar chipped in. "How can your stomach be closed? You should be grateful you've got food to eat," he grunted, attracting a click of disapproval from his wife's tongue. He huffed in annoyance at Esme and turned back to his kipper. Esme glared at him. He rustled his newspaper in defence, muttered, and then disappeared behind it.

"You make it so she doesn't want to eat, Oscar, the way you scoff your food down like you're starving. It's enough to turn anyone's stomach."

Oscar dropped the newspaper to reveal a full mouth and scowled at his wife. "I just enjoy good food," he mumbled.

"That's obvious," she said, showing her disgust. "But we don't want to see it."

Oscar growled and sank behind his newspaper. Mia smiled. When her father growled, it reminded her of a lion. He had the same grizzled looking features and crinkly hair as the entrepreneur Alan Sugar, or her mum's favourite old-time movie star, Sid James. It amused her how the noise fit their faces.

"Now, love, just ignore your dad. Let me make you one small piece of toast — just one thin slice?" Esme held up her hand to show just how thin she would make it and smiled at Mia encouragingly, as you would a child.

Grey-haired and slight in stature, Esme Barone epitomised the stereotypical homemaker and over-indulgent mother or grandmother. Meals were homemade from raw ingredients (no packets or jars in Esme's cupboard) apart from the low-calorie items to tempt Mia. Esme loved being organised, too. The items on the kitchen pin-board were a constant reference point for her lists and reminders. Mealtimes were religiously observed. Not one speck of dust or grime was allowed to remain longer than a nanosecond anywhere in their immaculate three-bedroom semi. But Mia was her primary focus. Nothing was too much trouble if it was for Mia. Esme fussed and worried about everything and anything concerning her wellbeing. Her husband came a poor third, and he knew it, but as he was as bad as his wife about Mia, he didn't mind. It was the fanatical tidying and cleaning of the house that drove him mad.

Mia cringed, but she was careful not to show her irritation. She was so familiar with the relentless theme of the lecture her parents took turns to deliver daily: "You should eat. Look how skinny you are! You don't understand how lucky you are. Some people would love the crumbs from your plate." She wondered how her parents got like that. When did someone change from being a reasonable person to a nagging parent? Would she end up like a stuck record if she had kids? Lisa and her other friends told similar stories, but none were as bad as Mia's parents. Time to deflect the interest away from her, she thought. It was a technique she often employed, and it was usually successful.

"That kipper smells disgusting, Dad. How can you eat that first thing in the morning? My clothes stink now. Great, smoked fish — such an attractive aroma. It really goes with my outfit. Perfect."

Esme looked alarmed and came over to sniff Mia's clothing. "They seem alright, love," she said, brushing Mia's shoulder as though it would help.

"You can't smell it here, Mum," Mia complained, "because it's permeated the whole room. It'll be when I get to work with fresher air; that's when it'll be noticeable."

"That's highly unlikely, Mia," said Oscar. "With the amount of perfume you've ladled on, you'll knock 'em dead at fifty paces. I can almost taste it as I eat my yummy kipper."

"Dad, I love my perfume — a lot more than the smell of that kipper."

"Are you sure you don't want a little off the side here? I've removed all the bones. Go on, have a tiny piece."

"Nah, you're alright, Dad."

"You wouldn't have refused when you were a little girl." Oscar held up his fork with a small piece of fish on the end. "Look, Mia. I've found you a delicious piece. No bones."

Esme looked on hopefully.

Mia shook her head. "No, really, Dad. Fish breath doesn't go with my image. It might now, though, given the smell I'm probably carrying around." Mia smiled fondly at her dad while loading her response with sarcasm and raising her eyebrows.

Esme swung into action. "Oscar, take that fish out into the conservatory to finish it. We don't want Mia arriving at work smelling like smoked fish." Esme opened the windows and sprayed air freshener liberally around the kitchen.

"Oh, for pity's sake, Esme, you've sprayed it all over my kipper. I'm trying to eat here." Oscar grabbed his plate and walked out into the conservatory, throwing his wife an angry glance. He was used to the way Esme fussed and clucked; he loved it most of the time. But he particularly enjoyed a grilled kipper and would have liked to have eaten it in peace. The smoky smell reminded him of his childhood — well, the happy years, anyway.

Esme ignored her husband's protestations and switched the ceiling fan on high. She then opened the back door and wafted it furiously to increase the airflow.

"And now she's trying to freeze us out," said Oscar from the conservatory. He was perched on a high stool with his long legs dangling. Esme had stripped all the covers off the conservatory furniture earlier and planned to oil the oak coffee table. He knew it would be suicidal to sit on uncovered cushions or put his fishy dish on the table. But he found it impossible to eat his kipper, avoid the bones, and balance on a wobbly bar stool. After a few mouthfuls of fish with bones, he sighed in resignation and took his half-eaten breakfast to the kitchen bin.

"Well, that was a waste of good food," Esme scolded.

"I've never liked lavender flavoured kipper with bones."

Mia smiled, amused at the kipper crisis, and finished her coffee in peace.

But Esme was not finished. "I could boil you an egg?" She was always hopeful that her various low-carbohydrate ideas would result in Mia eating something, anything.

"Coffee is great, Mum. It's just what I needed, frothy and creamy."

"But it's not even real cream," Esme protested. "Just that foul, low-calorie frother you insist I buy. It would be more nutritious if you let me make it with whole cream milk."

Mia grabbed her bag as her parents were about to enter a new nagging phase about food. "Bye, be back around six," she said, then kissed and hugged them both. She loved them dearly, but they went on a bit. They smiled at her, a weary, worried smile, making them look more like eighty-plus than their sixty-something years.

Esme adjusted Mia's work scarf unnecessarily, and Oscar commented on her unsuitable shoes for the dreadful weather. And why, he added, did she need all that 'muck' to enhance her already beautiful brown eyes? She had long since stopped resisting their last-minute administrations and expressions of concern. Mia realised they needed to go through the process. The upset she caused on one occasion by her insistence that they stop fussing was not worth seeing them so hurt. So, she tolerated it, tossed her hair over her shoulders and threw them one of her best smiles before she walked to the door with another cheery farewell.

Esme was quicker. "Mia?"

"What, Mum?" Her patience was wearing thin.

"What are you having for lunch? Shall I make you a sandwich? I hate to think of you buying junk when I can give you something homemade and more nourishing."

"No, that's okay, Mum. I'm getting sushi."

Oscar looked to the heavens as though seeking guidance.

Esme's face screwed up with concern. "'Sushi', 'sushi', she says. What's that?" She turned to Oscar, who shrugged.

"A Japanese meal, I think."

Mia was already gone, relieved to be out of the house.

CHAPTER 2

"How's it going, Mia?" Lucas asked as he slumped into one of Mia's customer chairs. As usual, he seemed to have emptied a bottle of what Mia called 'that disgusting cologne' over his entire body. Mia winced and waved her hand back and forth as though clearing the air. Then held her fingers under her wrinkled nose, shielding it from the onslaught.

"Sod off, Lucas. I don't want to lose the next sale that comes through the door because you're littering up my customer area." She flicked her perfectly manicured nails at him to shoo him away. "And please put less of the essence of stale male on, or whatever it is. You'll choke a customer one of these days and be done for murder by lethal pong."

"Ha ha. Amusing. Did we get out of the wrong side of bed this morning? Anyway, you can talk. There's a trail of fumes following you around, stinking something rotten. Fish, if I'm not mistaken."

Mia was annoyed that the smell of her father's kipper had indeed clung to her clothing. But she didn't rise to Lucas' bait or even look up. She waved her hand in dismissal again and then concentrated on opening her browser. "Just go, would you? My perfume probably costs ten times as much as the disgusting stuff you slap on."

"Fish-smelling perfume? Now there's an interesting concept." He chortled and continued to sit in Mia's area, gazing idly around the sales floor. "I reckon she has this month in the bag," he said, his eyes settling on their boss. "There you go. They're about to put a deposit down on their holiday of a lifetime," he said, gloating and nodding toward the branch manager. "And that 'stuff', as you call it, cost me an arm and a leg."

"You were robbed. Lucas, it reeks something awful." Mia retrieved her perfume from her bag and sprayed it all over her. "Just surrounding myself and my desk with a sweeter aroma," she teased.

"Well, anything is better than fish. Is that what you ate for brekkie?"

"Just bugger off, Lucas."

"There you go. The flights are booked. Now she's putting the final touches to the itinerary. Watch and weep, Mia Barone. You're about to be shoved off your pedestal," Lucas smirked at her, enjoying the discomfort he was causing his nearest rival in the sales team.

Mia shot an evil glance at the branch manager. "Yeah, the less said about Mr and Mrs Bryant, the better. I spoke to them on the phone last week. She knows they should be my sale," Mia declared, but kept her voice low.

It wasn't a good idea to challenge their new boss. Despite only being in place for two weeks, Sherri ensured they were well aware that she had been the top salesperson at the Sydney TopTravel branch. And she intended to repeat that achievement in Perth. Not long after her arrival, she had threatened the staff, warning that they wouldn't last long if anyone stood in her way. She was determined to be top of the sales scoreboard by any means and would probably maim anyone who tried to stop her. Maiming was a distinct possibility, given the length of her false nails and the way she slashed them through the air while doing the weekly team talk.

The team meeting was a misleading name. The sharp-clawed branch manager was as far removed from a team player as could be found. When she wasn't showing off about her impeccable sales achievements, she would strut around the shop, nit-picking about everything and anything — never any encouragement or team camaraderie. Come back, Brian, Mia thought many times, wishing she had fought harder to stop her previous boss from getting the boot. Ironically, she was pleased when they got a female boss. She thought they would become friends and even dared to hope it would be fun, but she was wrong. As cutbacks loomed, Mia was fearful of losing her job, one which suited her, especially with the discount travel perks and the location right in Perth's city centre. She could indulge in her favourite occupation of shopping during her lunch break or meet her friends for coffee and a chat. There was also the kudos of working for TopTravel — the biggest travel agency chain in Australia and streets ahead of any outfit in Western Australia.

She loved the company uniform, too, which was no surprise, as she had helped Brian choose the style to ensure it would complement her figure. It didn't suit all the female staff. In Mia's opinion, most of them needed to lose some weight or shape up, probably both. Mia knew she stood head and shoulders above all the girls in the branch in looks, even if she said so herself. Susan liked to think she was on a par, but with Susan's ginger hair, Mia doubted it. Susan called it red, but it was carrot orange. That was a fact. Susan had the nerve to comment that she and Mia were in a league of their own: the premier league. How could she compare herself to Mia? The girl was unreal.

"Well, you didn't close the deal, did you? Our glorious leader beat you to it," said Lucas, milking the situation as much as possible. He knew, as did everyone else, that it should have been Mia's sale. She had posted Mr and Mrs Bryant's name on the 'Contact Made Board' after she had taken their call, but strangely, it had been wiped off.

"Thank you so much for your booking. May I call you Hilary and Bob?" Pleased with the couple's acceptance of her proffered first name relationship, Sherri opened the shop door with a flourish. She assured the smiling pair of her continued attention until they departed on their holiday. As the door closed, Sherri did a little victory dance, which was an achievement in her skin-tight pencil skirt. Then she strutted back to her desk, her high heels drumming the wooden floor. She raised her fist in triumph two or three times before reaching her desk, ensuring every staff member witnessed her celebratory walk. Every strike of Sherri's heels hit Mia like a slap in the face.

"Bitch. Thieving bitch," Mia mouthed with venom towards Susan, who grinned in agreement and then dropped her head below her screen so the 'bitch' couldn't see her smirk. Susan worked hard at being friends with Mia. She wanted to be more than just a workmate. Susan desperately wanted to become a senior Paintball Puma like Mia. Mia's boyfriend was 'Invincible,'

AKA Vince Price, the paintball king of the west. His female Pumas were legendary.

They were all good-looking, shapely girls who glamorised Australia's biggest and most famous paintball site in their skin-tight puma costumes.

Like Mia, Susan had a weekend job at the paintball site and wore the figure-hugging jumpsuit of a Puma. However, much to her annoyance, she was still on less visible duties. She worked out regularly in the gym, determined to be fit and shapely. She was also learning the rules and advanced tactics of paintball. That way, she stood a chance of becoming a regular Puma who accompanied Vince and the other pumas into the stadium. Mia was, of course, the Puma Princess, as Vince called her, and she led the troupe. Susan often watched her in action from the sidelines in the stadium. Mia had the paintballers almost drooling as she went through the motions of the safety briefing while Vince delivered the speech. It was akin to being an entertainer's assistant. Mia stroked the demo gun, took up various shooting positions in sexy poses and then blew a marshal's whistle while looking at the paintballers seductively. It was a class act that ensured players came back to play paintball and see the sexy Puma Princess. Susan admired and envied Mia, who seemed to have it all: she was a crack saleswoman at work, the centre of their social circle, and the Puma Princess. Susan and her friends talked about Mia as though she was a celebrity, which to them, she was. She was beautiful, popular, confident, and had a body to die for. Mia also had Vince, and Susan coveted that more than anything.

The shop door pinged, and before anyone could flex a muscle, Mia leapt from her seat and ran to greet a young family. They were shocked at the speed of her approach but impressed with the level of service they were receiving.

"How can I help you today?" said Mia, loud enough for most of the sales team to hear.

"We're looking for a cheap weekend away," the man responded with equal volume.

Mia didn't look in Lucas' direction. She knew he would be amused by her very public attempt to grab what looked like a big sale. In fact, it was unlikely to earn her more than a few commission points. She would miss out on other customers because she was tied up with these cheapskates. Mia reluctantly switched her phone to busy and started trawling through endless options for cost-conscious customers. She saw Susan smiling encouragingly and found it irksome. Much of what Susan did irritated Mia. She thought she was such a cling-on.

Despite being annoyed with herself for misjudging the group's potential, Mia plastered a smile on her face and gave the family her full attention. She thought she would be the next one to get her marching orders at this rate.

CHAPTER 3

After dumping her bag in the hall, Mia called out to her parents. There was no reply.

"They'll be in the garden."

Her parents seeded, weeded, trimmed, and tended the garden until they achieved perfection. It was as organised and tidy as the house. From the kitchen, Mia saw them both through the window.

It was dusk. Oscar was busy ferrying his gardening tools back to his shed, and Esme was taking washing from the clothesline. She left the clothes basket for Oscar to collect and lifted a box loaded with fresh vegetables on her way back to the house. Mia could see one of her parents' friends on her knees by the shed, still working on the garden. The light was fading, making it difficult to see the woman's face clearly. Mia opened the door for Esme and kissed her on the cheek.

"Dinner won't be ready for a bit, love."

"Fine. Look, Mum, I'm sorry about this morning. I had a rough night."

"That's okay. Bad dreams again?"

"Yeah . . . keep having them."

Esme sat down to remove her garden shoes, and Mia moved to the window.

"Who's the woman in the garden, Mum?"

Esme took the vegetables over to the kitchen top and washed her hands.

"Is she a new neighbour?"

"Who?"

"The woman in the garden. God, it's like a drop-in centre for deadbeats in this house these days. She looks very shabby. You're a real waif-and-strays magnet. Is she from number twelve, you know, the new people?"

"Mia, what are you talking about?"

"The woman in the garden. By the old shed. You were dealing with the washing. She was bending your ear."

"I've no idea who you're referring to."

Mia was determined to have her say. She was convinced that her parents were being taken advantage of, and she needed to protect them. "I mean, look at the old bag next door. Alma. Now, what's she on, I ask you? She's always banging on about nothing important. It was her husband I used to feel sorry for. She probably talked him to death. He was a bit of a twerp, too, if I'm honest." Mia picked up one of her magazines and flicked idly through the pages.

"Mia, don't talk about Alma like that. She is one of my oldest and dearest friends. You don't know what the poor woman has gone through. And to talk of the dead like that, it's not right."

Mia scoffed. "I've got a fair idea what she's been through, 'cos she's always going on about something or other. How much can one person suffer in one lifetime, for God's sake?"

"Enough, Mia! Sometimes you've a cruel mouth on you. Some people have a lot to contend with. You don't know the half of it; you really don't."

Mia looked up, shocked by Esme's retort. It was so angry. She had joked about Alma before and hadn't got such a severe reaction.

"Look, love, I'm sorry about that. I'm on edge, that's all," said Esme.

"Well, if you will let these people unburden themselves to you, Mum." Mia stopped as she saw Esme's warning stare and held up her hands in submission. "Okay, if you want to be the local drop-in-centre for the old and needy, that's your lookout. Damn sure I wouldn't bother."

"No, I don't suppose you would," Esme whispered. Her mind was elsewhere. Esme put her knife down. "What did this woman look like? Alma was here a bit earlier. You may not have recognised her. She's had a blue rinse and was all rugged-up because she was feeling under the weather."

Mia laughed at the image of Alma. "Nah, it wasn't Alma. I told you."

"You haven't explained properly, Mia," said Esme, losing her patience. "What did she look like? Tell me. Was she small, tall, fat, thin, dark, fair?" Esme became agitated.

Mia looked up from her magazine again, taken aback by another outburst from her usually calm Mother. "Look, it's no big deal, Mum. You can socialise with who you like, but I'd give her a wide berth. She looks extremely needy. You can never shake off those sorts, if you know what I mean. Well, you do 'cos you seem to be like Mother Teresa around here. I think the lost and forlorn are attracted to you somehow. You're just too nice, Mum." Mia prattled on, without taking a breath, "Tell 'em to get lost. It's what I'd do."

"Yes, I think you would," said Esme. "But I wish you wouldn't talk about our friends that way, Mia."

Mia shrugged.

Esme continued to prepare the vegetables. Mia got a diet drink from the fridge and continued to flick idly through her magazine.

"It must have been Alma," said Esme quietly, but Mia caught it.

"I saw the woman just now, and it wasn't Alma. I told you that already." Hesitating only momentarily, Mia continued to harangue Esme with her views about some of the ne'er-do-wells her parents called friends. She didn't know much — or want to know — about any of them. To her, they were just a bunch of oldies that littered up the lounge from time to time. Sometimes she didn't get out of the house fast enough, and they would try to engage her in conversation. Their questions were often intrusive and too personal. She would make excuses and leave as quickly as she could. Once, she had caught her dad looking on fondly, like the person was important. That baffled her. Another time, one of them called her Ruth. Her mother was so angry when that happened. Mia didn't think it was that terrible. Old people often got confused. She supposed that as she was an only daughter, her mother had been offended that they got her name wrong.

"It wasn't Alma," said Mia. "I'd recognise garrulous Alma, with her wispy, flyaway hair. Who could mistake her? Crazy old bird." Mia laughed again. "It was probably the light playing tricks. Now, move, Mia, and let me get on." Esme wanted Mia to drop the subject.

Mia moved to the window again. The woman was gone, but Mia could still see her in her mind. It made her feel uneasy.

"Look, I care about you both. I don't want people taking advantage, especially by the likes of that one. I mean, the outfit she had on — a ridiculous-looking shift that was filthy. Maybe she hasn't gone at all, but just slipped into the old shed to bed down for the night."

Esme zoned out from Mia's chatter. She was pleased Mia was joining them for dinner. It was a constant battle to get her to eat. She had been such an easy child, not a picky eater at all. Now she was all but starving herself because she feared she would get fat. They weren't an overweight family, and they never piled her plate. It was a continual worry. But she was also shaken by what Mia said. She had felt uneasy about going in the garden recently, anyway. So uncomfortable, in fact, that she had been drying most of the washing indoors. Then this happens — a stranger in their garden. Maybe the poor old dear came round the side, and she just didn't see her. With the wind, she had been fully occupied trying to untangle the washing on the line. But what unsettled Esme more was Mia mentioning the old shed. They didn't have that shed anymore; Oscar had taken it down some months back and put up a new one in another part of the garden. Esme's thoughts were deep and troubled.

"Mum, you okay?"

"Yes, yes." Esme rallied. "I'll just get the veg on, and then we're ready. Can you call your dad?"

Esme had lost her appetite, but she tried to eat, anyway. Mia looked at her, puzzled, but Esme avoided engaging Mia in further conversation. She knew Mia was a person who didn't let things drop. She was their pride and joy, but she had her faults — they were well aware of that. They spoilt her rotten, resulting in her being self-centred and materialistic. Mia's escapades with her friends were a worry, too. Then there was that boy who owned a paintball site. He was not the type of person they envisaged Mia taking up with. Oscar questioned Mia about her boyfriend several times. They had no idea what paintball was until Mia explained. And they didn't like it any more when she did. It was hardly something a responsible husband should do, so they hoped this wasn't a long-term relationship. But Mia seemed serious about him.

"If there's any more of that fish pie, love, I wouldn't mind another spoonful," said a hopeful Oscar. His request was met by silence. "Esme. Esme, love?"

"Oh, sorry — I was miles away."

"Look, Mum, I've got half an hour before I need to go out," said Mia. "Why don't you tell us about that woman? It's obviously bothering you. I went on a bit earlier, but I was just trying to help."

"Woman? What woman?" Oscar stopped eating and was all attention.

"I said I didn't want to talk about it, Mia, so that's an end to it." Esme's tone was fierce and uncompromising. She finished it with a warning stare at Oscar, which he met with bewilderment.

Mia looked at Oscar, perplexed.

Esme got away from the table and scraped her dinner in the bin.

"Mum?" Mia began, trying to be firm, but Oscar put his hand on her arm and shook his head.

"Go and get ready, love. Your mum and I will have a little chat."

Reluctantly, Mia agreed and left the table. She glanced at Esme, who had her head bowed and was gripping the kettle with such ferocity that her knuckles were white. She was controlling her emotions, or she was in pain. That much was evident to her family. Oscar nodded at Mia encouragingly. She smiled at him and went to change.

"I won't be back late," Mia called from the hall on her way out. Oscar shouted an acknowledgement, but not Esme. Mia turned back and opened the lounge door. The sound of Esme weeping greeted her.

"I'm not going out if I've upset you, Mum. I shouldn't have gone on about your friends and the woman in the garden."

"Oh, Mia, I'm sorry," said Esme, drying her eyes.

"Someone needs to tell me what's going on," said Oscar. "Your mother keeps crying and making no sense. Talking about that shed I took down months ago."

Mia swung around and looked at Oscar. "You took the shed down, Dad? Of course you did. I remember now." Mia slumped down on a chair and grabbed her head. "I was awake, yet I saw the shed and the woman . . . It was *that* woman. Oh, God . . ." Mia shook her head from side to side, moaning.

"Now, both of you are at it." Oscar strode across to where Mia was sitting. "Come on, love. What's wrong? You can tell your old dad."

Mia looked at Oscar, pain written in her eyes and across her face.

"It's my dreams, Dad. They're coming to life."

Oscar glanced at Esme with a questioning look. She looked terrified and shook her head. He turned back to Mia.

"Look, love, when you lose sleep, you can imagine things. You're tired, and your mind is playing tricks."

Mia trembled. "I'm tired because of the dreams, Dad. They're awful. People get killed, and I think I'm in danger too. And now the woman from my dreams is right here in our garden. I'm sure of it now."

Esme let out a sob.

Oscar did a double-take. "Esme, do you know about this?"

Esme shook her head and wiped a fresh spill of tears from her face.

"Here?" Oscar asked Mia. "In our garden? When?"

"Yes, Dad, here. I saw her when I got back from work."

"Love, if there was someone in the garden, don't you think we would have seen her?"

"She was out there. I saw her. I didn't imagine it," Mia shrieked. "Mum wouldn't believe me either."

"Calm down, Mia. I *do* believe you," said Esme. "But now, you're also overwrought." Esme got up from the sofa. "I'm not sure you should go out, really. How about I make you some warm milk? And you can take one of my sleeping tablets tonight."

"I'm supposed to be meeting Vince," Mia sobbed.

"Call him, love. You can't go out in this state. I'm sure he'll understand," said Oscar.

"Yeah, okay. He'll freak out if I turn up like this. My make-up's ruined, and I'm seeing him at the weekend, anyway."

Mia left the room to make the call.

"What's to be done, Esme? She's dreaming just like Ruth."

"Shh, don't mention Ruth." Esme shook her head. "We're doing nothing, Oscar, other than getting her through this. We can help her."

"Esme, if this is a repeat of Ruth's experience, we must do more than we did for Ruth. We must act now."

"No, she mustn't know about that."

"Not even if——" Oscar stopped as Mia came back into the room.

"Not even if what, Dad?"

Oscar was silent.

"There you go again, clamming-up when I come in the room. I'm not a kid anymore."

"Look, I think we should all sit down and chat. Then I want you to take that sleeping tablet, Mia," said Esme, making it clear she would brook no argument.

Mia glanced at the folding doors that led to the kitchen.

Oscar caught the fear in her eyes. "I've locked all the outside doors, Mia. No one can come in without us letting them in," Oscar reassured her.

Mia wiped a tear from her cheek and looked up.

"I don't think you can't stop them, Dad."

CHAPTER 4

Esme and Mia sat side by side on the sofa. Oscar closed the curtains and the lounge door.

"There, now it's just us," said Oscar.

A car backfired outside, and Mia jumped and looked around wildly.

"That's the idiot next door," said Oscar. "He's bought himself an old car and keeps testing it. Nothing to worry about, love."

Mia nodded, looked down into her lap, and picked at her nail varnish.

Oscar found the situation unsettling, so he paced back and forth. He felt he should say something to ease the tension. "Well, let's look at the evidence——"

"Oscar, stop! Let Mia tell us herself. You'll put thoughts into her head. And sit down, for goodness' sake."

Oscar shrugged and slumped down into an armchair. "I'm only trying to help."

Esme gave him a lingering look of warning. He shrugged again.

As Oscar saw it, Esme had become bossy over the years. Always in the belief she knew best, of course.

Esme turned back to Mia and smiled. "Now, love, in your own time. If you're not going to take one of my tablets, have this whisky. I've put a little ginger ale in it."

Mia took a big gulp and then coughed violently.

"Esme, that drink is far too strong for her. Look what you've done," said Oscar, leaping to his feet.

Mia spluttered and gasped. "It's fine, Dad. I drink it neat sometimes. Just went down the wrong way."

Oscar was about to react, but Esme held up her hand. Irritated, Oscar took a deep breath, sighed, and sat back down.

Silence prevailed . . . until Mia cleared her throat.

"Are you sure you want to know all this stuff? It's pretty awful."

"Start at the beginning, Mia," Esme coaxed. "Your dad won't interrupt anymore."

"It's all weird. You'll think I'm going crazy." Mia looked from one to the other.

"We want you to tell us everything so we can help you, love," said Oscar.

Mia settled back on the sofa. "Well, I'm in this apartment."

Esme held Mia's hand.

Mia responded with a weak smile. "I'm someone else in the dream. I live in Italy with my husband and son."

Esme became dreamy. "Ah, Italia. What a lovely dream. And a boy. Ahh."

"I haven't even started yet, Mum."

"Esme, you told me not to interrupt. Now you're doing it."

Esme gave Oscar a surly look.

"Maybe this is a bad idea," said Mia.

"No, you carry on, Mia," said Oscar.

"It's fine at first. Peaceful. It feels as if we're in a small, quiet town."

"Not a city, then?" Esme asks.

"No, though I heard a couple of names mentioned . . . Trento? . . . Trieste? . . . They *are* cities, aren't they? People around us talk about going there, so I think they mustn't be too far away."

"Yes," said Oscar. "They're cities in the north of Italy," and he and Esme exchanged glances.

Mia just nodded, as if expecting this confirmation. Then her expression became dark. "But slowly the atmosphere changes. Mussolini brought in new laws that marginalised the Jewish community. Some of our friends became distant and made excuses not to socialise with us. I was fearful, but my husband, Isaac, was more optimistic and reassured me that everything would be fine. But then everything changed — big time." Mia stopped to wipe her tears. Oscar and Esme remained quiet. Clearly stunned by what they were hearing. Mia continued. "We're all in bed one night when we hear banging on our apartment door. My husband went to answer it, and I rushed to my son's room."

Esme gasps.

"They didn't wait for the door to be opened. Just kicked it down."

"Bastards," whispered Oscar.

"They were nasty. Pushed us around and demanded we get dressed. I grabbed what I could. But they didn't give us a chance to get much — just kept shoving us towards the door. If I hadn't picked up my son before they broke in, I'm not sure they'd have let me get to him."

"Better not to fight. Thugs like that only understand violence," said Oscar.

"Carry on, Mia. Did you escape?" asked Esme.

"No, we didn't. We were bundled into a waiting truck with others. People were crying and begging. But none of it made any difference. There were several trucks, all full of people."

"Did they take everyone?" asked Oscar.

"No, I saw people looking out of windows. They were our neighbours — people we knew well — but I believe one of them must have reported us." Mia stopped and wept.

"Now, now, love. Don't get so distressed. You're safe here with us," said Esme, hugging Mia.

"They took him, Mum."

"Your son. Oh no, not the boy."

Oscar threw Esme a questioning look.

"No, Isaac. He was amongst a group of men pulled out of the truck. We tried to follow him, but they pushed us back in. He squeezed my hand and told me he loved me, and then he tried to speak to Sarid, but they dragged him out. I thought my heart would break."

Mia sobbed. Oscar's and Esme's cheeks were wet with tears.

"Sarid . . . Sarid," Esme whispered, shaking her head. "Rachel's boy."

Oscar and Mia didn't hear Esme.

"Here, love, have a little more whisky," said Oscar, handing Mia the drink while looking at Esme, who shook her head from side to side.

They sat and waited for Mia to regain her composure. Esme cried quietly.

"Do you want to stop, Mia?" asked Oscar.

"If you don't mind, I want to get it all out. I need to tell someone."

"And we're here for you," said Esme, sniffing and mopping her cheeks.

"Each dream seems to be a part of that story. It's like a series on telly, and I'm one of the main characters. I'm not called Mia in the dreams. Everyone keeps calling me Rachel."

"Rachel? Are you sure?" asked Oscar.

"Why? Is it important, do you think, Dad?"

Esme looked at Oscar, her face drained of colour.

"No, no. You carry on, love." Oscar was now worried about Esme, too. She looked as though she might faint.

Mia stared into the distance as though she could see the scenes she was about to describe.

"Then we're on a train. That's me and Sarid, my son. Not a carriage with seats — a wagon like those that carried goods."

"And animals," Oscar whispered.

"We can hardly move. We're in there for days. No food or water, and it's airless. Some people die."

Esme grabbed her throat and looked at Oscar, horrified.

"I got into a corner with Sarid. There was a small gap in the wood to the outside so we could breathe. I also loosened one of the planks on the floor so we could use the gap as a toilet. Others used it too, but not everyone did, so the smell was disgusting."

Esme and Oscar stared at Mia.

"I told my boy that there had been a mistake and that his daddy would free us. But the longer the train ran, I felt the possibility of a rescue fade. I knew we were moving away from my husband." Mia then lifted her hand, stroked the air, and spoke in Italian as though she were comforting her dream child. Then she stopped, as she couldn't hold back her anguish. She wept.

"No wonder you get upset, love. That's awful!" said Esme, spluttering through her own tears.

"That's not the end of it. The dreams get worse. But I don't want to go on. I feel as though my heart is breaking, and I'm really upsetting you, Mum."

Oscar swiped his eyes as he tried to hold on to his emotions. "And you don't need to carry on tonight, Mia. You can tell us more tomorrow. That's if you're up to it." His voice was thick.

"I think I'll grab a shower. Clear my head."

Esme handed her a small bottle of lavender oil. "Put that on your flannel in the shower, love. The steam will lift it into the air, and it'll calm you a little."

Mia gave a weak smile and hugged Esme. "Sorry if I'm upsetting you, Mum."

"Come here, you," said Oscar, sweeping Mia off her feet in a bear hug. "Never forget how much we love you, my darling. We're going to help you through this."

Esme looked on with affection, with more tears tumbling down her face.

Once Mia left the room, Esme and Oscar sat and stared into space.

"She spoke Italian, Esme."

"I know. It sounded perfect to me. She's had no lessons that I know of."

"I always thought we should have taught her."

"We didn't want her burdened with the Italian migrant label. You know that," said Esme. "Or any other label." She looked meaningfully at Oscar. "We wanted her to integrate here in Australia. The same as Ruth."

"Unless she went off and got lessons and didn't tell us," said Oscar. "Maybe she felt drawn to the language after hearing us use it over the years." Esme saw Oscar working something through in his mind.

"No, Oscar. I know what you're thinking."

"Esme, we need to tell her."

"Absolutely not. As far as she knows, she just has bad dreams."

"In which she's Rachel," said Oscar, throwing his arms up in frustration.

Esme looked at the door in alarm. "Shh, keep your voice down." She walked over to the door, opened it, listened, and closed it again. "She won't understand what it all means. They don't do World War II in Australian schools."

Oscar raised his eyes towards the ceiling. "Of course, they do. Australia was heavily involved in that war, too. Maybe they don't cover the Holocaust in so much detail, but Mia isn't stupid, Esme."

Esme dropped onto the sofa and shook her head from side to side. "No, I won't accept it."

"Remember, Esme; Ruth died because of the same dreams. Are you willing to take the risk of another tragedy?"

"Oscar, please keep your voice down. You know Ruth had no support; she was on her own with a young baby. If she'd just come home to Perth . . . " Esme shook her head again slowly.

"And the scary thing is, Mia looks just like Rachel, as did Ruth."

Esme huffed in irritation. "Do you think I don't know that? She's the spit of my sister, as was Ruth."

"We owe it to our daughter to help Mia through this, love," said Oscar. "Ruth would want us to do that for her daughter."

"Yes, with therapy," Esme answered quickly. "If you keep making those references, and she hears, you will blow everything wide open. That she's really our grandchild. That her mother died horribly——"

Oscar slammed his hand down on the coffee table. "Well, I don't agree with you."

Esme shrieked. "Oscar, for God's sake. This has been traumatic enough without you losing it. There are good therapists."

"No. She needs to know."

"She's strong. Not like Ruth," insisted Esme.

"She should meet her relatives. Enough lies. It's ridiculous that she's never met them."

"She has many times, but we didn't reveal their identity."

"That doesn't count, Esme."

Esme went to the door again to check that Mia wasn't about to walk in on them, and then she returned to the fray. "No, that's madness. We've protected her from all that . . . Jewish stuff."

Oscar had never been happy with the deception. "Jewish stuff," Oscar repeated incredulously. "We *are* Jews. You can't——"

"Shh, she's coming."

"Rachel was her flesh and blood. We've written Ruth, her own mother, out of her life too — and ours. I won't be silenced anymore." Oscar was shouting now.

Mia walked into the room from the kitchen, surprising both Oscar and Esme, who immediately stopped talking.

"Why won't you be silenced, Dad? And I won't accept anything but the truth."

Oscar knew he couldn't betray Esme. He wanted her to come to the realisation herself that Mia should not be kept in the dark any longer. She was living the nightmares just like their daughter. She needed to know about her past — their past.

"Did you know, Mia, that Alma was my childhood friend?" said Esme, surprising Oscar.

"Seriously? Alma next door?"

"Yes, we played together as children."

"Wow, I didn't know that."

Esme was confident that the news had effectively diverted Mia's attention away from her initial question. But she knew it would only be a matter of time before they would run out of 'other' things to say. There were too many moments over the years when Mia had caught them talking and they would stop as soon as she entered the room. Esme was sure Mia had her suspicions.

It was a tiny revelation, Oscar thought. A miniscule fragment of information that would fit into the overall picture when Esme decided to open up about the past. But for him, it was a breakthrough nonetheless.

"Get up, I said, get up. I can't cover for you again — I won't, not anymore. They'll notice, and we'll both go on the short walk to eternity." Mia was being prodded on her shoulder, and it hurt.

It was only one of them this time. A sour, sweaty smell came with her, mixed with something else equally disgusting. Mia was angry. She was back in this horrible place against her will. She tried to force herself to wake up. But nothing worked. After glancing around the big, gloomy hut with roughly hewn bunk beds lining the walls, her eyes returned to the woman who hovered over her, holding a child. Her own bunk had lost its sides, so she could now see where she was with more clarity.

"What do you want?" Mia snapped, but it came out as weak and whiney.

"Have you gone mad? What are you talking about? Take him. *You* hide him," the woman said. "We hid you both as best we could, but now it's time for you to get up and take responsibility for yourself."

"I didn't ask you——"

"Huh! I've taken so many risks for you, and this is the gratitude I get."

The woman dumped the child on her bed. Mia flinched as the grubby little boy moved up close to her. She guessed he was five or six years old. His face was etched with grime and wore a constant frown. He stank, too. Stale urine and faeces were the prevalent smells. It reminded Mia of the time a tramp bumped into her outside a nightclub. She recoiled and gagged. It threatened to overpower her; it was too revolting, and he was so near. She tried to sit up, wake up — anything to remove herself from the smell, the little boy and the dream. An overwhelming weakness pinned her to the bed. She could only manage a slight movement of her shoulders. She tried again, giving it as much effort as she could muster. Despite that, she still failed. Why was she so feeble?

"I'm sorry, but I don't know who you are, or this little boy," she gasped, breathless after her exertions. Squeezing her eyes tight, she blotted them out. When she opened them again, she was still lying on the hard surface that had formed part of the wooden box bed. The bed from hell, with no mattress, no bedding, and a little boy who smelled more revolting with every passing second. The boy continued to gaze at her.

"You've lost your mind," the woman said sadly. "You need to look out for yourself and manage as best you can. We all do. God help us."

Too tired to deal with the madwoman, Mia sighed and turned her head away. The woman left, shaking her head and muttering something Mia didn't catch. What should she do about the boy? He looked at her passively, unaffected by the hostile interchange. She smiled at him with a sudden pang of compassion. He was only a kid and unlikely to be responsible for any of this. His face broke into a smile, and he snuggled down beside her. While she was taken aback by his nearness, it suddenly seemed right. She wrapped her arms around him and drew him close. A strange song came to her, a lullaby. She sang quietly as she rocked him back and forth. The woman looked back at her with a slight smile playing around her lips.

43

Chapter 5

"Mia, your alarm went off at least fifteen minutes ago. Are you up?" Oscar asked through her closed bedroom door. "You're sleeping through it so often these days."

Mia woke with a start. "Dad?" she shouted.

Oscar heard the panic in Mia's voice and wanted to rush into the room, but his own measures of propriety stopped him. "Are you okay? Mia? Mia? Answer me. Are you okay?"

Mia hugged her pillow tight as she looked around the bedroom in a daze. Yes, it was her room, and she was wide awake, but the rank smell of the little dream-boy lingered. The pillow was a link. She was hugging it when she awoke, but moments earlier, the pillow was a boy, her boy. "Yes, Dad, I'm fine," she mumbled and then buried her face in the pillow and wept.

"You don't sound fine, Mia. I'll get Mum."

"No, really, Dad, I'm okay. Just a bad dream."

She stumbled out of bed, feeling dizzy and confused. Mia looked back at the pillow, willing it to become the boy again because she could still feel him near her, but the room was clearing, and the strength of the memory faded.

"Mia. I'm not leaving until you show me your face."

She walked over to the door and leant her head against it. It was cool, comforting, and familiar. "Dad. I'm alright now."

Oscar wasn't happy. He knew Mia was far from alright because she sounded awful. He went to alert his wife. She could find out what was happening.

The water from the shower pounded on Mia's head, and it felt good. She enjoyed the wonderfully clean smell of her herbal soap more than usual. She would be late, but she needed to wash away the dream. Momentarily, she remembered holding the little boy close to her and singing the strange melody. The memory made her smile. But then she burst into tears as a tremendous sense of loss and longing swept over her. The woman in her dream said she was going mad; maybe she was.

Mia fought the emotions that were threatening to overwhelm her again. A sob caught in her throat, and tears flowed until she howled into the water as it splashed down on her. Being parted from her little boy made her chest ache.

"It was my son," she wailed. "Sarid, I'm so sorry I didn't recognise you, my sweet boy."

Finally, the warmth of the shower and the aromatic smells eased her distress and calmed her turbulent mind. She towelled her body vigorously and took several deep breaths to steady herself. As she wrapped herself in a clean, warm towel, she visualised wrapping the towel, with its warmth and comfort, around her little boy, and it felt good.

Mia, snap out of this woman! You're going crazy. You don't have a little boy. It's a dream, just a dream.

Still sniffling a little, she was determined to take control of her thoughts. "Right, sales targets," she said in a loud voice. She forced other thoughts to the back of her mind. "I'll win the monthly sales award or die doing it." Not the best choice of words, given the woman was close to death in her dreams. Her mind flashed back to the dream. Still, she persevered despite the threat of the images resurfacing. She was rewarded with a glimmer of motivation about the day ahead. The dream world was fading as she concentrated hard on her recent increase in sales. She had landed a few big travel itineraries in the last week. She was in the running for the top spot. If she completed the deals with two of her more promising customers this week, she might just pip her boss at the post.

She was going to be late now. Her parents would be angry as she planned to skip her cup of coffee. It would be fewer calories today, so Mia saw it as a plus. Her parents didn't appreciate that she needed to be very careful about what she ate and drank; she couldn't afford to gain an ounce of weight. Her work uniform was tailored to fit her figure. The Lycra Puma jumpsuit was just as unforgiving; it showed the slightest bulge. She was Vince's princess. She needed to set an example. She accepted the coffee Esme made every day, providing she didn't make it with whole cream milk or slip in a bit of cream to 'nourish' her, as her mum put it. Esme's sneaky tricks had caused two or three unpleasant scenes in the past, as Mia refused the coffee altogether and left for work in a huff. She finished straightening her hair and was carefully applying her makeup when her mum knocked and came straight in.

"Here you are, love. Drink this while you finish your makeup. Your dad said you were running late. I've made it frothy just the way you like it."

"Thanks, Mum. I may not finish it. I mustn't be late."

"Yes, I know, but do your best, Mia. You can't operate on an empty stomach. I've put one of my bran biscuits on the saucer. Made without fat or sugar, so no risk of any calories."

Mia forced herself to smile and thank Esme. It was kind, but her constant attempts to make her eat were annoying. Mia wished Esme would just back off. She saw in the mirror that her mum was now tidying the room. God, Mia thought, the woman is a paragon of cleanliness and tidiness. Watching her, Mia then regretted getting annoyed. Even though she said nothing, she was sure Esme could sense it sometimes in her offhand manner. She felt like a first-class cow because her parents were so loving and invariably forgave her. But they had made her the way she was; they had spoilt her.

Once Esme left her room, Mia called her friend Lisa. "Hi, you coming out later?" Mia sipped her coffee and tried to sound light-hearted, feeling anything but.

"Mia, it's mid-week. You know I'm strapped. If I go out tonight, I won't have enough for the weekend."

"Well, if you didn't drink like a fish, you could afford it," Mia bit back.

"What's your problem, Mia? Vince giving you the run-around again?"

"No, it isn't Vince. Look, I'm sorry. I'm feeling a bit rubbish right now, that's all."

"Well, I should think so. Anyway, you've got no room to talk. When was the last time you got home before midnight on a Saturday night sober?"

"Look, Lisa, I need to talk. Can you make Thursday?" Mia took the phone away from her ear to shout a farewell to her parents as she left the house. She put it back under her chin, hunching her shoulder to pin it in position as she struggled with the front door latch. She didn't wait for their reply.

"Yeah, but about what? I can't make Vince toe the line, mate. He can be a prick."

"Yeah, yeah, Lise, I know what you think of him, but it's not him. I said it wasn't Vince, didn't I? Look, Lise, I need to talk. Please, I'll pay for the drinks. I can't stay out long, anyway. Pressure at work at the mo. I don't want to lose my job."

"So, it's about the new bitch of a boss?" Lisa hesitated. "Oh, my God, you're not——?"

"No and no, stop trying to guess. I'll pick you up at eight on Thursday. Okay?"

"Yeah, okay. Laters," said Lisa, sighing. "Wish you'd give me a clue."

"No! See you at eight on Thursday. Bye." Mia wondered if talking to Lisa was a good idea after all. Lisa had a flappy mouth, and this was something Mia didn't want to broadcast to all and sundry.

###

Mia's reticence about talking to Lisa had not been misplaced. They were hardly in their seats when Lisa made it clear she was not taking Mia seriously. She even suggested Mia talk to Vince and their other friends about her dreams.

"I'm talking to you in confidence, Lisa. So, I hope you won't mention this to anyone."

"I reckon they'll think I'm as crazy as you if I did."

"Thanks for nothing," said Mia.

"Well, all this fuss about dreams. Come on, Mia! Everyone has dreams. I keep dreaming of a large house, and I'm lounging by this big blue pool. Amazing it is, and then I wake up, and I'm in my tatty little bedsit. Bit of a comedown. I feel pissed off every time."

"Lisa, can you stop wibbling on about your stupid dreams?"

"Nice, I must say."

"Sorry, Lise, but my dreams are very different."

"Of course they would be." Lisa's sarcasm was not lost on Mia. "Everyone's dreams are different."

This was a huge mistake. Mia could now see that clearly. Lisa was her best friend, but it wasn't because of her razor-sharp mind. She was a good laugh, and they had been friends since junior school. It didn't make her an ideal person to talk to about something so serious. But, against her better judgement, she ploughed on.

"Can you smell and touch things? Can people hurt you in your dreams, Lisa, can they?"

"What, you can smell your dreams?" said Lisa. "No, that's weird. And people can't hurt you in a dream." Lisa looked at her friend with fear. She was talking about mad stuff, and Lisa didn't like crazies at the best of times. She couldn't get her head around what Mia said, the good-time girl talking about whacko dreams. It didn't add up at all. Unless she was taking something.

Mia saw the doubt on Lisa's face. But she needed someone to talk to, apart from her parents. She continued. "In my dreams, people see me, touch me, and talk to me. When I woke the other morning, I could still smell my little boy."

"Little boy?" said Lisa, incredulously. "What little boy?"

"He was so real, and I could smell him. Well, he stank, but he was cute in his own way. He's my son in that world." Mia smiled and had a faraway look in her eyes.

"You've got to stop guzzling AlcoBlues, Mia. There're loads of chemicals in those. It's affecting you. Don't you remember how sick you were that night after a few bottles?" Lisa saw another friend at the bar and waved. The temptation to ditch Mia was strong. Her friend wasn't acting normal: she had just called a smelly little dream kid cute. This was not like Mia at all. She didn't even like kids, and she had a thing about foul smells. The Mia Lisa knew only cared about how she looked, who was dating who, and her sales targets. And, of course, Vince. She often bad-mouthed their friends who already had kids, so her comment about some cute dream kid was way off the mark. The night out with her was a bit of a flop.

Mia felt weary. Trying to get her friend to listen, really listen, and to stop looking around the place seemed impossible. It was nothing to do with AlcoBlues or anything else she was drinking or smoking. Well, at least she didn't think it was. And why was it happening to her? She never used to dream at all. Perhaps, as a new dreamer, the experience was more unsettling. She was getting nervous about falling asleep. Mia had never heard of anyone smelling anything in a dream; talking, yes, she had heard about that. She could see Lisa had lost interest. She probably thought initially that Mia had a juicy bit of gossip, and now she was disappointed.

"You'll never guess what happened at ShopDeal, Mia."

Mia usually loved these stories. Lisa explained how she had stood up to a snotty sales assistant who was left cringing. But today, Mia barely listened. Her friend carried on at a pace, hardly noticing Mia's monosyllabic responses. Only when Mia made her excuse to leave did Lisa finally register the frown on her best friend's face.

"Well, if I'm boring you, why didn't you say? You wanted to come out, Mia, not me." Lisa pouted as she gathered her things together, sweeping her long, blonde hair back in a huff.

"Sorry, Lisa, it's just these dreams; they're seriously freaking me out. I feel like I'm being haunted, and you know I can't stand horrible smells."

Lisa suddenly shrieked with laughter. It was completely unnecessary, Mia thought. It made people look in their direction. Lisa enjoyed the sudden attention, even taking the time to hold the gaze of a nice-looking bloke who was appreciating her skimpy outfit.

"Haunting! You're a laugh, Mia. They're dreams, girl, nothing else." She was no longer listening to Mia. "What are you like?" Lisa continued to giggle, fanning her face with her fake-tanned hands and long nails, as though it would help cool her after so much hilarity. It was a practised affectation, and it was attracting even more attention. Two men were staring at her. Lisa played the situation even more by laughing and tossing her head, enjoying their appreciative looks. She tried to pull her impossibly short skirt down while glancing provocatively in their direction.

Lisa was beautiful, Mia acknowledged to herself as she watched her friend putting on a show. But she was also an airhead who suffered from many 'blonde moments'. This, she thought, was definitely one of them.

Mia didn't want to spoil her friend's evening entirely, so she agreed she was a silly moo, and they laughed together, the laughter forced on Mia's side of the table. The night out with Lisa was supposed to help, but it made Mia feel more alone and desperate about her situation.

After a while, Mia apologised and said she had to go. She had suffered an additional hour of her friend flirting and talking about the usual stuff — blokes, shopping, clothes — and she couldn't take any more. Mia thought she had put on a good show, but that was all it was. In reality, she had to be at work early in the morning. It was a good excuse. She had an exclusive appointment with a customer who was a big spender. Like all premier customers, he had been invited to come in before the shop opened to the public. It was a clever idea and one that worked well. People with money liked special treatment as though they were more important than the regular customers. And, of course, they were to the sales consultants chasing commission points. The boss from hell, Sherri, would be there, too. She had another whopper of a sale on the go.

Mia dropped her friend off and then drove home, her head buzzing with the same questions and no answers. Lisa was probably right; they were simply dreams, and she needed to stop attaching so much importance to them. No more AlcoBlues or weed for a while; see if it helped. Her friend might not be so stupid after all. When she got home, the house was in darkness, apart from the porch and hall light left on for her.

CHAPTER 6

Mia and Vince parked outside the Go Ballistic site office. This would be a big day, and Vince was all fired up about the record number of players. Five hundred paintballers could be accommodated at the site. That figure had been reached two days earlier for both Saturday and Sunday. It was a first, and everyone was excited. Vince invited the press, as it would be terrific publicity, but he noticed Mia wasn't her usual bubbly self. He needed her to be on top form as he wanted the players roaring in the stadium and totally wired for the games. She was an essential part of the warm-up show, but the way she looked right now, he wasn't convinced she could raise a smile, let alone a cheer from his paintballers.

"What's up, Mia?"

"I feel really rough. Not sleeping too well."

"No kidding. It looks like you've got shopping bags under those lovely eyes today."

Mia gave Vince a withering look and stared out of the windscreen.

"Look, Mia, this is a massive weekend for me. I could do with your support. I suppose you've been out with Lisa."

"Yes, but we hardly drank anything. I was telling her about my dreams. Which, for your information, is the reason I'm not sleeping. Not alcohol."

"That doesn't help me, Mia. You look awful."

"Thanks for your concern."

"Well, what can I do? People dream."

"Not these dreams, I bet."

Exasperated, Vince breathed deeply, closed his eyes and leant back against his headrest, trying to stay calm. "Maybe one of the other girls should take your spot today."

A volley of paintballs slammed against Mia's window. She screamed and ducked down, holding her head.

Vince jumped out of the car.

"Ah, sorry, mate. Didn't see you there. The windows were all steamed up . . ." Three of his staff laughed and whooped suggestively, holding their paintball guns up in submission.

"Fuck off, the lot of yah! And get ready. You'd be off the site for that stunt on any other day."

Vince got back in the car to find Mia crying and taking headache tablets.

"Bloody idiots. They could get me shut down fooling with paintballs out here."

Mia put her head back on her headrest and closed her eyes.

"You know I meant nothing by it, Mia. You're my best girl — my Puma Princess."

"Yeah, whatever," said Mia. "I'll go to the Puma cabin and check all the girls have turned up," she added in a deadpan voice.

"If you aren't up to it, let one of the other girls take the lead. Give yourself a bit of a break." The way Mia was acting offhand annoyed Vince. This was his big chance to get some incredible publicity. He felt that she should have made an effort to get some shut-eye instead of hitting the town with her mates — or whatever she had been doing.

"I don't want any of the giddy girls," said Vince. "Give Susan a chance. She has a nice little body and fiery red hair. She'd look great for the cameras."

"Yeah, yeah, carrot-top cling-on it is, then." Mia was furious that Vince had chosen her replacement. Should the need ever arise, she thought that was her prerogative. Choosing sickly sweet Susan made it worse.

"For Fuck's sake, Mia, show a bit more interest."

"Yeah, yeah, laters." Mia climbed out of the car and walked away from a fuming Vince. "Huh, who am I kidding? It's all about his precious paintball."

Vince didn't hear her as he stomped off in the opposite direction.

Mia found the girls ready and waiting for her as she entered the Puma cabin. They all looked great. The air was thick with perfume, chat, and laughter. She felt like the proverbial wet blanket and probably looked like one. The chatting died down, followed by a few whispers. She ignored the critical glances and walked straight over to Susan. In a monotone voice, Mia informed her she was to do the briefing alongside Vince. She then allocated duties to the rest of the troupe in a bored tone of voice. She thought about changing into her Puma suit, but decided she would be strictly 'backstage' today.

"Thank you sooo much, Mia. You won't regret it," squeaked an ecstatic Susan.

"Well, you'd better get it right. Vince is uptight about everything going well today. You blow it, and it's your first and last appearance in the stadium. For the record, Vince chose you, not me." Mia regretted imparting that information as soon as the words were out of her mouth.

Susan suddenly leapt forward and hugged a surprised Mia.

"Yeah, yeah, whatever," Mia droned. "Now, as you're leading Pumas today, you can do the motivational speech in here too." As Mia's enthusiasm was nil, she knew she couldn't hope to instil any fervour into this giggling gang of girls. She turned away to leave as Susan pranced about at the front of the cabin. Like a ginger cat on a hot tin roof, Mia thought unkindly. In an excited, squeaky voice, Susan cajoled the girls until some sort of order prevailed.

"Paintball Pumas, are we ready? Susan called.

"Meow," they replied, stretching their arms up and clawing the air.

As Mia shut them in, she could hear Susan continue the chant.

"What do paintballers do?"

"Go ballistic!" came the response.

"If you didn't go ballistic," Susan prompted.

"You didn't go paintballing," the Pumas yelled in response.

Mia walked over to the canteen to check they were ready. Vince would make a lot of money on food and drink over the weekend. If the canteen team achieved their target, they would get a big bonus and a night out.

As the Pumas streaked past her, the boys in the canteen whistled. The Pumas waved, some with their hands and others flicking their tails. It earned them a roar of approval and more whistling. Susan was glowing at the head of the troupe, and Mia grudgingly thought they looked good. She purposely didn't refer to Susan as the Puma Princess because that was her title and hers alone. Mia was glad she was not leading them today, though. She felt rotten, really ill, in fact.

Susan led the Pumas to the stadium to practice their moves before their real performance began. This provided an early morning show for members of the public who would already be in the car park. It was all good publicity, and it built the Go Ballistic brand.

"I see the biscuit is leading the girls today, eh Mia?" a bloke from the canteen said.

"Yeah, she is, and she'd better not crumble, or Vince will have her little ginger guts for garters." Mia enjoyed her own wit and the fact she left the canteen boys laughing at Susan's expense.

Paintballers were arriving for the first games of the day. A deep tribal thrumming blasted out over the loudspeakers that mingled with the battle cries from the Puma troupe in the stadium. As the tension and expectation ratcheted up a notch, Mia could feel the excitement. It was a carnival atmosphere with a slight edginess that precedes any battle. An impressive set-up and one Mia helped Vince to create over the last four years. The powerfully illuminated stadium, enclosed by chain-link fencing, was strategically placed so players and spectators could see the pre-game performance from as many positions around the site as possible. It smacked of a warm-up for a Roman gladiatorial contest, such was the hype and the build-up to the paintball battles that followed.

No other paintball site in Australia had such a theatrical start to their games. It worked. As a result, Vince was a wealthy man. The Pumas were an essential part of the set-up, and Mia knew she was letting her boyfriend down by not being on top form today. But it was hardly her fault. The nightmares were haunting her sleep, and last night was one of the worst. She woke in the early hours, out of breath, terrified, and determined not to go back to sleep and get dragged back to that awful place again. It was the first time she had been directly threatened with extreme violence in a dream, and her heart still raced with fear when she thought about it. Now, she was high from endless cups of coffee but exhausted from lack of sleep. It wasn't a comfortable mental state, and she didn't present a pretty picture either. She had done Vince a favour by stepping back and letting Susan take her place. But, of course, he wasn't grateful for her self-sacrifice; he was too bloody self-centred, she thought bitterly.

Mia grabbed yet another cup of coffee and walked to the stadium. She checked that the Go Ballistic banners were not drooping on the walkways, and the flags were flying free from the poles at each corner of the site. Everything was in place. The buzz of excitement was palpable as the final few paintballers took their seats in the stadium for the first briefing of the day. The noise level was deafening from over two hundred players who stamped in unison as they awaited the arrival of Vince and his Pumas. Mia watched from a safe distance, unseen, but she could see everything. The invited members of the press sat in the front row with the best view of the action. They were chatting, smiling and giving the occasional nervous glance at the crazy mob of paintballers behind them.

Vince strutted into the stadium and posed with his legs wide apart and arms crossed. He stood still in the front of the tiered seating, then dropped his head to his chest. The crowd went quiet; everyone stopped talking and watched. But a roar went up when the Pumas ran in and surrounded him, their empty guns pointing at his head. As he threw his head back and raised his arms in the air, the Puma guns lifted as though he had pushed them all away. He bellowed, "I'm in . . . vin . . . cible, and this is my kingdom." He paused dramatically, then yelled, "Go Ballistic!"

The players shouted and stamped their feet in response. The Pumas turned on the seated paintballers, crouched, and then opened fire, but the sound effects came from the speakers. Players, new to Go Ballistic, ducked the non-existent paintballs, then laughed with embarrassment. The shocked reaction from the uninitiated journalists almost made Mia smile — almost. They not only ducked as a group, but one of them fell to the floor and held his arms over his head for protection. Totally embarrassed, the poor man sat back down after being tapped on the shoulder by a colleague. The Pumas then strutted about as dry ice was pumped into the stadium. Then they all adopted various sexy poses, using their guns as props. Players whistled and roared their approval. The Pumas' finale saw the girls standing in formation, legs akimbo, guns on hips, ready to go through their practised chants. They wore mikes, so their voices carried across the entire site:

"Have you got the balls?" the Pumas yelled.

The paintballers leapt to their feet and, with Vince, who thrust his fist in the air, shouted, "Yes!"

"Will you surrender?"

"No, never!" The cries got louder, with paintballers remaining on their feet and punching the air.

"Are you ready to do battle?" the Pumas taunted, pointing their guns at different parts of the seating area.

"Yes!"

The Puma Troupe finished with the all-important:

"If you didn't go ballistic," to the tumultuous response.

"You didn't go paintballing!"

The loudspeakers boomed to the beat of drums, ratcheting up the battle atmosphere. Paintballers, led by Vince, stamped, whooped, cheered, yelled and clapped. The Pumas then dropped back and sat on a bench behind Vince. Susan remained by his side. It looked like an impromptu performance. However, Mia had choreographed every move, carefully synchronising the drums, battle music, and special effects. She varied it a little every week to keep it fresh for regular players.

The music stopped. Vince stood, head bowed, waiting for silence. Susan held her gun aloft and waved it slowly from side to side, holding her finger to her lips. The Pumas on the bench mimicked her actions. Gradually, the commotion died down. Theatrically, Vince raised his head.

"Now, we come to the serious part of the day. You need to pay attention or pay with exclusion from the battle zones." His face was stern, and no one would doubt his threat. Those who played regularly at Go Ballistic knew Vince and his marshals would throw them out of any battle if they broke the rules. Once Vince had control, Susan took her position. As Vince outlined the dos and don'ts of gameplay, safety rules and details of the various missions they would play, Susan demonstrated his every instruction with her paintball gun. While the players needed to take the rules seriously, Vince wanted them to enjoy every aspect of their experience at Go Ballistic. Seeing a beautiful girl acting-out the rules during the pre-battle briefing softened and reinforced its impact simultaneously. The audience was mainly male, but the female paintballers enjoyed the spectacle just as much. They often stood and mimicked the Pumas.

Susan was perfect, Mia noted; she even brought her tail into play in a sexy, alluring manner, which Mia never did. Vince seemed pleased with his new Puma Princess, and the paintballers gave their seal of approval with the odd wolf-whistle during the briefing. Vince repeated each of the rules and safety requirements to ensure everyone heard and understood. Then he lifted the mood. "Now, go do battle . . . and . . . go ballistic!" He roared over the loudspeakers.

The drumming and music resumed, and, almost to the beat, each team jogged to line up behind their Puma, holding up their team's chosen name on a plaque. Cheering and shouting, they filed out to head for the safety enclosure, where they would load up on paintballs and smoke grenades before being sent into the various battle zones. Vince talked to the press before joining Susan for a photo shoot. Happily, and with practised ease, they wrapped their arms around each other for a few cheeky shots.

Mia had seen enough. She left her hiding place, making sure she was unseen. Obviously, Susan had stood and watched her and Vince for weeks from this very spot. She had Mia's moves off to perfection. Before this performance, Susan had only performed with the troupe once, so watching her and Vince was the only way she could have given such a flawless performance. Mia felt rejected and miserable. She went to the canteen for another coffee. Feeling sure she looked as she felt, she didn't want Vince to see her. She would get one of the blokes to run her home without telling Vince she was going. She wasn't needed here. Susan could copy Mia's performance perfectly, with a few clever touches of her own. And she would undoubtedly be splashed all over the press — the local TV too.

Bitch. Ginger-haired bitch, Mia thought, surprising herself with the intensity of her dislike of Susan.

She's after Vince. Well, he can have her, and good luck to them.

She didn't mean it, even as it marched angrily across her mind. She was feeling tired and very sorry for herself. As she sipped her coffee, she thought of ways she would make Susan pay for her actions. Susan the cling-on was now Susan the arch-enemy. And, she would make Vince regret his leering looks at her new rival. No one crossed Mia Barone — well, not without getting a few nasty battle scars.

CHAPTER 7

Only one more week to the end of the month, and Mia was nipping at the heels of Sherri for the top spot on the scoreboard. Just an additional five hundred commission points; then she would be neck and neck with the boss. If Mia's two pending sales, together with a deposit from a premier customer, came in, it would put her in the lead.

Mia wasn't sure why she couldn't hit it off with her boss. She liked to brag about her sales performance too, but this Sherri was something else. Her clothing and makeup were all that power stuff, which was yesterday's news in the fashion stakes. She looked like something straight out of the eighties with her big hair, padded shoulders, startling red lipstick and nails to match.

Mia, by comparison, knew she looked cool. Everyone remarked about how good she looked and could have any bloke she fancied. Vince was her boyfriend right now — well, only just, given his behaviour at the weekend. If all it took was for that devious cow, Susan, to flutter her eyes and wag her tail to have him drooling over her, she would think hard about their relationship.

But Mia was no fool. Vince was a good-looking bloke with a lot of money. Paintball operators coined it in, but Vince made most other sites look like they were taking home pocket money. To be fair, though, Go Ballistic paintballers got a day like no other. Vince also crammed the site with unique features and props to make the paintball games in each zone challenging and exciting. Mia enjoyed her position as Puma Princess and jealously guarded it. And she did a damn good job. Many of the site development ideas and marketing could be attributed to her, too. Mia suggested having girl pumas, and she trained them with routines she had devised.

When she thought about it, she contributed big time to the success of Go Ballistic. But Vince showed his appreciation. Her sporty little car was a gift from him, as was most of her expensive jewellery. An upstart like Susan would not steal her man. That, she thought viciously, was a fact.

"Susan," Mia barked, "I'm expecting a customer at any moment. A Mrs Harvard. Can you get her coffee and sit her in the waiting area? I'm just going to pop upstairs for a brochure."

"Get stuffed, Mia," Lucas put in. "While she's doing your dirty work to increase your sales, she'll be missing out on online enquiries and shop customers."

"Did I ask you to put yer beak in, Lucas? Sue doesn't mind, do you?" said Mia in her best syrupy voice while staring meaningfully at Susan. Mia knew very well that Susan was feeling awkward after the weekend.

"Oh, Sue, is it now?" Lucas scoffed. "You do it for the great saleswoman, 'Sue', and she will put a bit more dosh in your leaving collection next week. You know you're trailing behind everyone else?"

Susan was torn. She wanted to help Mia, knowing she was angry with her, but Mia should be grateful. None of the other girls would have performed as well as she had. She loved the attention, especially from Vince. He invited her for a drink after and made a move on her. She was so shocked that she fluffed it, but hoped he would try again. He was so dishy, and he had a Porsche and everything. She would get her eyes scratched out if Mia knew, but she thought Vince was worth it. If he chose her as his next girlfriend, none of the gang would dream of going against him. But all that aside, Susan knew Sherri would sack her if she didn't reach the base level of commission points, at the very least. One decent sale and she would get there, even if she was still the month's lowest scorer. Three strikes, Sherri liked to remind them, and you were gone, and the two previous months, she had missed base level by a few points. She couldn't let it happen this month.

"Sorry, Mia, but I've got to get to base, and I can't afford to risk missing out on potential sales."

"Oh, suit yerself." Mia stuck her head in the air and strutted over to the stairs. "Not much team spirit in this office anymore. Everyone's out for themselves," she added. It wasn't a smart remark, as it would needle Sherri, who talked about teamwork all the time. Even she was the complete opposite. Not surprising, then, that Mia's comment hit a nerve, and she got a knock-back glare from her boss. "Shit," she whispered to herself as she lowered her head and dashed for the storeroom up the stairs.

The shop door pinged. Mia was undecided if she should pop back down and see if it was Mrs Harvard or grab the brochure first. She took off her shoes and ran the rest of the way, opting to collect the brochure, or she would have to leave her customer in the shop while she got it later. Why they put the brochures on the second floor, she couldn't fathom. She mentioned it at a few staff meetings, but nothing was done. It was such a trek, and staff left piles on the steps, making it a hazard, getting up and down the already narrow stairs. She had better be quick, grab the one she needed, and get back to the shop. As long as she took a couple of minutes on the last step to catch her breath. She could then make a dignified entrance. There was laughter coming up the stairs from the sales floor; at least no one was getting angry, Mia thought.

After moving several boxes, she finally reached the small attic room where the brochures were stored. It was stuffy at the top of the building. It made her head swim with a lack of air after rushing up the stairs. She breathed heavily to catch her breath.

There was no logic to the storage. It was a jumble, and it needed to be organised. It was an old building, but she felt there was no need for such a mess. Some brochures were old and way out of date. New brochures were being dumped on top. It annoyed her. Then she had a brainwave. Susan was hopeless at sales. She could suggest to Sherri that Susan's time might be better spent getting all this lot in some sort of order. Her plan made her smile.

Mia was sure Mrs Harvard would get impatient before long if it was her she had heard arriving. She tried to push the door open. It was stiff and wouldn't budge. Losing her temper, she shoved it with all her strength. She didn't care if it came off its hinges because they couldn't operate efficiently with this set-up. And it would draw attention to the situation.

The final push sent her stumbling headlong into the room, sending her shoes flying out of her hand. "Damn, damn," she said as she stubbed her toe on a pile of boxes. She swore again and then stifled a scream as an intense pain shot up her leg. She squeezed her eyes closed and dropped to the floor to grab her wounded toe, pressing it until the wave of pain subsided. "Bloody hell," she cursed, "that really hurt. What numpty left those right by the door?"

She opened her watering eyes to inspect the damage and was utterly confused. Her bleeding foot was resting on mud; it was filthy with chipped toenails packed with grime. The confusion lasted momentarily because she knew she was back there again. She screamed long and loud. A hand slapped her face hard, knocking her backwards.

"Do as you're told, bitch, or you will get worse."

Mia looked up fearfully at her assailant. A large uniformed woman looked down at her before grabbing her hair and hauling her to her feet.

"Did you hear me, you dirty Jew?"

"Aargh, my hair. Yes, yes, sorry," she heard herself say.

"Now get back in there and work, or you'll feel the butt of my rifle in your disgusting Jewish face."

Mia stumbled towards a shed where another woman grabbed her arm and helped her into the dark interior. Piles of clothing and shoes were heaped on the floor. There were groups of men and women at wooden tables, sorting them and putting them in different boxes. Others were tying sorted clothing into bundles.

"Walk properly. You can't limp," the woman hissed at a terrified Mia. "If they think you can't work, you know you will go. Do as you're told, when you're told, or you will not last much longer here. Think of your little boy. Think of Sarid. He needs you. Now get to work, Rachel, and don't keep annoying them. I don't know what's got into you, but you'd better stop this now. You're acting crazy, and it'll get you killed, and you may just take some of us with you." The woman pushed Mia towards a stack of suitcases.

"I'm sorry, but I stubbed my toe and——"

"Lucky it was only your toe. You nearly got a bullet in your head."

Mia glanced around at the other women nearest her. They were like tramps, filthy with either shaved heads or grubby-looking hair scraped back from their lifeless faces. Their clothing was soiled, and they moved like sacks of potatoes. It reminded Mia of drug addicts. She looked at her own arms as she reached for a suitcase. They were brown with dirt. Her stomach rumbled, and her head ached from the earlier hair-pulling. She gagged with the reek of the unwashed bodies of her companions. That, together with the suffocating smell of the fusty clothes piled in front of her, was almost unbearable. She worked hard and kept quiet, as did her fellow workers. The woman beside her whispered that her name was Esther, and she was new. She looked like a friendly woman and even took some of Mia's clothes to sort as she was getting behind. Esther pointed at a woman opposite, who looked beautiful even under the grime. Tears silently rolled down her pretty face, making tracks in the dirt.

"Her name is Augustyna. Polish. Poor girl, it doesn't pay to be attractive in here. Her work doesn't stop in the sheds," she whispered meaningfully.

"God, that's awful. Can't anyone help her?"

"What, in here?" said Esther, incredulously. "I thought you'd been here for a while." The guard was walking in their direction, so Esther stopped talking immediately and looked busy.

"Well, I, for one, wouldn't stand for it. We've got rights."

Another woman scoffed. Then glanced around to see if the guards heard her. "In here?"

"We can't just leave it. Now we know what's happening."

"Keep your voice down, you crazy woman. What's wrong with you? Just do your work," the other woman hissed.

Swallowing hard and trying to think of other things in her real world, Mia worked silently. She saw her old friend Ariella further down the line. They glanced at each other and allowed themselves a quick smile. Ariella was a close friend from her life in Italy before her family were snatched. Memories flooded her mind of sitting and chatting with Ariella and other friends and neighbours while her little sister, Naomi, and Ariella's niece, Alma, played with her son, Sarid. Lost in childish games, the three of them were so close. It was a beautiful memory. Remembering, Mia looked up again. Ariella gave her another smile behind a piece of clothing, lifted to hide her face. Warmth spread inside Mia, momentarily by the show of love and friendship. Mia's stomach rumbled as she thought of her lunch, tucked away in her desk, as meagre as it was.

The next case she opened was so small. She took out the clothing of a young girl, neatly folded. Mia found a teddy bear wrapped in a jumper. A kaleidoscope of raw emotions bubbled to the surface. A little girl had worn the clothes she held in her hands. She had hugged the teddy, then wrapped it in her jumper, like a shawl. She would have been someone's precious little girl. Loved dearly by her family, just like she loved her son, Sarid. Where was that little girl now? — as if she didn't know! Tears fell, but she continued her work. The other women moved away from her and gave her furtive and worried glances, hoping the guards wouldn't notice, but that hope was in vain.

A burly looking guard marched towards the group. The Polish girl swiped her face to remove her tears and glanced at the guard, expecting retribution. Another guard fell in line, joining the first. It looked like they were coming for Mia. Almost imperceptibly, the other workers moved even further away. But they were careful not to make any sudden moves and continued seamlessly with their work. Mia's hands shook uncontrollably. There had been too many chances, too many near misses recently. Someone was going to get a beating, or worse. As the guard lifted his hand, Mia crouched out of reach. A hand gripped the back of her clothes.

"Mia Barone, what the hell are you playing at? Mrs Harvard has been waiting downstairs for a full ten minutes. I've a good mind to give the sale to Susan. She has been fussing around, making sure your customer doesn't want for anything. Mia, are you listening?"

"Sorry, sorry, don't hit me. I'll work. Please. Please."

"What in the name of God are you going on about, woman? Hit you? You're talking gibberish." Sherri stepped back, feeling nervous. Mia was acting strange. She turned on the light and saw Mia grovelling on the floor amongst the brochure boxes, her hands above her head in supplication. Sherri was at a loss and embarrassed by the situation. She gasped as Mia's head snapped back and stared at her with a crazed look. Sherri backed up further towards the door.

Through a haze of tears, Mia saw the glamorous figure of her boss, wide-eyed and staring at her. The shed had become the attic room at TopTravel again, and she was sprawled on the floor.

"Oh shit, I must have slipped. Sorry, Sherri. I think I banged my head cos it really hurts." Mia stuttered out another apology and an attempted explanation. Her heart was beating fast, and she was wet with perspiration. After trying to get up, she abandoned the effort, slumped down across the nearest box, put her head in her hands and wept. "They just won't leave me alone."

Sherri was stunned into silence. Mia wiped her eyes, trying to behave normally. She saw the look of fear in Sherri's eyes. "Sherri, I'm a bit worse for that experience," Mia snivelled.

"Susan can have that sale — Mrs Harvard. I don't think I can talk to anyone right now. I need to sit in the staff room for a while, if you don't mind."

Sherri could see that Mia was acting like some sort of loon. But, couldn't believe she would give away a high commission sale, especially not to Susan. Like Sherri, Mia was desperately trying to get the top score for the month. Giving away these points would ruin her chances. Sherri's heart gave a little leap of joy. She would now be at the top of the scoreboard again. But she had a nagging doubt that Mia must be planning something underhand. Otherwise, this made no sense to Sherri. Being the top salesperson was everything, and she thought Mia was the same.

"Well, yes, yes, you look ill," said Sherri. "Go to the staff room and make yourself a coffee. I'd best get someone in to have a look at the carpet; we don't need any accident claims." This now looked like a priority to Sherri. She didn't want any black marks against her during her time as manager at this branch.

Sherri still couldn't take it in that Mia was giving her sale away — and to Susan. This generosity was way out of character. "Anyway, just . . . er . . . take your time," said Sherri, trying in vain to sound solicitous for Mia's welfare. She looked with uncertainty at her best saleswoman and fierce rival. As Sherri didn't know what else to say, she simply walked away.

Mia waited until Sherri was out of earshot, sank to the floor and allowed her tears and distress free rein. Nightmares in the day and at work. "What's happening to me?" she sobbed.

Sherri heard Mia crying as she rapidly descended the stairs. She glanced back fearfully to check Mia wasn't following her. She hated the people management side of her role as a manager; it didn't come naturally to her. Mia lived with her parents. They could deal with this, Sherri decided. She would call them and get them to collect Mia. After racing downstairs, Sherri burst breathlessly onto the sales floor. She stopped, took a deep breath, smoothed her clothing, and then walked purposely and calmly to Susan's desk. She handed Susan the brochures and made a big show of her good fortune in the customer transfer, as though she was giving it to her personally. Most of the staff looked toward the stairs in astonishment. They fully expected Mia to appear at any moment and demand her customer back. Other customers at the desks, realising something was happening, looked around expectantly. An uncomfortable silence forced Sherri to act.

"Right, let's get back to it, shall we?" Sherri clapped her hands in the affected way she did — not really clapping at all. Her hands touched gently together. Then she swept a syrupy smile around the shop. Slowly, the talking resumed: consultants launched into their travel-speak; customers murmured with delight at proffered brochures showing their chosen holiday. All was back to normal in the busy, bright interior of TopTravel. Except for Lucas. He wasn't convinced. He was sure that Sherri would need to kill Mia to prise a sale away from her. Lucas looked towards the stairs again as he heard the staff room door close. He found it all very peculiar.

CHAPTER 8

Oscar insisted Mia stay in bed for another day. "You've had a nasty shock and hit your head, my love. You need to rest up," he said, tenderly stroking her troubled brow. The love and affection that shone from his deep brown eyes caused Mia's tears to flow hot and salty, stinging her already sore eyes. It disturbed him to see her being so emotional. It wasn't like her at all. His Mia was usually such a little tough nut.

"Can you tell me a little more about your dreams?"

"Dad, they terrify me. Look." Mia showed Oscar her face. He lifted her chin to see better.

"That's where that animal hit me."

"What animal?"

"In my dream."

"Mia, it's a dream. No one can hurt you. Look, love, perhaps you should sleep now."

"I can't sleep, Dad. I don't want to sleep. They usually come when I sleep or when it gets dark, and believe me, Dad, they're so real.

"As real as I am right now?"

"Yes."

"Surely that's an exaggeration, Mia. I mean——"

"No, Dad, it's not. I can even smell them, and, God, they all stink like crazy. The people, not the soldiers. The soldiers are mindless brutes who beat us on a whim and kill without cause." She touched the mark on her head.

What Mia said was shocking, but Oscar didn't think it would help if he said so.

"Rest, Mia. Try not to dwell on it."

Mia broke down. "They seem to know me, although they call me Rachel. But I told you that already." She sobbed until snot and tears flowed. Oscar wiped it away gently with his big cotton hankie.

"Don't cry, my love. Please don't cry. Try to rationalise it. Where is it? Do you know?"

"It's some kind of detention centre, I think. But we're sorting things from people's suitcases." Mia sniffled and wiped her eyes again. "Why would there be so many suitcases?" Mia searched her memory. I think the people who owned those suitcases died. It's hardly lost property in a place like that. She clutched her head, remembering the little girl's suitcase and the much-loved teddy lovingly swaddled in her jumper.

Oscar looked at her with mounting concern. As she spoke, long-buried, ghastly memories and fears surfaced for him. Had she been there? It was a question that was constantly on his mind. But it made little sense that it should be Mia. It was long ago, so long ago — even though his memories were as fresh as if it had all happened yesterday.

He closed the curtains. Mia needed to sleep, and he wanted to think. His own memories were flooding back, threatening to overwhelm him. She mustn't see the apprehension on his face. He was sure she knew where the dream place was. The events she had witnessed were so explicit. And they studied WWII in school; he was sure of that.

"No, Dad. Don't close the curtains," Mia shouted. "They come in the dark." She sat up, panic-stricken.

"Okay, love, okay," Oscar soothed, pulling the curtains back quickly. "Look, Mia, I'll make an appointment with the doctor for you tomorrow. If you don't sleep, you'll get very ill."

"No, Dad. The doctor will think I'm a nut job. I'm not going," Mia screeched hysterically; her dark-rimmed, frightened eyes stared at him from her pallid face.

"Mum will be home soon, Mia. She'll know what to do. He was defeated by so much anguish.

Mia pulled her doona up under her chin and glanced apprehensively around the room. "Dad, leave the door open, would you? Don't shut me in. They shut me in a tiny shed once. It was awful — no windows and nothing to eat or drink for days."

Oscar wanted to pursue Mia's last comment, but he thought better of it. It would only cause her more distress. So, instead, he smiled reassuringly. "Of course, love, there you go. Look, I've put a chair in front of the door, so it can't close, even if there's a breeze. See?" Oscar's mind was racing. The past had come back to haunt them again — well, Mia. And why Mia? She wasn't even born when it happened. But then, neither was their daughter, Ruth. He mustn't risk putting anything into her head that wasn't there already.

"Mia?"

"Dad. I don't want to talk about it anymore."

Oscar pulled up a chair beside the bed.

"I think perhaps you must. You can't deal with something unless you understand it."

Mia nodded. "Okay, but when I need to stop, I want to stop."

"Agreed. The first thing we need to establish is where the dream place is."

"I told you."

"Mia, you did history at school — European history. I think you know what that place is.

Mia looked small and frightened, peering over the top of her bedclothes. "It's a concentration camp, and the people being held are mainly Jews."

Oscar smiled encouragingly. "Well, that's a start."

"Why am I dreaming of a concentration camp? . . . and why do they call me Rachel there?"

"Rachel is——"

"What's going on?" Esme had just walked into the room. "Mia, why are you in bed?"

"She had another one of those nightmares, Esme. At work this time. I had to fetch her. We were just talking about it."

Esme rushed to Mia's side. "Talking about it?" Esme gave Oscar a look of fear.

"Mum, Dad is trying to help."

"What, by dragging up unpleasant details and poring over them? I don't think so." Esme turned to Oscar. "She'll see a therapist. Something has triggered this, and it needs to be stopped. Dwelling on it will just make it worse. She'll see a therapist, and that's that."

Oscar shook his head at his wife's outburst. He crossed the room and took his wife in his arms. "Look, love. You can't hide these things forever."

Esme pulled away from Oscar and took a deep breath. "It's all unravelling again. After all these years of protecting her."

Mia sat up in her bed. "What do you mean, Mum?"

Esme walked over and gazed out of the window. "I wouldn't know where to start, Mia."

"Come on, love. We can do this," said Oscar. "We're a family. Maybe you need to sleep a little, Mia, and we can talk later."

Mia got out of bed to embrace Esme.

"Mum, if there's something you can tell me that will help, please say it."

"You don't deserve this, my darling girl."

"Deserve the dreams? No, I don't. But, Mum, I don't deserve to be kept in the dark, either."

"What's your father been saying?"

"You didn't give him a chance to finish, Mum. But I know there's something. You and Dad stop talking when I come into the room, so often. You did that when I was younger, but it's happening such a lot recently."

Esme looked at Oscar, who smiled and nodded encouragingly. He hoped this was the moment.

"I think this is better discussed at another time," said Esme.

Oscar was disappointed that his wife still didn't feel able to open up about things, things he knew would help Mia.

"Give me another hug, Mia," said her mother. "Hugs are what we need right now."

Mia embraced her mother. She didn't want to let go. The warmth and familiarity felt like an anchor to reality. The slight scent of lavender was the smell of security and comfort since childhood. "I could do with one of your special cups of tea, Mum, with heaps of sugar."

"That's easy, Mia. How about a couple of bickies?" said Esme, returning the warmth of Mia's embrace.

"One." Mia agreed and laughed at her mother's continued attempts at feeding her, regardless of what was happening. "You're the best, you two." Mia looked from one parent to another with love.

"I still want you to see a therapist, Mia," said Esme.

Oscar shook his head sadly. Their deception about their past had gone on for too long. Like him, Esme probably didn't know how to tell the truth now.

CHAPTER 9

The lights were flashing, and the music pounded. Mia was in the groove and enjoying the noise and the crowded dance floor. She was giving it her all, and the men dancing around her were enthralled by her energetic gyrations.

"Great to see you out and about again, Mia. Your mum and dad were dead worried about you," Lisa shouted over the music.

"Thanks, Lise. I'm fine now. Must have caught a bug," Mia yelled back. Then spun round to dance with a bloke who had sidled up to her. He was confident her suggestive dance moves were a "come on", especially given her scantily clad body and the "I dare you" smile. He dared and was rewarded with the sexiest dance he ever had with a girl.

Lisa left the heaving dance floor and returned to their table and friends. They were pleased to see Mia back out with the crowd, but they all agreed that she wasn't the same. She invariably embarrassed them these days with her erratic behaviour and excessive flirting. Her friends commented that she seemed to be trying to prove something, but they didn't know what. Lisa watched her friend on the dance floor. It was important to her that Mia had fun; now, it looked like she was doing just that. Seeing her closest friend so low when she called on Mia at home a few weeks ago was awful. Mia's dad had phoned and asked Lisa to pop in, which was unusual enough, but she was more than happy to oblige because she was worried. For days, she had rung Mia and just got her recorded message.

Mia weaved her way through other dancers on the dance floor and stood by Lisa's side.

"Look at those girls in the dance cage, Mia. Brilliant movers. Fancy getting up there later?"

"Why not? Show 'em a few moves, eh, Lise? But right now, I need another drink."

"Yeah, but lay off the AlcoBlues, ay?"

Mia ignored Lisa's comment. "Loved dancing with that guy," she shouted over the music. "He can really move. Did you see the way he slid me across the floor? It was like an old-time rock and roll move. Incredible feeling, Lise." Mia slumped down in a chair, breathing hard, but smiling.

"Yeah, I saw, Mia. You trying to make Vince jealous?"

Mia looked across the table at a sour-faced Vince. He glared at her and turned away. "Nah, not bothered. Nuffin to do with me, Lise. I'm out for a good time, and I'm not letting some miserable git like him spoil my fun. What's with 'im, anyway?" Mia sneered in Vince's general direction. "It looks like he lost a ten and found a five."

"Aw, come on, Mia. The bloke's hurting. It's not like you to be so cruel to yer mates."

"Well, maybe I just don't care." It was an honest, if seemingly cruel, response. Mia was tired of feeling. She wanted to throw all the deep, meaningful feelings off and get back to her old self. "C'mon, Lise, let's get a drink and then get back out there, eh?" Mia slid off her chair and was already dancing and singing as she moved toward the crowded dance floor.

"Look, those girls are getting out of the cage. Let's go, Lise. Quick."

Lisa glanced at her friends and shrugged in defeat. Lisa felt she had tried. But it was a balancing act between trying to have a good time with Mia and getting her to tone down her erratic behaviour. Vince gave the merest flicker of a glance towards a now disappearing Mia, tottering on her high heels. Definitely one too many, Lisa thought. Then she caught the worried look in Vince's eyes. She didn't blame him. Their friend was acting wild and out of control, and all they could do was wait for the Mia they used to know to come back. Lisa was pretty sure the dreams Mia kept talking about figured big time in this whole mess. Her friend seemed to be on a self-destruct mission, drinking night after night, partying, and getting off her head. She was a train wreck waiting to happen. Vince wasn't guilt-free — going out with Susan from Mia's work. There'd be trouble if Mia found out. Lisa questioned him about it, but he shrugged it off, saying it meant nothing to him. His excuse was that Susan was begging for it, and he was only a bloke, so what was he supposed to do while Mia kept giving him the cold shoulder? Blokes! thought Lisa.

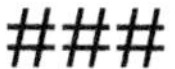

###

Mia was barely keeping her eyes open. Sherri hurled daggers at her from across the sales floor when she could catch her eye. Mia kept her head down, pretended she was busy on the computer and hoped she didn't get any customers. Every time the phone rang, she winced. The shop doorbell had the same effect. To discourage customers from choosing her, she had turned her customer chairs away from the door and placed them very close to the front of her desk. Stay away was the message. Sherri undoubtedly noticed, but Mia's head was splitting, and she could barely focus, let alone chat enthusiastically to a customer.

The layout of the sales floor was a semi-circle. The sales consultants' desks were arranged around the edge of a carpeted area emblazoned with a TopTravel logo between each desk. The centre of the office and the entrance area were wooden laminate. In the last few weeks, Sherri had taken to walking on the carpeted area to sneak up on her staff if she thought they were slacking. Not surprisingly, then, Mia didn't hear her approach.

"In my office, now," Sherri hissed.

Mia was caught with her head in her hands, hiding behind her computer screen. She sighed in resignation and then stumbled out of her chair to follow her boss. Unfortunately for Mia, the route to Sherri's office was across the wooden floor. Her boss's heels hammered out her angry march to her office. Each head-splitting strike delivered a blow to Mia's aching head. She loved high-heels, but right now, it was all she could do not to push Sherri to the floor and remove the offending noise-makers. It was torture. As she trailed behind the boss with her head bowed, she knew everyone was looking at her. *I must look like a right mess.* She caught Lucas' eye. He appeared startled and embarrassed and immediately looked back at his computer screen.

The door to Sherri's office closed with a loud bang. Mia winced.

"You look like death," Sherri shouted.

Oh, very original, Mia thought sarcastically. "Please, don't do that."

"What?"

"I accept you're going to have a go at me. I don't blame you, but please don't shout, or my head will explode, seriously. It'll just explode," Mia assured her irate-looking boss.

Sherri took a deep breath, as though she intended to continue her tirade, but thought better of it. "Mia," she said softly, exhaling the huge breath she had already taken to propel her next accusation. This made Mia's name come out in a huffy sound. "What's going on? We're nearly at the end of the second month of appalling sales from you. And today, you turn up for work hungover and unable to work at all!

Mia leant on the desk and put her head in her hands.

"You know full well it's three strikes and you're out," Sherri continued. "Or an official written warning at the very least. Did the last two verbal warnings have no effect on you whatsoever?" Sherri folded her arms on the desk and leaned her ample bosom on them. It pushed her breasts up, and they looked as though they would pop out of her uniform with little encouragement. "Well, what have you got to say for yourself?"

Mia couldn't justify her behaviour, or maybe if she was being truthful, she didn't intend to do anything of the sort. "Look, Sherri, it's personal, okay?"

Sherri needed to be careful. Mia was a shining star in the TopTravel Group, with many regional sales awards under her belt. This sudden change in her performance began when Sherri took over as manager, so Mia's decline may reflect on her. Despite other things in play, she couldn't take the risk. She tapped her nails, which she always did when she was thinking. That was, until she saw a pained expression cross Mia's face.

This woman gives either the floor or the desk a hammering, and both do my head in.

Sherri reached her decision, and not before time, as far as Mia was concerned.

I'm about to keel over off this chair.

"I'm going to send you home," Sherri said, finally. "You shouldn't be at work under the influence of alcohol. Today will be taken off your holiday entitlement, or it'll be unpaid leave. Which do you prefer?" Sherri felt confident her decision was both fair and firm, and she was proud of herself.

"Er, I'm not sure," Mia stuttered. She wanted to say, "I don't care. Just make a bloody decision, woman, and let me get out of here."

But Sherri wanted a proper response and a formal acceptance from Mia. She could then record it officially. God, how she hated this part of her job, Sherri thought. People management sucked.

"May I remind you, Mia, that being drunk at work is usually a case of instant dismissal. I'd be within my rights to sack you immediately. But I'm giving you another chance. Well, one of many. This isn't the first time. Your past performance as a saleswoman is why you still work here."

Thankful that the course of action had been decided, Mia smiled at her boss. "Okay, fair enough, thanks. I'll take it as holiday leave," said Mia in her most grateful voice. She felt genuinely indebted to Sherri for this break, and for all the other times she had been reasonable about her erratic behaviour. Whatever it took to go home. The details didn't matter.

Trying not to look anyone in the eye as she left, Mia collected her bag and jacket, made a quick call to her dad to pick her up, and left the shop without another word. Not fit to drive, she had come to work on the bus. But now her head hurt so badly that to have inquisitive people stare at her on public transport was something she could do without. Fortunately, Oscar was already out shopping in the city, so he was happy to swing by and pick her up. Mia knew he would have made a special trip regardless, but it was less guilt-ridden for her this way.

She called in at Espressos and got a large, strong coffee to wash down her migraine tablets and boost the pain-killing action. Then sat on a bench near the agreed pick-up point. She closed her eyes against the glare of the sunlight and periodically sipped at the hot, sweet coffee. Oscar arrived and called out from the car at the kerbside. Staggering and shielding her pain-racked eyes, she climbed in beside a worried-looking Oscar. Mia buckled up with Oscar's help and then sank back against the seat, feeling relieved to be out of the sun and in the quiet of her father's car.

"You can't carry on like this, love," said Oscar eventually.

Mia didn't respond.

"I want you to sit down with your mother and me and talk about your dreams because this is all about them, isn't it?" His momentary lack of attention brought a blast of a horn from the car behind when the lights changed.

"Oh hell," Mia mumbled. "What did they have to do that for? I swear my head will crack open, and my brains will explode."

"I really wish you wouldn't be so graphic, Mia," Oscar chided. He kept his voice low, out of consideration for her delicate state.

It started raining, and Mia groaned when the wiper blades squealed back and forth. Oscar drove an old classic. It was unreliable, but he wouldn't trade it for a newer model. Unlike new cars, everything thumped and clanked; even the gears were noisy. Mia hated his treasured car as it continued its relentless noise attack on her already battered senses. She cried quietly with self-pity. The tears stung her eyes, and her head hurt even more, if that was possible.

Oscar looked at her in alarm. "Okay, Mia, you're going straight to your bed when we get back to sleep this off, and then, when you're rested, we'll talk. No arguments." He couldn't stand by any longer and watch Mia destroy herself over these wretched dreams. He had come to terms with his nightmares, and they had faded over the years. Now he must help her do the same. But his dreams had never been as bad as Mia's. He didn't feel he was actually travelling back in time, and he certainly suffered no injuries.

Mia's eyes remained squeezed closed. She wiped the tears away but said nothing. She didn't want to talk, as moving anything was too painful. Eventually, she fell asleep.

Oscar gently woke her some twenty minutes later as they arrived home. She blinked and slowly opened her red, bloodshot eyes, kissed Oscar on the cheek in gratitude and then, without a word, got out of the car and walked into the house ahead of him. Even though she should have helped with the shopping as she usually did, Mia couldn't bear the glare of the daylight any longer.

The migraine pills had eased her headache a little, so she popped in to say hello to her mum before going to bed. That proved more difficult than she expected, as she couldn't find her. Just as she was about to give up, she saw her pulling the washing off the line in the garden. Mia thought her mother spent too much time processing the washing. She was unsure why Esme was bothering today. It must already be wet as it had been raining for a while. But Esme could never leave the washing out in wet weather. Mia smiled fondly at her mother, who was busy rescuing a large bedsheet. The wind had wound it around the line, and the end was flapping furiously, but her mother was winning. Mia turned to go when she saw the mystery woman in the garden again.

Fear rose from her stomach. "Dad? You there, Dad?" Mia called out, the effort sending a bolt of pain through her head. Her eyes ached but remained locked on the woman. There was no answer. She assumed he was still bringing the shopping into the porch. Esme was ignoring the woman — that much was obvious. The woman fell to her knees and held up her arms to Esme, pleading.

Mia then realised the woman wasn't looking at her mother at all. She followed the woman's gaze and the direction of her outstretched arms. There were others at the bottom of the garden. She stared, trying to see them through the rain and her bleary eyes. A man in uniform was holding the hand of a child. Yes, she was sure it was a man and a child. She shivered involuntarily but couldn't look away. The woman on the ground was joined by another, who looked like she was trying to comfort her. Mia felt the familiar panic, but remained glued to the scene playing out in her own back garden.

Recognition hit her. The woman on her knees was Rachel, and Ariella had her arms around her. Mia's eyes stung with the effort of not blinking as she switched her gaze to the back of the child's head. She needed to know. Suddenly, the child looked back at the distraught woman. Now Mia could see his face clearly. It was the little boy from her dreams. His face was set; there seemed to be no tears. In fact, he lacked any emotion — dead to the drama of the situation.

"No, no, it can't be. Sarid, my Sarid. They're taking him!" Mia screamed and then sank to the floor, sobbing. The last thing she remembered before passing out was the worried face of Oscar and his strong arms wrapping around her trembling body.

CHAPTER 10

Oscar thought there was a distinct possibility that TopTravel wouldn't hold Mia's position open for much longer. The Branch Manager had called several times for an update on Mia's health, and Oscar struggled to give her an optimistic outlook. The calls were less frequent now, as Mia had been off sick for three weeks. She was as bad, if not worse, this time. He decided he would speak to her, despite Mia's and his wife's continued protestations. He feared Mia would be sucked into such mental anguish that she would become unreachable. Or she would suffer from malnutrition, as she often refused food and just sipped water. She seemed locked inside her head. He had heard her chanting more than once. It was as though she were trying to ward off evil spirits.

Her light was rarely off as she was fearful of the dark and falling asleep. Occasionally, sleep was unavoidable through utter exhaustion, which resulted in her waking terrified, screaming and crying. Her usually perfectly groomed hair was a matted mess on her pillows, and her expensively manicured nails were bitten down and ragged. Esme was in a terrible state about it all, so Oscar felt he needed to protect her too, now.

Esme was convinced she was drawing the apparitions into the house and onto Mia. She sat by Mia's bedside for the first two nights and soothed her when she started shouting in her sleep, but then decided she would do better to keep her distance. It made no difference to Mia's level and frequency of dreams. Oscar knew it wasn't Esme who was causing the dreams. It was him. After all, it was him and then Ruth before Mia, not Esme. It was never Esme.

"Mia, love, drink this, would you?" he asked her. "It's a little homemade broth. It'll slip down easy, love. Just drink it, please, if only for your mother and me."

"K, Dad," said Mia, her voice child-like. She pulled herself up onto her pillows. Her hair stuck out at the sides and was flat on the back of her head. Oscar could have wept seeing Mia brought so low. She was uncharacteristically meek and mild, too. He longed to see and hear the stroppy, headstrong Mia back with them. Anything but this. She refused to see any of her friends, even Lisa, who came around several times.

"I know you don't want me to talk about this, but I must."

"Dad, please; we did this before." Mia's eyes filled with tears as she begged him not to torture her further.

"No, Mia, I must. Your mother stopped me before we finished last time." He held her hand tight. "I used to have dreams, and they were upsetting, too. I need to know if you're having the same dreams. Can you tell me more? Perhaps a few more details? Then I think I could help you." This was met with more tears. Oscar was struggling now and was no longer sure what he should say. Despite being so confident initially. He found he was dumbstruck when it came to following through. Then it occurred to him. "What if I tell you about my dreams?"

Mia reluctantly agreed, but her eyes showed absolute dread at the prospect. She held the edge of the doona to her face as though it would protect her from what she didn't want to hear.

"My dreams were about a man who was a prisoner," Oscar began slowly.

Mia interrupted Oscar immediately. "No, Dad, no, that's not it. It's a woman and a child, not a man, and they're not in prison. Remember, we decided it was a concentration camp. I thought it was a prison at first," she said, hoping it would stop Oscar from saying any more. While she wanted an explanation, she also feared the possibility that Oscar's dreams were the same and somehow, in the telling, would validate her own. It was enough to be tormented by them without the possibility that they were some sort of family legacy she was destined to experience.

Oscar was torn between allowing Mia to enjoy the relief she evidently felt or pressing on. He was confident their dreams were linked. Mia leaned back against the pillows and gave a deep sigh of relief. She had finished Esme's broth and that delighted Oscar, as she had eaten nothing much for days. But he must be strong, or the dreams would continue to bring her down if she didn't get help to cope.

"The man I dreamed about was not in prison either — well, not a traditional prison." Mia's eyes darted from side to side as though this new information would cause a manifestation right there in her room. She grabbed the doona tighter for protection. "He was in a concentration camp, too," said Oscar gently, as he felt sure it would register like the crash of thunder.

"A concentration camp, like Rachel and Sarid?" Mia's eyes widened.

"Yes."

"Why, Dad, why?"

"I wish I knew, Mia. There's no sense to it."

"The people I see will be killed, won't they? Oh God, I'll be there when they die. I can't take this. I don't want to see them die. There are children, Dad, little kids. Babies. Those bloody Nazis are bastards. Utter bastards! Why isn't anyone trying to save them, Dad?" Mia was now sitting bolt upright, and hysteria had taken over.

Oscar slumped. He wasn't sleeping very well either. But he had to continue for her sake, for all their sakes. His own nightmares, the memories of which he had locked away, were creeping back into his dreams. He only saw flashes, but that's how they started before. They were pushing their way back in.

"I never understood why it happened. And not because I didn't want to. I came to terms with it all with the help of others. Your mum was never troubled by the dreams. But she saw me and someone else close to us going through all this as you are, and now she's so afraid for you. She's got the idea she's attracting the dreams."

"Why?

"Because the apparitions often appear near or around her." Oscar didn't add: and because Rachel is related to your mother.

"Dad, what happened to you?"

"Let's take it one step at a time. More importantly, I want you to know I understand, and you will get through this, just as I did." Oscar tucked the doona around Mia, laid his hand on her forehead and smiled at her, willing her to trust him and hold on.

Mia saw the pain and concern in Oscar's eyes. It frightened her, but she felt a sense of relief, knowing Oscar truly understood. She laid back against her pillows again and relaxed her exhausted body and mind as Oscar stroked her forehead. He sang a lullaby that she vaguely remembered from her childhood. She had never understood the words. It was certainly not Italian, her parents' mother tongue. But its lilting melody always soothed her as a young child. She often wished they had taught her Italian. But they were very resistant to the idea when she had raised it — particularly her mother. Mia slept untroubled by the dreams for the first time in days.

###

Esme Barone felt as if she was taking a younger version of Mia shopping. Her granddaughter seemed to have regressed. Esme was back in charge again, guiding her from shop to shop. Before the dreams, Mia had taken on the role of fashion advisor because she didn't want Esme to look frumpy and embarrass her. Now, she was nothing like her usual ebullient, confident self. There was a childlike vulnerability about her. Esme could see Mia's torment through the furtive glances and the world-weary facial expressions she wore so much these days.

Esme thought about their early trips into the city together when Mia was a child. Back then, Esme had been very protective of her. They would make a whole day of it with Mia trying on endless outfits and shoes that Esme would buy if she showed the slightest sign of liking them. She wanted Mia to have everything she wanted. She knew from experience that life and happiness were tenuous. They could be taken away so easily, as had happened to both her parents and to Oscar's. A happy and carefree life, theirs to enjoy one moment, smashed the next, ground into the dust, and them with it.

Esme had worked in the city for many years in fashion retail. Her last job before she retired was at Myers. Their daughter Ruth loved to come to the store with her dad on weekends. Esme would spend a lunch break shopping with Ruth while Oscar met friends for a coffee and a chat. Then Oscar would take Ruth to the beach, to an event in the city or to a friend's party. They would all get back home for their dinner together.

Esme had retired by the time they took charge of Mia, but she still liked the shopping trips. Occasionally, the memory of shopping with Ruth would almost overwhelm her. Still, Mia was such a happy, outgoing child; her disposition helped Esme and Oscar get over the heartbreak of losing their precious daughter.

Esme would often call into Myers to see her past colleagues, and they would make a fuss of Mia. But that was when Mia was a little girl, and most of them had long since retired. So now Esme and Mia were just another couple of customers. Life moves on, Esme thought wistfully.

She linked arms with Mia in a companionable way and felt her granddaughter's body tense and then tremble on what was a gloriously sunny day. It made Esme angry that her once carefree Mia was now living in fear. Esme didn't react outwardly, but she cried, yelled, and screamed deep inside. Why Mia? Why couldn't she be left in peace? This had nothing to do with her? She and Oscar paid a high personal price for their life and freedom in

Australia. Then they had to face the tragedy of losing their own daughter to the dreams when Mia was just a baby. But the past seemed relentless in its pursuit of them, and Esme was unsure why.

Suddenly Mia cringed and increased her pace, glancing fearfully toward a shop they passed with a gloomy window display. Aptly named 'Times Gone By', the dark colours and sepia prints were a perfect setting for the antiques and memorabilia on sale. But to Mia, it was threatening and potentially a portal back to her dreaded dreams.

Esme immediately chatted about the first things that came into her head to distract Mia. "Shall we go for a coffee, just to warm up a bit before hitting the shops? You must help me find a pair of shoes for our neighbour's wedding. My outfit will be a light blue, so I think navy would be ideal. Alma suggested yellow shoes and a handbag to match, but I think I'd look like an IKEA advert, don't you?" Esme laughed without joy.

"I dunno, Mum. I can't think about shopping right now. Not sure why I came, really." Mia gave Esme a weak smile. Suddenly, Mia jolted Esme's arm. "Oh no, there's Lucas from work." Mia quickly steered Esme down a side street. "I don't want to see anyone, Mum. He's on the coffee run."

Esme glanced back at Lucas, who had raised his hand in greeting and was smiling enthusiastically. But he then dropped his arm and smile after being snubbed. Esme was in no doubt he would return to work and tell them he saw a pale-looking version of Mia clinging onto her arm. TopTravel was still prepared to keep Mia's position open at the moment. Still, Esme wondered how long it would last with reports being received about such incidents. Mia had been diagnosed with stress-related exhaustion. Well, she was stressed and exhausted, so it was appropriate. Of course, it wasn't the entire story.

Oscar called into the doctor's surgery to pick up Mia's sick note extension and asked if he could refer her for therapy. He explained briefly, and the doctor was sympathetic. However, he wasn't prepared to do a referral without seeing Mia himself. Mia had insisted she was not sick, so seeing a doctor was ridiculous. "What will he give me?" she said cynically when Oscar raised the subject again. "Anti-nightmare pills?"

Mia's back ached, and her head hurt unbearably. Maybe she should see the doctor if only to get something for her aches and pains. She turned in bed, reached for the bedside lamp, and found nothing. Opening her eyes, she still couldn't see anything. When she groped further, she found a head lying alongside her. Momentarily confused, she stared into the darkness, felt the head some more, and then a face. The little face of her son.

"*Mamma, mamma, coccolami.* (Mummy, Mummy, cuddle me.)"

Mia pulled her son close to her and hugged him tightly. He was shivering. She reached for the doona to wrap it around him. There was no doona; there were no bedclothes. Mia buried her face in her son's hair and kissed him repeatedly. "*Dormi, il mio bambino, dormi e non temere. Mamma è qui. Mamma è qui.* (Sleep, my baby, sleep and do not be frightened. Mummy is here. Mummy is here.)"

A siren wailed, causing sudden activity around Mia and her son; feet hit the floor, and urgent cries rang out to hurry. In the dark, a woman stifled a cry of pain as others coughed and wheezed. Mia nudged her son gently and urged him to be quick. "*Presto. Torna tuoi alloggi.* (Quickly, back to your quarters.)" Mia snatched Sarid's hand and rushed to the back of the hut, where she pushed a panel aside underneath a bunk bed, pulled herself under the bed, and dropped outside. Sarid followed. She gently lifted him down, kissing him again as he came level with her. Another mother, Rebekah, followed her with her son, Dieter. They exchanged a nervous smile before inching forwards on their bellies to the edge of the hut. There was only just enough space between the hut and the ground, so their clothing was filthy. Running inmates sped past them as they waited for the right time to show themselves. Everyone was heading for the parade ground.

The two women ran from hut to hut, lost in the hubbub. Dust rose into the air with every footfall, coating their legs and making the boys cough. Sarid and Dieter moved as one with their mothers, with skills gained from practice. The hope was they wouldn't be identified as individuals by some eagle-eyed sentry. Once they arrived at the furthest reaches of the camp, Rachel and Rebekah hid behind a hut. They shooed the children off to join others in the relative safety of Hut 66. Even though they were exhausted, the women needed to run back as fast as possible to join the others for the morning inspection and roll call on the parade ground. Mia jarred her back just as they came to a halt. The pain was intense. It took all her willpower not to show it.

"Argh."

"Are you alright?"

"Shh, don't draw attention to us."

"Mia?"

Mia ignored the pain. She mustn't look unwell. So, she stood to attention and pushed her shoulders back to ensure she looked ready and willing to work.

"Mia, speak to me. Mia?"

"He's safe. That's all that matters," Mia whispered. "I have to see him occasionally, or my heart aches to hold him."

"Mia, who is safe?"

"Sarid. He's back in Hut 66 next to the hospital block. The Germans don't go there because of the risk of disease. They have a little room for the kids. They'll take care of him there. Those men and women are saints, heroes; the kids even get extra food." She smiled. "One day, I'll repay them a thousand-fold." Mia was still whispering, so the guards couldn't hear her.

Oscar held Mia's hand as tears coursed down his cheeks. He couldn't reach her.

CHAPTER 11

Lisa was nervous about seeing her friend. Mia's mum told her bits and pieces about what was going on. Instead of making it more likely that she wanted to help, it made her want to back off. Mia was really weird now and insisted her dreams were real life and she needed to act on them. They were messages from beyond, she said, or something equally strange. Her parents told Lisa they wanted Mia to get back to her real life in the present day and not dwell on the nightmares. If the truth was told, Lisa was spooked by it, but Mia's mum pleaded with her to pop in and stay for dinner. Mrs Barone was an incredible cook, so that was no problem, but facing an odd-acting Mia would be a lot harder.

"Just act yourself," whispered Mia's dad as he took Lisa's coat in the hall. He gave her a beaming smile and an encouraging nod towards the lounge.

"Hi Mia, how's it going?" Lisa stammered, flicking back her hair.

Mia looked up at her friend, who was all smiles and fresh from the world outside. She gave her an uncertain smile, making Lisa want to run straight back out of the house. Mia was slouched against a pile of cushions, covered with a blanket. She looked very sick, like an ailing elderly person, with her dull hair, dark shadows around her eyes and no makeup. Unheard of for Mia. Lisa didn't know what to say. It was like meeting a stranger. It certainly wasn't the Mia she grew up with and had fun with. This had to be her older, unattractive sister.

"It's okay, Lise. You don't have to stay. I know I look like a weirdo. To be honest, I think I'm well on my way to the local loony bin. Mum and Dad mean well, but you're okay to leave." Mia spoke with resignation and exhaustion.

As Lisa looked anxiously from one parent to the other, both smiled reassuringly. She felt trapped, as they were lovely people, if a little overprotective of Mia. Lisa didn't want to be a part of this charade, but before she could say she couldn't stay much longer, a glass of orange juice was thrust into her hand. "No, Mia, I wanted to see you," she said haltingly. "All the gang are asking after you. When are you coming out?" Lisa felt better once she started talking and sat on the chair next to a disinterested Mia.

Her inane chatter was music to the ears of Oscar and Esme; it usually drove them mad, but not today.

"You ought to see what Mandy looks like with her new hairdo. My God, Mia, she's such a mess. It's bright red. Can you believe that? Red frizzy hair on a skinny girl." Lisa chuckled. "She looks like a crazy matchstick. Seriously, it's hilarious." Lisa laughed.

Mia just looked at her passively.

Realising she was getting no feedback, Lisa looked around, fell quiet, and fidgeted with her bag.

"Is that Mandy Warton?" said Oscar, trying to keep the momentum going. He wouldn't have dreamed of joining their conversations in the past.

Faced with a silent Mia, Lisa looked stumped. Mia even closed her eyes and sighed while Lisa was still talking and looked like she was falling asleep. "Yeah, yeah," said Lisa, unsure of how to respond to the situation. She wasn't used to talking to Mia's parents and was sure they weren't the least bit interested in Mandy's red hair, but then — looking back at her friend — neither was Mia.

Lisa and Oscar continued to talk about anything they could think of to fill the silent void. It was uncomfortable for them both. Esme had left them to attend to the meal. She wasn't much help when she was in the room, anyway.

Moments later, Esme put her head around the door and breezily called them through for dinner. Thank goodness, Oscar thought. Lisa looked at her friend, then fled to the dining room with relief written all over her pretty, if heavily made-up face. Oscar helped Mia to her feet and held her in his arms. "Love, make a bit of effort. The poor girl is struggling."

"Sorry, Dad, I can't. I know I said I'd try. I was really looking forward to seeing her, but I don't know how anymore. She's just a juvenile airhead who loves to tittle-tattle. Why couldn't I see that before?"

"Shh, she'll hear you, Mia. Let's talk about it after, but try to be pleasant over dinner. She's your best friend, after all." Oscar could see the radical change in Mia. It was like talking to an older person, not Mia, who — just like her friend — had definitely been someone you could call an airhead before all this happened.

"Okay, Dad, I'll really try. But, as you say, she's my best friend, and she'll probably see straight through it." Mia leaned on Oscar for support and kissed his cheek lightly. Oscar felt his heart wrench at the tender moment. If wishing and praying could spirit all this away, the hours on his knees begging God for mercy would have long since released Mia from this torment.

Mia and Lisa sat in silence while Esme and Oscar chattered to fill the gaping chasm between the two friends. Mia's parents had watched the girls grow up together and become as close as any sisters. They shared everything, had the inevitable rows, and made up with the same fervour that two people who truly cared about each other did. They looked very different, however. Mia was very dark with olive skin, and Lisa was fair-skinned with blonde hair, although initially, it was a mousy blonde. Lately, peroxide had taken care of any less than blonde strands.

Mia ate steadily with her head bent over her plate until every morsel was gone and then took a piece of bread and wiped the plate until it was thoroughly clean. Lisa picked at her food and swallowed a couple of mouthfuls. She furtively glanced at Mia from time to time, as she had never witnessed her eating with such gusto. Mia seemed oblivious of her fellow diners until she had finished.

"More wine, Mia?" said Oscar with the same fake smile he had worn since Lisa's arrival.

"Yes, thanks, Dad," Mia replied, holding out the glass she had slurped from throughout her eating marathon to help push the food down. Mia glanced surreptitiously about the table and noticed they were all looking at her.

"What?"

Esme immediately broke into a smile and said something about the dessert. Lisa dropped her head to stare at her plate, where she had pushed the food from one place to another.

"It's good to see you eat so well, Mia," said Oscar.

Mia gave her dad a winsome smile.

"You going to eat that, Lisa?" said Mia, pointing her knife at Lisa's plate.

"She doesn't have to finish it, said Esme, disappointed with Mia's aggression. Here, let me take your plate, Lisa. Do you have room for dessert?"

"She can't want, or should I say, need, dessert if she can't finish what's in front of her," Mia muttered.

Lisa's eyes filled with tears. She would have eaten a little more, but when she was upset, she couldn't eat. "Sorry, Mrs Barone, it was delicious, but I'm not very hungry now." She sniffed.

"That's alright, love. Don't——"

"No, it's not alright," Mia cut in. "If you had no intention of eating your food, why did you say yes to more meat? And what was all that pushing the food around your plate about? Such a waste of good food. I hope you're not going to throw it away, Mum. Lisa can take it away with her and eat it later, when she's hungry, whenever that's likely to be," she added, piling her words with sarcasm.

"Mia, that's enough," said Oscar, kicking his chair back suddenly and standing up. "Lisa's our guest."

Mia jumped at the unexpected movement, but was undeterred. "Well, you're right there; it's enough," stormed Mia.

"She doesn't get dessert, as she didn't finish her food. There are starving people out there."

Oscar and Esme glanced at each other. Mia was parroting them with her reference to starving people. She had never paid attention to such things before. They both realised that her experiences in the concentration camp, where she witnessed starvation daily, had made her acutely aware of the value of food.

Lisa got to her feet, tears streaming down her cheeks. "Thanks for having me for dinner, but I must go now." Her breath caught in her throat.

"Huh," said Mia. "Got important things to do, like paint your nails?"

"Mia, that's bad-mannered, and you know it is," said Esme.

Esme and Oscar walked with Lisa into the hall with their arms around her shoulders. They ignored Mia and shut the dining-room door.

"We're so sorry, Lisa. We thought your visit would help Mia, but you've just been abused," said Oscar.

"Yes," agreed Esme. "But please, please don't judge her too harshly. She's not well. We're going to get her some help. Shall we let you know how it goes?" Lisa didn't answer.

"Thanks so much for coming, Lisa," said Oscar, desperately hoping it wasn't the last time they would see her. Lisa and Mia's other friends were a lifeline, Mia's way back to normality. But at that moment, he was sure that Lisa didn't give a damn about how Mia's treatment went, and who could blame her?

"Thanks for dinner," she said and dashed out without another word as she dabbed her eyes.

"Well, that went well, didn't it?" Oscar sighed. "She has to meet the relatives, Esme. It's the only way."

"Don't keep bringing that up as though it's an answer to everything.

"It's the answer for Mia."

"We can get professional help to get her through it. Our relatives will make matters worse," Esme hissed. "What effect do you think it'll have if she knows the unspeakable truth of our family's past, the torture, degradation, and murder? We've spent her whole life shielding her from those horrors. Now you propose we let her have all the gory details."

"We kept it all from her mother, too. That didn't end well, did it?" said Oscar.

"Shh. For pity's sake, be quiet. You keep referring to Ruth. Mia will hear you."

"I'm whispering, Esme, so that's unlikely. But to be honest, she needs to know about her mother and her other relatives and our past. Her fear is fed by her lack of understanding. Can't you see that?"

"I won't allow it. No."

Oscar wanted to raise his voice and shout at his stubborn wife, but Mia would hear. "I'll give it two more weeks, tops, Esme, and if there isn't a marked change after treatment, I'll speak to her myself and ask the relatives to come and see her. I think it's the kindest thing to do. Look at her, for God's sake. I'll not listen to any further arguments on the matter."

Esme huffed with annoyance.
"The clock is ticking, Esme. Two weeks and that's it."

CHAPTER 12

Mia sat with her eyes firmly fixed on her lap and fiddled with her fingers. The therapist, Jonathon Weaks, positioned himself behind his desk and waited. Esme looked at her watch and worried the session would be over before it began. She coughed, hoping it would trigger something, anything. Then she sighed, realising it made no difference.

"Would you like to start the session, Mia?" the therapist offered again.

"I think my parents have already told you what's going on."

"They said you have nasty dreams."

"Yes."

"And how can I help you, Mia?"

"Well, you're the expert. You tell me. I have dreams, and I want them to stop."

"Mia, be a bit more cooperative, please," said Esme.

"Mum, this won't help. He treats nut jobs, and I'm not crazy."

"Perhaps you could give me a chance, Mia. What are the dreams like?"

Mia took a deep breath. Rolled her eyes and sat forward, staring at the therapist. "Nasty, horrible, dangerous, threatening and bloody scary — how's that for a list?" She then sat back in her chair and closed her eyes.

Esme took a breath to speak, but the therapist held up his hand to stop her — smiling to show no offence.

"Are you in one location or multiple?"

At first, Mia did not respond but then answered as though she was bored. "A couple of other locations to start, but now just a Nazi death camp." Her eyes flew wide open, and she smiled. "Crazy, huh?"

"She comes back to us with cuts and bruises, and is often filthy."

Jonathon was shocked, but managed not to show it. The parents were obviously encouraging Mia to believe in the reality of the nightmares.

"Thanks, Mrs Barone, but it's probably best if Mia tells me in her own words."

"Yes, so you can hear from the lunatic herself," said Mia.

"I'm going to wait outside," said Esme. "Maybe it's better if I'm not in the room." Mia looked up and gave Esme a pained expression.

"What, Mia? Do you want me to stay?" No answer. Mia just dropped her head again. Esme left the room.

"Your parents are extremely worried about you, Mia. Perhaps you owe it to them to at least speak to me. They're paying for these sessions." Jonathon was a man in his forties, intelligent and smartly dressed. He was an experienced therapist and had dealt with people like Mia before. They also believed in the reality of their dreams. He was a patient and empathetic person, but could be stern when the situation required it.

"Money doesn't matter. Nothing like that matters. In reality, material things are unimportant," said Mia.

"Perhaps if it was your money, you could say that."

"I didn't ask them to bring me here. I *am* an adult."

"Try acting like one, Mia, and give this a shot."

Mia looked at the therapist with undisguised mistrust. "What do you know? I mean, really know? Have you any idea what I'm going through? What I'm putting my parents through? Have you? No, you've no idea. You're the man who supposedly has all the answers. But you learned those at university, not by going through anything yourself. So, you only have an academic understanding."

"Well, you've judged and condemned me before finding out anything about me. But I know what's been happening to you because your parents informed me. However, what they can't do is tell me the details; only you can do that."

"What? So you can get me banged up in a loony bin and throw away the key?"

"I'm not in the habit of getting my patients banged up in loony bins," he said calmly.

Despite herself, Mia laughed. Dry and without humour.

"So, tell me in your own words, what's happening?"

"There's little point in going over things my parents have told you. You know I'm having nightmares, they're becoming more frequent, and I can smell, touch and feel things during them."

"Smell?"

"Yes, I can smell during my dreams, and it isn't pleasant, let me tell you."

"A concentration camp?"

"Yes, I think it is."

"Is it the smell that's particularly bothering you?"

"Well, I detest awful smells, but it's hardly the main point?"

"Is it possible that elements of your dreams are excerpts from a film you've seen or from a book?"

"What?" Mia was annoyed. "No. I've never read a book or seen a film like it. Look, this is more than dreams or nightmares. This is a reality for me. I go there. It's so strong that I could even sense my little boy in my bedroom when I woke up."

"Your little boy? I wasn't aware you had a child. Your parents didn't mention this."

"I don't have a child in this world, but I do in that world." Mia became more agitated with the line of questioning. Not to mention the way the therapist kept repeating things. This man was humouring her, probably laughing at her.

"Mia, could you go through one dream for me, from start to finish, giving me as much detail as you can? Choose the more frequent dream."

"The dreams are not repetitive. Their lives in the camp move on each time I visit. That's one reason it's so frightening. It's leading to a tragic end. Something will happen to my son and me; I know it will."

"Shall we go for the latest instalment then?"

Mia hesitated. She didn't like the word instalment either; it smacked of a reference to a story, film, something that wasn't real. She sat hunched in her chair, looking at her hands as she twisted a disintegrating tissue repeatedly.

"Mia?"

"Look, this isn't a story or the re-run of a film. I don't want to be patronised."

"That's not what's happening here. If I'm using the wrong words, I apologise. But I'm trying to help you."

Moments passed in silence. Then Mia uttered a barely audible "ok" and, after drawing a deep breath, talked about one of her experiences. She explained how she felt, including the all-pervading cold and her state of weakness, that she could speak and understand other languages and experienced the cruelty exacted against her and others. The therapist sat and listened patiently, interjecting to encourage Mia to continue when she faltered. When Mia finished, she was sweating, crying, and shaking.

Handing her more tissues, the therapist waited until Mia gained a measure of control before proceeding with his summing-up of his thoughts about the session. "I think you experience lucid dreams with false awakenings. Some people call them night terrors. But I can assure you, Mia, you don't actually go to that place."

"Okay, so how do you explain the dirt under my nails and the injuries?"

"I can't explain the dirt, but you said you thrash about in your dreams, which could cause bruising."

"And the tattooed number on my arm that fades as I come out of the dream?"

"Hallucination, I should think. Has anyone else seen this number?"

"I said it fades."

"Mia, would you mind if I did a small relaxation exercise with you?"

"Just to relax me? Nothing else?"

"Yes, you'll then be able to rationalise this experience more readily in a more relaxed state."

Mia agreed with a nod.

In the reception area, Esme was finishing her coffee when she heard Mia scream. She rushed into the therapist's office and found Mia weeping.

Jonathon was pleased to see Esme. It was wiser to let her be the one to comfort Mia. He had made that mistake before. His heart went out to a patient, allowing a young woman to fall into his arms, weeping. The patient's instability and subsequent misinterpretation of his actions, deliberate in his view, resulted in her accusing him of being over-friendly. She even suggested he had a hard-on when he hugged her. The inquiry that followed was lengthy and worrying. At one point, he thought he may lose his licence. He wasn't about to make the same mistake again. Because he really felt sorry for this young woman, too. But he was no longer young and impulsive where his work was concerned.

"Oh Mia, love, are you alright?" Esme was distressed to see Mia in such a state.

"The bastard took me back to that place. Huge dogs chased us, and one of them bit Sarid."

"Please, Mia, there's no need to swear," said Esme.

"A dog bites my son, and I should be cool about it?"

"It would have happened, anyway," said Esme. "Even if you were not there to see it, Mia. The dreams are about the past.

Everything you experience has already happened, and you're just a witness."

Again, the mother's comment made it clear to Jonathon that the parents endorsed Mia's belief in the reality of the dreams. It wasn't helpful.

"*Not* a witness, Mum. I don't *just* witness these events. I'm *part* of it. I *experience* them.

"I'm sorry, Mia," said Jonathon. "It was not my intention for you to dream. I just wanted to help you relax a little."

"Well, that's what happened. Have you listened to nothing I've said? I told you when I sleep, I get taken back there. What did you think would happen?"

"Every time you sleep?"

"No, not every time," Mia had to admit.

"The good news is: I *can* help. But I think that's enough for today. The main thing is we've made progress."

Esme looked at the therapist in disbelief. "Progress? Look at her."

Jonathon smiled reassuringly and advised Esme that genuine progress had been achieved, despite Mia's current state. He explained that recalling such frightening events was bound to be upsetting. Esme wrapped her arms around Mia and rocked her as you would a child.

The therapist left the room momentarily. He found Mia almost asleep when he returned, enclosed in Esme's arms. "Mrs Barone, I'll prescribe Mia a mild sedative, but I think we can deal with this further through therapy. Please see my receptionist on your way out to make another appointment. I recommend one week from now."

Esme agreed, and he handed her the prescription. Mia stirred and shivered, so Esme put her coat around her shoulders and held her close again.

"Now, don't worry, Mia, this isn't an uncommon phenomenon," said Jonathon confidently. "I can help you with this. I've prescribed a sedative that'll help you sleep. I also need you to be a little calmer at our next session, so take one tablet two hours before you set off. You'll need to be driven here, and you mustn't drive at other times when you're taking the tablets. Thank you for sharing your experiences with me, and I'll see you in a week."

Sheepishly, Mia nodded in acknowledgement, embarrassed by her lack of control. She hated being so helpless and needy, but she was, and she had to accept that. Her appearance was dreadful. She had her hair tucked tight behind her ears, and she knew how swollen and red her eyes must look. She hoped this was the lifeline that would rescue her from the purgatory that was now hers.

PART TWO

Our immortality comes through our children and their children. Through our roots and branches. The family is immortality. And Hitler has destroyed not just branches and roots, but entire family trees, forests. All of them, gone.
Amy Harmon, *Sand and Ash*

Seventy-six years after seeing her mother gunned down by the Nazis, Hannah says she finds the concept of forgiveness difficult. 'I'm not empowered to forgive for the people they murdered. I don't speak for them. I don't have forgiveness because for the life of me, I can't understand why we were selected. I don't have forgiveness, but I have acceptance. I can't change it. Hannah Lewis, Holocaust survivor

CHAPTER 13

Go Ballistic had another record number of players booked in for the weekend, and Mia was genuinely pleased for Vince. They had made up after their recent fallout. Susan was still playing the role of Puma Princess — with Mia's reluctant approval. She didn't want Susan at Go Ballistic at all, but she didn't feel up to getting back into her suit yet. She blamed the lack of energy and enthusiasm on the sedatives. But being back at Go Ballistic felt good, even though Mia was relieved to be off work for another two weeks. It made her feel more like her old self. The staff at the paintball site were lovely, too: tough paintballers who gave out hugs and made her sweet cups of tea. Mia was genuinely touched by it all. She felt a little guilty, too, as she had often been a total bitch when dealing with them previously. Susan seriously annoyed her, probably because she was infatuated with Vince and made no secret of it. It threatened Mia's position as Puma Princess and as his girlfriend. She was acting a bit too cocky for Mia's liking. She had even made a snide remark about Mia not being fit enough to go back to work, but could still make it to Go Ballistic at the weekends. It wasn't said to her face — one of the other Pumas passed it on. She told herself that Susan had another thought coming if she believed she held the hearts and minds of the Puma troupe, even if she was her stand-in. One word from Mia, and they knew they would be out on their ears. It was well known that there was a long waiting list to become a Puma. Yet, Mia felt sure that Vince must have given

Susan enough encouragement to make her confident in slagging Mia off. She would watch the performance today and see if she had anything to worry about.

Mia tucked herself in behind a hoarding as the performance in the stadium began. Vince made a show of giving Mia a long, sexy kiss before he went in. Much to Mia's delight, Susan saw it. But was Vince two-timing her? Because Susan looked devastated. Perhaps Susan was kidding herself, but Mia wanted to know for sure. The day was overcast, and with dry ice swirling around the front of the arena, it took on a menacing atmosphere. Mia observed both of their faces. Vince seemed to ignore Susan at first, but then as she bounced over to him, like the good little Puma she was, his eyes lingered a bit too long on her crouched body. Susan then raised her eyes as though sensing it and gave him a long and significant look.

She bloody knows I'm watching, and that bastard's definitely two-timing me.

Yes, she decided, Vince was lost to her. The kiss was just an act to placate his nutty ex-girlfriend. As the last part of the routine came to a close, Vince stepped forward and shouted to the players, 'Name your teams.' This was new. She kept her eyes fixed on Susan, who, along with the troupe, collected her team from the stadium. A great addition to the performance, this, Mia had to agree. One after the other, the teams stood and shouted their names. "The Untouchables," one group yelled. A Puma rushed to their side and held their captain's hand aloft. There were cheers and a few boos. "The Hustlers," another team shouted. The Nasties, The Killers, The Barbarians and The

Spartans were named, cheered and allocated a Puma. They then followed their Pumas out of the stadium to loud marching music.

Susan was last and flicked her tail at Vince as she led The Barbarians out and towards the safe area. Vince responded by winking and watching Susan as she left the arena. Susan turned her head, smiled, and blew him a kiss. Mia put her head in her hands and cried.

As the last team to leave the arena, Susan's group was delayed reaching the safe area. She led them to a piece of rough ground to mess around with their empty guns to fill time. Susan continued to perform, enjoying the attention as she adopted her various poses. The paintballers cheered and egged her on, shouting and cheering and playing at mock battles. Susan giggled as she lapped it all up. As Mia watched her rival, she became more incensed with every passing minute. First, the flirting in the arena, and now this. *She's taunting me.* Mia's head ached, and her eyes streamed with red hot tears until she could barely see. Something snapped deep within her mind. Running to the safe area, Mia pushed her way to the front of the queue for paintballs, grabbed a gun, and filled it. The marshals were taken aback, but as it was Mia, they did nothing. Mia strode back to Susan and her team, pulling her mask down over her face as she moved.

"Bastards!" she screamed and pulled her gun up, ready to fire. Shoshana was right there laughing and joking with those Nazi bastards. She would show them.

Terrified, Susan pulled down her mask after shouting at the paintballers to do the same. They all turned their backs to Mia and crouched down defensively. With no ammo, they couldn't retaliate other than to yell and curse the mad woman who sprayed them with paint. Mia knew she must act fast before they opened fire on her. The paintballs hammered into the crouching players as Mia shot them repeatedly at point-blank range. Screaming, "you bastards" and "you bitch, die!" Mia was oblivious to the protestations and swearing from her victims and the shouts from the soldiers closing in on her. She made sure she shot more into Shoshana than the others. She hated her more than these killers. The bitch wouldn't think twice about betraying anyone in the camp to save her skin.

"Christ, she's gone crazy. Keep your masks down and turn away from the mad bitch," Susan shouted.

"Bitch, am I? Well, from one bitch to another, take that. Die, die, die."

Mia swung around and saw the commandant running towards her. She swung her gun towards him. "Take that, you murdering rapist!"

"What the fuck?" Vince yelled.

"This is for Augustyna, you animal!"

Susan screamed as Mia turned her gun on her again. Gasping from the pain, she yelled, "Vince, can't you stop her? It bloody hurts at this range."

Vince pulled his mask down and ran at Mia, and grabbed her. "I've got her, sweetie," he yelled. "Someone, anyone, get her legs, or she'll kick me to pieces. And for God's sake, call the cops."

"Already called 'em, Vince, a marshal replied. "And the ambulance. She needs help."

Mia's gun was snatched away, and the cowering paintballers got to their feet.

"Let me go, you cowards." Mia then turned and snarled at Susan. "And you'll get your comeuppance, you simpering bitch."

"Come on, Mia, give it a rest," said Vince, struggling to hold on to a very determined Mia.

"I fucking hate you, you and your sort. Hitler loses, you know. You're all going to die."

"Hitler?"

Mia kicked Vince as he wrestled her to the ground.

"Mia, just hold still. You're sick. The medics are on their way."

"Let go of me, you bastard! I know what your medics do." Mia kicked and screamed.

"Help me hold her. Be careful. Don't hurt her. She's not well," said Vince.

"They're here," said Susan. "Paramedics too." Mia glared at her, and Susan backed off, frightened by the manic look in Mia's eyes.

As the police took over and Mia was released, she immediately started fighting, scratching, and screaming until someone slapped her across the face. Defeated and spent, Mia collapsed in a heap on the ground.

"I got them. I got them," she whimpered. "You can do what you like to me now. They've paid.

At the far end of the camp, several women were being led away. "No, don't take them; it was me. I did it. Please listen." Mia stretched her hand out towards the women and beseeched the guards to release them. But it was pointless. They disappeared from view.

No one came back from the other side of the bridge. Mia knew that. She saw the resignation in the women's slumped shoulders and hanging heads. They painted a picture of hopeless acceptance of what they knew was inevitable.

Someone was pulling her to her feet. She accepted their help, feeling unable to fight further. "The short walk to eternity. Oh no, please no! I failed them . . . I failed. Oh God, I failed!" She felt herself being lifted. She tried to escape, but where? There was nowhere to run. Then a sharp stab in her arm and darkness enveloped her.

CHAPTER 14

Esme was delighted. "The therapist is still confident he can help her." She kept repeating this as though doing so made it true.

But Oscar was not convinced at all. He continued to tend his plants in the greenhouse while his wife chatted happily at the door.

"You're forgetting about the episode at the paintball site."

"Oh, that was just a blip. Susan upset Mia by flirting with Vince."

"It's a waste of time and money. Don't you remember, Esme, how I reacted to therapy?" he said. He wished his wife would see sense and not throw good money after bad in the vain hope it would actually help.

"You were unwilling to see it through, Oscar."

"Because it made it worse. It's opened up the portals to the nightmares and made them even stronger. Just like it has for Mia."

"You were different, Oscar, and you know that. To begin with, you were older, more entrenched in your thinking. Anyway, it was many years ago. Things have advanced since then."

Oscar looked at his wife and raised his eyebrows in response. "So, you think she's getting better? Does she look better to you? Didn't the incident at the paintball site make you doubt the value of what you're doing?"

"Oscar, don't stare at me like that. There's been an improvement. She hasn't had one episode for a week now. You were stubborn, Oscar. Remember, I was there."

"She could see how upset we were after the paintball incident," said Oscar. "So, she's probably trying to avoid saying anything. She's also sedated most of the time."

"You're determined to be negative about the therapy."

"Because it didn't help me, and my dreams were nowhere near as bad as Mia's," said Oscar. "And what's the value of delaying the meeting with the relatives? Mia knows most of the facts, anyway. They'll just fill in the gaps. Make sense of it for her."

"Knows everything? Everything?" Esme raised her voice. "Are you insane?" Oscar had angered her now, just when she had started to feel more upbeat and optimistic. "Do you want to risk her knowing all the details, every rotten, life-destroying detail? Because I don't. If only I had insisted that Ruth see a therapist, our daughter might still be with us today."

Oscar fell silent, finished potting his herbs, and brushed his hands on his overalls. Then he stood facing her. "I think we'll live to regret this delay. Talking to our relatives helped me enormously," he said. "They are better than any therapist because they have first-hand experience or, at the very least, relatives that died in the Holocaust."

"Well, we do too. What makes them better than us at helping her?"

"Because they helped me. That's why."

"That makes little sense," said Esme.

"You've got one more week, Esme, and that's an end to it. No more therapy, and Mia meets her extended family."

"Oscar, look at the mess on the floor?" said Esme, deliberately ignoring Oscar's threat.

Oscar did not react, but allowed his wife to change the subject. There was little value in pursuing the matter further. Esme would see the treatment through to the end of the deadline and keep hoping she was right. But she wasn't blind; stubborn, yes, but not blind. He was sure she must have her doubts now. "Esme, we agreed! This is my greenhouse and greenhouses get dirty. No, please. Don't start sweeping. Leave me one place I can treat as I wish."

"Okay. Alright, but don't ask me to tidy it up later."

"I won't," he said, smiling at his wife.

Esme continued to wax lyrical about the success of the therapy and, despite her promise, lined up a few pots in a more orderly fashion. He sighed. He knew she did it automatically and wasn't trying to be awkward, but he removed some seed packets from her hand. He knew they were about to be tidied away, too. Oscar was convinced Esme was in denial because she desperately wanted the therapy to work. But what puzzled him was that she knew it had made him much worse. Only when he faced the demons, assisted by relatives who understood what he was going through, did the nightmares reduce and then stop. He brushed the potting compost from the sides of the newly planted pots and placed them in the sun on the patio. Esme trailed behind him, chatting and pointing out new blooms in the garden.

Oscar broke into her conversation. "Where's Mia, Esme?"

Esme looked up at Mia's bedroom. The curtains and windows were closed. "We won't disturb her if you keep your voice down, Oscar."

Oscar laughed the deep, throaty laugh of a big man. "As I've hardly said a word compared to you, Esme, I think you should take that advice." Before his wife could object to his sarcasm, Oscar suggested they take a cup of tea to the summerhouse and talk about other things. Their lives had narrowed down so much since Mia's nightmares. They rarely did or talked about anything else. They kept telling Mia to get back to her everyday life. Maybe it would help if they did, too.

Esme huffed with irritation at being effectively silenced, but she agreed to a change of location for their chat and went to get the tea. Oscar looked up at Mia's window as he caught a movement. Mia's gaunt, pale face gave him a lukewarm smile as she opened her curtains. He waved and got another hesitant smile before she moved back into the room. If this was the outcome of her therapy, he would not allow it to continue. Mia seemed to be sinking deeper and deeper into herself. Despite his wife's enthusiasm and the therapist's assurances, he couldn't see any discernible improvement.

Esme reappeared with a tray of tea and biscuits and headed down the garden. She tipped her head towards the summerhouse in a gesture of invitation. Oscar obediently followed, leaving his beloved gardening. He thought it was best to get Esme in a reasonable frame of mind before he insisted on ending the therapy after seeing Mia at the window. Now, he was not prepared to wait — not even a week.

The late afternoon winter sun was shining brightly and flooding the summerhouse with light and a little warmth. This was one of their favourite spots in the garden. They spent many occasions with a cup of tea, soaking up the beauty of the garden; they often took a glass of wine and a light supper out there on warm summer evenings. Fixed to the outside of the summerhouse were hanging baskets and troughs of assorted geraniums. They were an easy and colourful choice, and the profusion of flowers reminded him of the chalet in Alto Adige, where he spent many childhood holidays. The perfume from the many and varied flowers was intoxicating in the spring and summer, attracting the bees and butterflies. Oscar's garden displays were impressive even in the winter, so there was always something to feast their senses on. During the colder months, this was still their preferred place to relax, where they could be rugged up against the autumn and winter chill and 'chew the fat', as Esme called it.

Besides being a haven for Esme and Oscar, the garden had a special significance for him. He had been a gardener at Perth's world-famous Kings Park for thirty-five years. After his retirement, he put all his energy and knowledge into their own garden. He was sure it added value to the property or, at the very least, gave it a fall-in-love factor. He felt people underestimated the importance of a well-maintained garden. His mum used to say that you could tell the state of mind of the inhabitants of a house by how tidy their front garden was. Oscar had never forgotten that, and thanks to him their front garden was always immaculate. He would have loved a visit from his parents to his Australian home and garden, but it would never happen. The Holocaust had taken care of that.

Their neighbours undoubtedly thought they were slightly unhinged, sitting outside as often as they did, especially on wintry days, with a mug of something hot clasped between their icy fingers. Mulled wine was another favourite when there was a nip in the air, and Esme liked a hot whisky. It looked a bit crazy, Oscar admitted to himself. After all, they had a perfectly comfortable, warm house and even a big conservatory, yet they huddled in the summerhouse with coats on and rugs over their knees. It made them feel more in touch with nature and the reality of life. It was always a good place to sort things, too. When Ruth was little, she would join them after racing around the garden or trying to help (but usually causing more work). It was the same with Mia. The thought of his beautiful daughter taking her own life because of the dreams brought on a wave of familiar sadness. But she had left them a beautiful gift of her own daughter. In a twist of fate, her daughter was also being driven to distraction by the same dreams. Tears sprung to his eyes. Would the sadness ever go, he wondered.

Mia differed from her mother, Ruth, in many respects. They were both so alike when they were young, Oscar mused. They were full of unbridled enthusiasm and vitality, which they carried into their adult years. However, Ruth had been a practical and down-to-earth girl. In contrast, Mia was a superficial young woman before she became haunted by the same dreams as her mother. They overindulged Mia, but they couldn't help themselves. She was a gift from a heartbreak that should never have happened, and so she was incredibly precious to them. As a result, they couldn't bring themselves to exert much discipline. He was sure Mia must wonder about their ages. It was never discussed. They had allowed her to continue with the assumption that she was a late child, as she knew nothing about her mother. They thought it best that she didn't have her mother's suicide hanging over her. Oscar's heart felt heavy. They had tried so hard to protect their grandchild from the sadness of her mother's death and their brutal family history. Now, she was suffering the same terrors that had plagued her mother's dreams — and, to a certain extent, his own, too. Not only that, but now she was experiencing the brutality of their family history first-hand and without the benefit of understanding any of it. He resolved to discuss meeting the relatives with Esme just as soon as they finished their tea.

Both busy with their own thoughts, Oscar and Esme sat and sipped, gazing out over their spring garden. The blossom was just breaking through on the damson and apple trees, and the cherry was in full bloom. Oscar was savouring the peace before he confronted his wife and shattered the tranquillity of this moment. He was tired after spending most of the day in the garden. So, he was enjoying the sit-down and strong tea. His eyes wandered around the garden appraising the day's handy work. Esme pointed out that she liked the new bedding plants, which were a striking yellow. Oscar agreed and was just about to point out other flowers when he caught a movement from Mia's window. He was jolted out of his reverie. Mia was screaming with one rigid arm pointing at the greenhouse. The closed, triple-glazed windows, the birds' evensong and their distance from the house was muffling the sound of her screams.

"Quick," he said, spilling his drink as he threw his mug on the tray.

"Steady, Oscar, those are the mugs Mia gave us for Christmas. They have beautiful flowers, and——" Esme stopped short; Oscar was not staying to listen.

"Mia," Oscar yelled as he sped across the lawn. "I'm coming. I'm coming!"

Esme saw Oscar running faster than she thought he was capable of towards the house. She looked up at Mia's window and saw her gasping for breath and grabbing her throat. She was pointing at something in the garden. Fearful of what she might see if she looked in that direction, Esme looked straight ahead. She hurried towards the house, skirting the identified area. The sun was still shining, and the birds continued to sing; nothing seemed amiss. But, just as Esme passed the side of Oscar's greenhouse, an icy wind blew in her face together with an unpleasant smell. She would also describe later how time "paused" and that she wasn't in their garden for a fleeting moment, but somewhere dark and threatening, and there was no birdsong. Frightened and confused, she quickened her pace. She glanced back up at Mia's window before stumbling towards the door. Mia continued to point while looking desperately at Esme with fear in her wide eyes. Esme crashed through the door, feeling a cold, dark threat tugging at her back.

CHAPTER 15

It was Mia's last therapy session.

The therapist had done his best to convince Esme to continue a little longer. He assured her that Mia was going through a necessary process. Part of that, he said, might see the manifestations grow stronger as they discussed them in more detail. Mia would, he assured her, learn how to manage them. He also suggested more potent drugs, but Esme still insisted they wouldn't be continuing. He then attempted to appeal to Mia and asked if she felt the benefit of the sessions.

"It helps to talk about the dreams in one way, but it also seems to give them more strength," said Mia.

"What happened at the paintball site was serious. I can vouch for you to the police, Mia, but they'll be more sympathetic if they know therapy is ongoing."

"We've decided to end the sessions, Jonathon," said Esme. "We'll stick to that decision. The police are not pressing charges, and we're hoping Mia's boyfriend will accept that she was unwell when the incident occurred." Esme turned to Mia. "Isn't that how you feel, too, Mia?"

"Yes, yes, I do."

"Mia is a sick young woman who needs professional help, Mrs Barone. Would you deny her that? Do you have money worries? Perhaps we can get help to cover some of the cost."

Esme didn't want to be confrontational with the therapist. Still, she now agreed with Oscar that the therapy made Mia worse. "I know you mean well, but this process exacerbates the situation. At first, I didn't think so, but the dreams are more defined and have increased in frequency."

"I advised you that sometimes this can happen," Jonathon explained. He was exasperated now. "She's opening up and confronting these manifestations. They seem real, but, of course, they're imaginary."

"Imaginary!" Mia was aghast. "After everything I've told you. You wouldn't say that if you were in my place. There's nothing imaginary about these nightmares, I can assure you. I actually experience the world I'm being taken back into. I've already told you that. After I wake, the smells linger and I have dirty clothes and injuries. Also, I've a tattoo on my arm, which my dad saw once before it faded. And, and how do you explain what happened in our garden? Answer me that?"

"Mia, only you saw that."

"Not strictly true, doctor," said Esme. "I caught the smell too; something was there. I felt threatened and afraid. There was an icy wind that blew in my face. The air was different in that part of the garden. It came with an oppressive atmosphere, from what felt like a threatening and dismal place. It was awful."

"It's still spring, Mrs Barone; we still get the occasional chilly wind." Jonathon was trying to be as patient as he could. It didn't help that Mia's mother was endorsing the reality of the manifestations. It was clear that these elderly parents were getting caught up in the hysteria. He hadn't met Mia's father, but from what he'd heard, Mr Barone believed in the whole thing too. Jonathon liked Mia. But more than that, he would feel that he had failed if they left now. He must deliver Mia back to good mental health, or he would be a failure in the eyes of his peers and, more importantly, in his own eyes.

Mia snapped. "You haven't stopped these nightmares, dreams, or whatever they are. If anything, they've increased. And I'm not crazy. I've never been the kind of person to imagine things. I think I'm being sent messages." Mia looked fearfully at both Esme and the therapist. What she said was new, and such voices were definitely a symptom of mental illness — she checked that on Google. "Look, I haven't got voices telling me to do things. Rachel, who I become in my dreams, needs me to know something significant. It's troubling her. I think she's using me to get her message into the living world by taking me through her everyday experiences in the concentration camp."

Esme stared at Mia.

The therapist shrugged, looked at Esme, and shook his head knowingly. "If you still think you can deal with this yourselves, Mrs Barone, then fine. But what you've just heard Mia say must give you considerable doubt."

"No, no. Quite the opposite," said Esme, still staring at Mia as though in a trance.

"Mum, are you alright?" Mia got to her feet and went to Esme. "Come on, let's go home. Thanks for all you've done, Jonathon," said Mia, as she guided a stunned Esme out the door.

Jonathon Weaks was not given to bouts of anger or temper tantrums. But after sitting for a few moments in his empty consulting room, he flung his notepad across the room and swore. This case was shaping up to be very interesting. He was writing it up and was hoping to submit a paper to the

Association of Academic Psychiatrists. But now, the opportunity had been snatched away from him. Mia's mother's strange reaction was fascinating. He wanted to know more. He would leave the situation dormant and contact the family later. Hopefully, he could eventually finish his paper.

###

Mia's parents had been acting strangely ever since she and Esme returned from the therapist two days previously. She found them having whispered and very animated discussions. They stopped talking when she asked them if they were okay. Then they just said "yes" and smiled at her sympathetically. The snippets of conversation she caught made it clear that her comment at the therapy session had stunned Esme. She knew it, had seen it for herself, the way Esme's eyes had widened as though she had been struck. Mia did not say it to shock. She truly believed what she said.

By dragging Mia back to the war in her own body, Rachel had effectively made her a witness to the life in the camp and the suffering at the hands of the Nazis. Or so Mia believed. Thus, while Mia was Rachel, the message would become apparent. Maybe blurting this out in the therapist's room was not the cleverest move, but he frustrated her with his constant disbelief.

She was glad it was out, as verbalising her suspicions felt like a release. The realisation and acceptance gave Mia a measure of peace and control. When she entered her dream last night, she concentrated on determining what message Rachel wanted to give her rather than struggling to come out of the dream. The possibility that the dreams had a purpose almost made the trauma they caused her worthwhile. Yes, they were terrible, but perhaps that was part of it. Mia had already witnessed unspeakable acts of torture and suffering, and she was constantly fearful of what was to come.

"Mia, love?" her dad cut into her thoughts. "Your mum and I have decided we need you to know a few things about our past to help you understand what's happening to you."

"How can your past help?"

"We're not without our own unpleasant experiences, Mia," said Esme.

"And your past relates to my dreams?"

"Yes, indirectly, love," Esme replied.

"So, we've invited some people to see you. Hopefully, your dreams will make more sense when they tell you about their own experiences."

"What people, Dad? Why would their experiences or yours help me?"

Oscar took a deep breath. "They're relatives," he said. "They're part of your past, or our past, to be more accurate."

Esme looked on apprehensively, unsure what she should do. Then she did what she always did when she was stressed — busied herself with organising and tidying.

"Relatives? But you told me we don't have relatives." Mia looked at Esme and Oscar suspiciously. "Mum, Dad, what's this all about? Who are these so-called relatives?"

Oscar was hesitant. He was about to unravel a lifetime of lies and half-truths. He looked at Esme, but saw his uncertainty reflected in her anxious eyes. So many secrets. So much deception. How should he begin? Oscar had pushed for this truth-telling, even though he was sure they were about to disturb a hornet's nest full of lies, many of which would sting them. Weaving a new story for Ruth and then Mia over the years had become routine. Their carefully constructed lives were now their reality. How did you dismantle such an extensive web of lies? He didn't know.

"Mia, I'll make tea and set it out in the conservatory," Esme interjected, seeing Oscar struggle. "I suggest we sit in there, make ourselves comfortable, and then discuss this with you properly. How does that sound?"

"Yes, yes," said Oscar. His relief was palpable. "Why don't we do that? Have you put out some of your homemade shortbread? I love those biscuits, Esme."

He knew he was deluding himself. He had saved himself a few minutes, only a few minutes before Mia realised that her entire life was a lie created by them, her grandparents. What would she think of them for their dishonesty?

"It sounds as though you two are crazier than I am, but I don't exactly have much choice in the matter, do I? If this is something you've cooked up between you to make me feel better, it's unnecessary. I think I can handle this now."

Her parents exchanged worried glances as they walked through to the conservatory.

After many cups of tea and a few shots of brandy to treat the shock that came with one revelation after another, Mia discovered that her life was based on fiction. Most shocking of all was the revelation that her parents were her grandparents and her mother had taken her own life because of the dreams. Her mother, who she now knew was called Ruth, had never revealed who her father was — her birth certificate registered him as unknown. Now she knew why she had never seen it.

Mia wept and shouted, and Esme and Oscar took the onslaught as payment for their deceit. Their emotions swung from guilt to justification and back. They had lied to their granddaughter with the best intentions. Still, they questioned their actions in denying her the knowledge of her mother.

They had tried to find Mia's father after Ruth's death, but without success. Their search led them to the UK, where the trail went cold. They showed Mia photos of her mother and told her all about Ruth before suicide cut her life short. They had only one photo of her father.

"So, she too suffered as I'm suffering. And you thought it wouldn't help me to know that?"

"To be honest, we didn't know," said Oscar.

"I feared it could make it worse," said Esme.

"You mean I'd take my life too?"

"It's our biggest fear, Mia," said Esme.

Her parents' — or rather, her grandparents' — background and ancestry were pure inventions. She did, in fact, have actual relatives, though she had always believed she had none. They visited, but were introduced as her grandparents' friends.

Mia listened to their protestations about protecting her from racial and religious prejudice. And to achieve that, they had felt the need to raise her in a bubble of lies. It made her angry and sad, feelings that were accompanied by a deep sense of loss.

The relatives had continued to receive photographs and snippets of news about Mia. So, while they were news to her, she was not unknown to them.

They sat quietly as darkness fell outside. Esme cried intermittently, and Oscar sniffed a great deal as Mia looked through photographs she had never seen. Many were of her mother, Ruth. Others were strangers who cradled her in their arms and looked at her with such love. After a while, Mia was spent. Her anger subsided; her tears were gone. All three of them were left red-eyed and gazing at the night sky through the conservatory roof — all lost in their own misery.

Mia broke the silence. "So, I'm your granddaughter. I've a dead mother, two elderly aunts, one uncle and several cousins. There are people who visit us who were your childhood friends, and who are an important part of your life. I've met all my adult relatives, but you called them your friends, correct?" Confusion, anger, and sadness still simmered beneath her words.

"Yes," said Oscar sheepishly.

"And none of them have been allowed to be a part of my life – even those around my age. Obviously, my mother couldn't be."

"Mia, we decided it wouldn't be in your best interests," said Esme. "We wanted you to be an all-Australian girl without the baggage of our past." Her pleading tone irked Mia.

"I don't know what to think," said Mia.

"But we want to correct it now," said Oscar. "Everyone has respected our wishes for your sake. Now they're prepared to speak to you. We believe they can help you cope with your dreams."

Mia was reluctant to relieve her parents of their discomfort. She was too angry. "I feel I've been dropped into a mystery drama without a script. I was getting to grips with the dreams, finally getting my head around them. Now this! Do they know what I'm going through? Have I been a hot topic of gossip with these strangers? Do they know about the dream world that haunts me? Do they know Rachel and if she died in that place? Did Sarid die?"

"Mia, love," Oscar pleaded. "One question at a time, please. We'll answer them all if we can, but give us a chance to explain properly."

"Our friends and relatives are all around us, and they've seen the change in you for themselves," said Esme.

Mia instinctively looked around the room. She was a little unnerved by the existence of these unknown people who knew her. She felt watched from afar and talked about — the subject of their conversations, but not a part of their lives. It was like living a life behind a one-way mirror. She was viewed, but she couldn't see them.

"As a starting point, Mia, Alma next door, as you know, is one such old and very dear friend. She has agreed to help if she can," said Oscar, fully expecting the reaction he got.

"I know Mum knew her as a child, but she's a crazy old bird. Not sure how she could help me."

"She may seem a bit dotty, but she's far from it. I think you will find she will be an enormous help to you," Esme chastised. *She knows a lot more than you give her credit for.*

"Steady, Esme," Oscar interjected. "This has been a terrible shock for Mia. Let's be considerate here."

Esme was contrite but restless. She went to make more tea.

"There's one last thing, Mia."

"Oh God, what bombshell have you been saving, Dad? I'm adopted, yeah?"

Esme rushed back into the conservatory. "You certainly are not adopted, young lady. We brought you home from the hospital where your mother died. You helped us through what was a very dark time." Esme sat on the chair, overcome with emotion.

"Yes," said Oscar. "Like the sunshine on a rainy day."

The tension in the room was still high. Mia felt shell-shocked, deceived and without an anchor. She felt that she had been set adrift: what she knew as reality was built on a tissue of lies. She had nothing to cling to.

"Do you want to continue to call us Mum and Dad? We would understand if you didn't," said Oscar.

"You're the only parents I've ever known. It would be strange to call you anything else."

"Did you ever wonder why we were so elderly?" asked Esme.

"Not really. Women have children late in life these days. Even if you're ninety-something, you're still just Mum and Dad.

That explains why you're such an old codger, though, Dad," joked Mia, her emotions causing a fresh spill of tears with hysterical giggling.

Oscar raised his eyebrows in mock horror. At that moment, he felt only relief that they had at last summoned up the courage to be truthful with Mia. Now she was joking despite it all. "Not quite ninety — not for a while yet," he said.

The mood lightened in the room, but it was short-lived.

"There's more, Mia," said Oscar gently.

"Not sure I can take much more."

"Can we tell you a little more," said Esme. "Just a little, and then we'll call it a day. What do you think?"

"Okay. Let me have it. It can't be any worse than the rest of it."

Esme looked at Oscar for reassurance before she spoke. He smiled. "We also assumed another identity," she said, "a Christian identity and new names. We wanted to be sure we were not linked to our past."

"Seriously? A completely new identity?"

"Well, yes. We felt we had to because we're Jews."

"I just can't see why."

They couldn't see why now, either. Hiding their true identity as persecuted Jews when they fled to Australia seemed like the right thing to do. They wanted to leave everything behind — the memories, mainly. But, of course, memories follow you.

"And Mum, we're Jewish, so what? I always thought you were like a Jewish mother because you fuss so much."

Esme looked startled at first, but then she decided she loved the image of being a doting Jewish mother. Her mother had been just the same, and while Esme complained like mad, as did Rachel and her brothers, they all adored her. Esme's breath caught in her throat when she remembered her family — gone, and such a savage end. She pulled another tissue out of the box on the coffee table and noted it was nearly empty. So many tears in one day.

Mia's head was swirling with all the new information, and she was exhausted. She yawned. Her world had been knocked sideways; it had changed colour and felt a little alien. Her beliefs and accepted normality were challenged, and she felt strange and muddled.

She looked at her nails, now cut short with a simple, clear gloss. She had loved her long nails, complete with nail art, which she used to change to match her outfit. Perfect nails were a part of who she was — or maybe she should say who she used to be — a smart, sassy dresser with nice clothes and makeup applied perfectly at all times. She never set foot outside the house any other way. Now life had changed irrevocably, and her with it. She couldn't remember when she had got dressed up in the last couple of months. Lisa was shocked when she met her outside the cinema in jeans, a baggy shirt, and the biggest sin of all, no makeup. Her friend said she was just glad it was dark inside and made sure they left via the fire exit so no one would see them. Mia didn't care. Such superficiality was insignificant compared with the enormity of the life and death scenarios being played out in her dreams.

"Sorry," said Mia, "this has worn me out. I'm tired, and I feel I don't know who I am anymore. I need to think about it all, try to take it in."

Her sudden change of mood worried Oscar. Maybe they had gone too fast. But no, they had hardly begun. How would she handle the rest of the information if she felt that way now? "Look, love, I think that's enough for one day," said Oscar. "I'm exhausted too, as I'm sure your mother is."

"Yes, I agree," said Esme as she collected the cups and tidied the conservatory.

"As you now know, we're old duffers, and it's way past our bedtime," said Oscar, smirking. "Shall we sleep on it, Mia, and speak again tomorrow? And remember, love, we did it for you. I hope you don't think any less of us because of it."

Esme was nervous. She could see Mia was struggling. She didn't want to let her go to bed in such a state. What they had done, albeit with the best intentions, may now backfire and affect Mia more profoundly than they could imagine. And with that thought came the memory of losing Ruth, which did nothing to allay Esme's fear for Mia. "Night, night, Mia. Please know how much we love you, my darling." Esme hugged Mia tight and let her tears fall on her hair, which she stroked with affection and trepidation. She quickly wiped her eyes as Mia turned to give Oscar a hug. Their plans to reveal the past might give Mia a better understanding of who she was and perhaps why she had the dreams, Esme thought. Of course, that was if Oscar was right about this big revelation, and Esme hoped he was. She had just one regret at that moment: she had resisted her husband's advice about this for too long, and, as a result, Mia had probably suffered longer than necessary.

Emotions were running high, and Esme was still panicking about Mia leaving their company too soon. To delay it a little, she offered to make cocoa before they retired.

Oscar looked at his wife with sympathy. He felt torn, too. So many times, he felt the frustration of not being able to protect his family from the curse of the dreams. He wished he could scoop Mia up and take her away to a place where nothing and no one could hurt her again. But all he could do now was try to be strong for her. "I think Mia is extremely tired."

"Yes, yes, of course she is," agreed Esme. "You go up, love, and get showered and changed, and I'll bring it up for you. Would you like marshmallows and cream like you had when you were little?"

"No, Mum, just the cocoa. That'll be great. Thank you." Mia smiled reassuringly at Esme. "Mum, for what it's worth, I think you and Dad are doing the right thing, but it'll take me a bit of time to take it all in. Can you understand that? You both know who you are and where you came from. I'm only just finding out. But I'm not upset anymore, just a little wonky."

"Of course you are, love, of course you are." Esme gushed. "Your Dad and I are very impressed by how well you're coping. Especially considering what you're dealing with right now. Aren't we, Oscar?"

Oscar nodded in response. "You're a very resilient young woman. But it's no surprise. You come from tough stock."

"But you haven't told me what connection my relatives have with the people in my dreams. After all these years, I assume that's what this truth-telling is all about."

"We haven't told you everything as yet," said Oscar.

"But we will," Esme assured her.

"Just get some rest, and we'll start again tomorrow," said Oscar. "Everything looks better after a night's sleep, love."

Mia gave a little backward glance and a weak smile as she left, leaving Oscar and Esme with many conflicting emotions. She was exhausted, and the thought of yet more revelations was weighing heavily on her.

But one thing she was determined about was that she would experience the dreams as calmly as she could. She wouldn't try to escape back to her real life. She needed to know more about that place and the messages she was sure Rachel wanted to pass to her. She would actively try to discover why the people in the dream were targeting her; what was the connection? Getting to know her relatives, people she suspected knew a lot about this desperate place, would help her more. They were Jews who came from Europe. As some of them were as old as her grandparents, it made sense that they knew more details, since they were alive during the war. But given her dreams were a direct line — first-hand information about actual events — they wouldn't know those details. Or would they?

Feeling resolute, she jutted her chin forwards and walked from the hut. Mia refused to be cowed by these brutes and bullies again. She was here as an observer with a purpose.

"What in the name of all that's sane do you think you're doing? Are you completely mad, Rachel?" Ariella grabbed Mia by the arm and pulled her into a space between the huts.

"I'm not——" Mia wanted to deny her name was Rachel, but stopped as Ariella pulled and pushed her further into their hiding place.

"I'm not mad, but I'm not frightened either."

"Then you certainly *are* completely insane."

"Listen, Ariella; we must try to be brave and strong. We need to be prepared to stand up to them. They've no right——"

Ariella cut her off. "Huh, we're strong, some might say brave, even, my dear friend Rachel, because we've survived so far and taken whatever these animals have dished out. That says a lot, wouldn't you say? So many others have died, and amongst them were the fools who thought they could outwit our captors or show them they were strong or brave. Being strong in here requires resilience and being acutely aware of everything and anything that threatens your personal survival. But, of course, avoiding those threats is a lot harder. As well you know, life here doesn't always follow a set pattern. Being one step ahead of whatever they're about to do is a valuable skill. That's why your beautiful son survived when you were sick. But we need to remain alert and ready for the unexpected. But brave? How would you define 'brave', my foolhardy friend?"

"Well, standing up for yourself and standing firm against their brutality," said Mia, but she was feeling less confident now; she wasn't sure about what she was saying. Ariella was right; her fellow prisoners were brave — they had survived so far.

"Don't be a fool, Rachel. You've been very sick, and we brought you through. You shouldn't have survived, but we took risks to save you and Sarid. Now, don't throw it all away," said Ariella firmly. "You've obviously been affected by your illness, but we can no longer protect you. You need to be very careful, very careful indeed."

Mia hung her head and mumbled an agreement.

"It's having the skill, wit and strength to survive until this madness ends and not showing any emotion, least of all a brave face. Most of the survivors have learned that lesson, some more brutally than others." As they emerged, Ariella looked with sadness at where they stood. It was a desolate, lifeless place of steel grey and dirty brown where fear ruled their lives without respite. She and Rachel had a wonderful life before this violation of their freedom. Like most people, they took such things for granted. Now they were in hell. Any life they had after this that wasn't this excuse for an existence would be a sweet and blessed one.

Ariella checked it was all clear. Turning back, she whispered. "And it *will* end, Rachel. It can't last indefinitely. Everything ends," she said in a softening voice and then clasped Rachel to her. "Be clever, not brave. Outwit these bastards. Play them at their own game. If God is willing, they'll pay for what they've done."

"Yes," said Mia, overcome with emotion. "It will end; everything must end. I'm sorry, Ariella, I don't know what came over me. I want to be here on that day of reckoning with my boy. That'll be a glorious day."

Before they could be seen, the two women embraced again with great affection, their tears flowing freely. Such emotions were frequently felt but rarely allowed to find expression, even between old friends. They needed to become numb to survive. They must suppress natural human emotions, which could get them into trouble or worse in the camp — a degrading, merciless place where they were treated like the lowest form of life on God's earth.

CHAPTER 16

Mia was excited and nervous about meeting the strangers she now knew to be her relatives. Having an extended family beyond their little unit of three was something she would have to get used to. She tried to remember the people who called at the house in the past. But, as she always made a point of being out, if possible, she rarely caught more than a fleeting glance as she left and they arrived. Her general lack of interest and her attempts to avoid them resulted in a poor recollection of the few occasions when she met them.

Her parents briefly listed them and their relationship with her, but they didn't say how Rachel and Sarid fit into the family. It was strange, as if they wanted to tell her everything but had practised their deception for so long that they couldn't release some details. They had bottled it all up, pushed it deep down inside and then got on with their lives. As a result, this was alien territory for her parents — telling the truth about the past. They still believed that their lies had protected Mia; in their minds, the notion lingered that telling all the truth might expose her to unknown risks.

The evening they told her about the fate of her great grandparents and other relatives was indescribably painful for them both. Mia asked them to stop many times; she wasn't sure they could cope with such an outpouring of raw grief. But they assured her they had remained too quiet about it all for too long, and it was a relief to express their genuine feelings.

She fared little better herself with all the truth-telling, feeling sympathy for her grandparents and self-pity for what might have been if she hadn't been living a lie. She was like a long-lost child who had been reunited with her family. She would have loved to know about her extended family sooner — particularly the younger family members.

To discover that the Nazis killed so many of her ancestors was shocking. And there were many similarities between her family's experiences and her dreams.

###

"Mum, are you sure you don't want me to help a little with preparing the food? There seems an awful lot to do, and it would keep me busy."

"I can manage, love, but if you're at a loose end and want to help, thanks."

Esme could see how agitated Mia was, and she was not surprised. Mia's life had switched from predictable and familiar to the opposite within a few months. It wasn't what they wanted for her, not in a million years. Their beautiful girl was now racked with anxiety and doubt about everything in her life. What was worse, they couldn't give her any reassurance. The secret was out about her true identity, so everything they said, Mia checked to ensure that it was true. Esme didn't like to be mistrusted.

"Mum, there's enough to feed the entire street. How many people are coming?"

"I'm not sure, Mia. I know at least fifteen people have confirmed.

Mia shuddered as she put yet another tray of jam tarts in the oven. *People are coming here because of me and my dreams.* She felt overwhelmed and wondered what her estranged family made of it all. Did they believe her or see her as some hysterical young woman who needed to tone down her over-active imagination? She would soon find out, she told herself as she heard the front doorbell echo through the house. Well, at least she had made a reasonable contribution to the buffet. As well as fetching and carrying for her whirlwind cook of a mother, she had also washed, chopped and mixed four bowls of salad. Along with her mother's baking and making, the salads added a healthy look to the enormous spread laid out on the kitchen table. Esme pointed out that some of the food was "Jewish", but although Mia had tasted a few of these dishes over the years, they were never identified as such.

"Well, where is she, our lovely Mia?"

A man's voice boomed out from the lounge. Mia froze. She was suddenly unsure if she could actually carry this through. Esme cradled her arm as they entered the lounge while she expertly removed her apron and adjusted her hair a little. My mother is a true multi-tasker, Mia thought. She clasped Esme's hand, and they exchanged smiles. The chime went again before they reached the lounge, and voices were raised in greeting out in the hall.

"That sounds like lots of people arriving, Mum," she said nervously, glancing at the door. "How will we fit them all in?"

"It'll all be fine, my darling, believe me."

She was barely in the room before she was pulled into a warm embrace by a tearful man as his wife laid a gentle hand against her back. Mia felt an immediate connection with them. More guests filed in, hugging each other and Mia while talking furiously. She saw her dad briefly as he showed each group into the room. She caught his eye, and they exchanged a brief smile. Oscar's look spoke volumes. Be brave, it said. She didn't feel brave. Very far from it. She gazed around the room and was acknowledged with smiles and nods. She was the star attraction, and her knees threatened to buckle. Rescue came from Esme again, her arm encircling Mia's waist as she guided her to two chairs in the corner.

"It's quite uncanny; she looks just like her. As Ruth did, too," Mia heard a man say.

"Shh, not so fast, Danny. Give the poor girl a chance to meet us before you scare her half to death," said a rather buxom woman. She then ignored her own advice, rushed towards Mia, lifted her up from the chair and gave her a long, lingering embrace. Mia was swamped with warmth, perfume and a brightly coloured scarf. She thought this would be the pattern of behaviour until she met everyone. Well, at least every woman anyway.

"Lovely to see you, Rochelle," said Esme with affection.

Dewey-eyed, Rochelle released Mia and transferred her hugging to Esme. "Naomi, it's been so long," Rochelle gushed.

"Esme, Rochelle, remember?" said Esme.

"Mum?"

"I'm so sorry," said Rochelle. "This is all so emotional."

"Mia, I used to be called Naomi. I just hadn't got round to telling you yet, love. You've had so much else to take in," said Esme, worry etching lines on her face.

"And Dad?"

"Your daddy is my brother, Edan," Rochelle cut in. "but we called him Ed." And then she looked at Esme with concern. She couldn't seem to help herself from blurting things out. She was so excited.

"Rochelle, can I get you a cup of tea, dear?" said Esme, taking a firm grip of Rochelle's arm and guiding her away from Mia.

Mia looked at them as they moved away. *My Great Aunt. Dad's sister.* Yes, she could see the likeness now. She quickly crossed the room to stand by Oscar. "Hello, Edan," she said, smiling.

"Rochelle could never keep her mouth from running away from her. It's a wonder we kept all this a secret for so long. I think it only worked because we forbade her to visit us here," said Oscar. "We always met her out somewhere or went to their place."

"It might have been better if she had visited. I hate the fact I've lived a lie, Dad. But I just can't believe that I didn't have an inkling. I mean, who has no family at all — not even distant relatives? Did I never question it, Dad?"

"You did a couple of times, Mia. Then you went through a phase of having imaginary siblings."

"Lots of kids have imaginary friends, Dad. How did you deal with my questions about family?"

"When you were a teenager, we told you we were Italian refugees and that our family died in the war. Not strictly a lie, but rather a bending of the truth. Because, of course, we *do* have family that survived the war." Oscar smiled and turned his hand towards the assembled.

"And that satisfied my curiosity?"

"Yes, as far as we could tell. At least you stopped asking about it." Oscar put his arm around Mia's shoulder. "We did it for all the right reasons, love. I hope you'll come to understand that. It would have stayed that way if it hadn't been for those wretched dreams. Being Jewish is not an advantage. History shows us that repeatedly. Yes, being Jewish in a family or your own community is wonderful. But we wanted to ensure that you'd be free of negative things that come with being a Jew — prejudice, suspicion and even hatred." Oscar paused with a faraway look in his eyes. Then he shrugged. "But today proves that we can never escape who we really are."

Oscar's impromptu speech was overheard by those nearest to them, and Mia saw heads nodding in agreement and others shaking sad faces. The subject was clearly a topic that didn't have a right or wrong answer. All these people, her relatives, were affected by the dilemma — that was obvious.

Esme and Rochelle came back into the lounge with trays of canapes. Mia's stomach was permanently clenched. She didn't think she could eat a thing. The room was buzzing with chatter and laughter. Hugging and crying were part of the mix, making it clear many of the assembled hadn't seen each other in a while. Mia counted twenty-five guests, which made the lounge seem tiny. Oscar obviously had the same thought as he swung open the conservatory doors and invited people to spread a little.

"Before we say much more, I want you all to know Mia has had a great deal to cope with lately," said Oscar. "So, this get-together needs to be as light-hearted as possible. I know you've a lot to tell Mia, but this is her first meeting with you all, and we need to take things gently." He looked from his wife to Mia, who each stood on either side of him. "If we can start by everyone introducing themselves, I think that would be a great way to begin, as Mia doesn't know anyone here." This was met with gasps and a few exclamations of 'shame', but Oscar ignored the disapproval. It was his job to hold this day together, and he was determined he would. Oscar had invited the whole family, most of whom came. Still, he knew that his and Esme's decision to turn their back on the Jewish faith and their family and friends did not have universal approval, whatever the motivation.

Held on both sides by her grandparents' loving arms, one by one, Mia's newly found family introduced themselves and outlined their relationship with her. Most were simple introductions. However, emotions ran hot in some quarters, and they spilt over into the proceedings.

"I married your Aunt Maya when we were released from Auschwitz," said a man called Izzie. "Don't ask me how we survived, because I don't know. We were lucky, I suppose, if you can call it luck. I prayed for death so many times, but I was spared so I could marry the most beautiful woman in the world and have four wonderful children." His eyes filled with tears as he swept his arm around the room to identify his family. The youngest of his grandchildren rushed to his side and put her arm around his shoulders.

"I'm Rachel," she explained, looking at Mia. "Named after a great aunt who didn't survive the Holocaust — my grandad's older sister. But people call me Rach."

"Rachel?" Mia whispered and looked at Esme.

Esme took a deep breath. "Rachel was my sister, too," she said, nodding sadly. "She was the eldest in the family. We all adored her and little Sarid."

Mia gasped

Izzie, together with other siblings, shook their heads. An awkward silence followed, with secretive and knowing glances passing around the room.

"Well, it's been raised," a woman sitting on the couch said bravely. "We may as well talk about Rachel now. As we all know, she features in Mia's dreams, and that's why we're all here, after all."

There was a general murmuring, and heads nodded in agreement. Izzie's granddaughter, Rach, gave Mia a broad smile. Mia noted she didn't look like her great aunt, Rachel. The mention of Rachel and knowing that she and Sarid were connected to everyone in this room was quite overpowering. She returned Rach's smile with tears in her eyes, which prompted Rach to cross the room and embrace her with affection.

"This must be so hard for you, Mia," she whispered, "but we truly believe we can help you with all this, and don't forget, you're family, and we love you. So, please trust us."

Mia nodded her head vigorously, unable to speak, but smiled in acknowledgement.

"Whether we talk about Rachel and Sarid is up to Edan and Naomi. Sorry, Oscar and Esme," said the man who had remarked earlier that Mia looked like Rachel.

He was a tall, kind-looking man with big hands and an unattractive, prominent Jewish nose. She felt ashamed as the thought crossed her mind that he was typically Jewish-looking. A stereotype that was part of the prejudice against Jews.

Mia jumped as Esme suddenly spoke. "As Rachel was my older sister, Mia, I thought I was attracting her ghost to this house. We were very close, you see. I was a late baby, so she was more like a second mother to me. I escaped the Holocaust because an Italian family took me in as their own child . . . but Isaac, Rachel and Sarid were taken." Esme was only just keeping her emotions in check. Now, she clearly couldn't continue. Under the sympathetic gaze of the assembled, Mia sat beside Esme and draped her arm around her shoulders to comfort her while she wept.

Esme's outpouring affected the entire group. Some bowed their heads; others prayed. Whispered conversations continued. Esme and Mia gazed into each other's eyes, painting a picture of confusion and misery. Esme continued. "And, my dear Mia, you look just like her. She was about your age when those savages murdered her and her sweet boy, Sarid, who was more like a brother to me as we were so near in age." Esme slumped in her chair, unable to control the raging emotions that tore through her heart. "Those brutes killed Rachel and Sarid when they had so much more living to do. Sarid was only five years old. I hate them. I truly, deeply hate them," she shouted. Tears streamed down her face. Supportive mumbling and head-shaking spread through the room like a noisy wave.

A *dank tsu got far rateven aundz,*" said a man who had not yet spoken.

"*Amn. geloybt gat!*" came the response from the older members of the assembled.

"Dad?"

"It's Yiddish. They're thanking God for keeping them alive," Oscar replied without enthusiasm.

Mia turned back to Esme. She had never seen her so angry or desperately sad. "Oh, Mum, why didn't you tell me? I've been banging on about my dreams, and Rachel, and you didn't give me a clue."

Esme looked at Mia with wet eyes and a hopeless expression, shrugged her shoulders, and shook her head slowly from side to side. "You had enough to contend with, my darling Mia."

"I've been so bloody selfish, and I thought you didn't care, Mum. Staying away from me, acting like the housework was more important than I was. But I've been torturing you, and you've been just trying to cope. I'm so sorry, Mum. Honestly, I am," said Mia.

CHAPTER 17

The sun continued to shine throughout the day on the first-ever open family meeting at the Barone household. Food was served as a rolling buffet, and Mia's newly found family wandered around the garden, drinks and plates in hand. Mia saw many of them pass the area where she had seen two apparitions of the concentration camp. It still made her shiver just looking in that direction. After many more revelations, tears, sympathy and calling on God to save them all, the event moved into an uneasy calm with regular outbursts of emotion mixed with laughter, love and hugs.

Mia's feelings were mixed. She was relieved to have finally met her relatives, but she was still reeling from shock. To think that the Rachel of her dreams was her great aunt — it was hard to take in. And Sarid was her cousin (first cousin once removed, if she was being exact). And yet the revelation seemed to bring them closer to her, physically and mentally. She relived snippets from her dreams, looking at Rachel and Sarid differently. She became distracted and distanced from those around her.

Although he hadn't told her, she knew, from the way Oscar responded to various questions, that he intended to hold some sort of question-and-answer session at the end of the day. It would lead to more highly charged exchanges, with tears and terrible recollections from family members who had survived as well as acknowledgements of their ancestors who hadn't. She could see Oscar ushering everyone back indoors.

"So, you become Rachel in your dreams?" said Lydia, a girl of around fifteen years old, as she sidled up next to Mia.

"Yes, sort of," Mia replied. "I'm still me. I know I'm me even when I'm there, but I look like Rachel, well I must, or it would seem strange to the other prisoners. They call me Rachel, and Sarid calls me mother." Mia looked into the distance as she thought of Sarid.

"So, how can Rachel give you any kind of message if you're her?" Lydia persisted.

"A good point," someone said nearby.

"I think she's showing me her message, or messages, by causing me to live her life inside the camp. I'm not sure, but I think that's what's happening."

Mia walked inside with Lydia to find some of her relatives recalling their own time in concentration camps or retelling the accounts of their parents' experiences. Those in the room who had first-hand experiences in the death camps would have been children or teenagers during the war.

Mia learned a great deal from several people's recollections, some of whom were actual camp inmates where Rachel and Sarid were held. However, as they were moved to other camps before the end of the war, they didn't witness Rachel and Sarid's demise.

A heartening story was told about children in the camp — babies and toddlers in particular — who were sometimes rescued from the processing centre by one particular guard. He was assisted by people who lived nearby. They all made a point of being present when the trains arrived. The children were pulled through a small gap in the fence to a safe house. They were then given to local families to hide. They were usually adopted later when their parents failed to track them down. This was not surprising: Mia knew no one survived that camp.

It was mentioned that some parents wouldn't hand over their children. But the woman telling the story sympathised, recognising that the parents would have no idea what fate awaited their little ones in the camp. The guard was nearly caught on one occasion because of the fuss one woman made when he tried to take her baby son. She paid the ultimate price, as they were both gassed within hours.

"She nearly exposed the entire operation," the woman said.

"Why didn't you get rescued?" one of Mia's younger relatives asked an elderly man.

"I wasn't born until after the war, thank God," he replied.

"*A dank got.* (Thanks be to God)," repeated the assembled.

"So, not all Germans are bad," said Mia.

"No, of course not, Mia," another man said, "but the Holocaust couldn't have happened without support and cooperation from the German people. We're not talking about a few deaths. The official figure is six million Jews. Unless enough of the population was involved, how could that happen? Many Nazi supporters betrayed their friends and neighbours, too. Such was the grip Hitler had on the German peoples' psyche."

"That happened to Rachel's family," said Mia.

Mia's comment drew a lot of astonished stares. It clearly validated knowledge that she could have only gained through her dreams. How else could she have known?

"Yes," said another. "We must concede there were undoubtedly good people, even amongst Germans. The story of those rescued children is just one of many brave acts. If they'd been caught, they would have suffered the same fate as the prisoners — remember that."

"And it wasn't just Jews who died at the hands of the Nazis," Lydia added. "Gypsies, handicapped German children, gays . . ."

"*Aoy ya, sharklike, shreklikh.* (Oh yes, terrible, terrible.)" Again, the assembled responded.

"*Der khurbn hot ibergelozt aoyf aundz ale an aumaoyfgemakhte simn.* (The Holocaust left an indelible mark on all of us.)"

Mia already knew where Rachel and Sarid had been imprisoned. Now she decided to undertake some research about the war and the Holocaust. Having covered it in school, she knew the basics, but she needed to know more. One thing that struck a personal chord with her was the way Hitler whipped up his followers at rallies. He had them cheering, stamping their feet and hanging on his every word when he finished. Inexplicably, it felt vaguely familiar, and that bothered her. But then it came to her: Go Ballistic. The similarity was unmistakable. Like Hitler's followers, paintballers were easily excited and motivated by the right words, common sense being sacrificed in the wake of being a part of the crowd. The many become one — voice, motivation, and action. Mob rule. But that meant that anyone could be influenced by the same method. The thought scared her that people anywhere, of all kinds, can be so easily led by clever propaganda and powerful speeches. Unless humans learnt from their mistakes and recognised their weakness in being easily led by unscrupulous leaders, the Holocaust and other atrocities against minorities would happen again and again. The remembrance words "lest we forget" were said in honour of those who lost their lives fighting in wars. Mia thought it should apply to the victims of war as well — people like Rachel and Sarid and the thousands of others who had suffered a similar fate.

"I think Mia is getting tired now," said Oscar when he felt the mood become too sombre.

Had he been privy to Mia's thoughts, he would realise just how right he was.

"She has answered so many questions, and you've all been wonderful about answering hers. We'll arrange a few more meet-ups if everyone is agreeable, but maybe with individual families."

There was a general murmur of agreement and a movement towards coats and bags. Mia was relieved. She found Esme by her side.

"All right, love?"

"Yes, Mum." Mia held Esme's hands firmly and looked into her eyes, smiling.

Esme felt so much closer to Mia. She was now genuinely pleased that Oscar had pushed for the family gathering.

They linked arms and went to say their goodbyes. It felt good to acknowledge these people as her family. But Mia was tired, as her father said, and she needed to rest.

After everyone left, Oscar poured them a drink. They exchanged their thoughts about the gathering — the emotions brought to the surface and the revelations shared. The atmosphere was soon heavy with each one's musings and feelings, which ultimately silenced all three into private contemplation.

CHAPTER 18

Vince looked and acted nervous as he stepped into the hallway, glancing from Mia to the now-closed door. His escape route.

"Hi Mia, how's it going?" He tried to be casual and act unperturbed about being alone with Mia.

Mia rushed forward and hugged her ex-boyfriend with genuine affection. Vince froze, but he relaxed and responded to her embrace as Mia continued to hold him. She felt and smelled great. But he would make a speedy retreat if she started acting strange again.

His girlfriend, Sue, was unhappy about him coming, but he owed Mia a lot, and he felt sorry for her. She had gone a bit bonkers, and it was such a pity.

"I'm well, Vince." She smiled. "Look, I just wanted you to know that I'm okay with you and Susan being together. I wasn't, but it's okay now, honestly. Sit down. I'll make us coffee in a minute."

"Good, well, that's good," he stammered. He didn't add "because we're engaged", just in case that was one step too far.

Vince sat on a single armchair. He was still wary. She had looked normal before at the paintball site, but then pulled off one of the most dramatic stunts he had ever seen, acting like a raving lunatic. Can someone actually come back from that? It resulted in the paintball site getting a lot of publicity. "Crazy Woman Attacks Nazis at Paintball Site", the headline in the local rag read. But it wasn't all positive. Some parents stopped their kids from coming for a while, and they were regulars. Sue helped him through all the fallout, and he was pleased she was around. With her help, he built it up again. In fact, they were pulling in even more players each weekend than ever before. Sue was responsible for the recent increase in business, but he knew Mia had put the foundations in place.

Mia was still attracted to Vince. He was a sexy bloke, but she had moved on, and there was a feeling of distance between them. Vince seemed like the past. And right now, he was obviously desperate to leave. These days, Mia's outlook on life took her way beyond the paintball site and the job at TopTravel. Once, she had thought of them both as critical to her self-worth. Not now. Susan was sitting at her former desk and doing well at the travel agency. A contender for the monthly prize for the most commission points. Quite a leap, given her performance when Mia worked there. *She has my old job and my boyfriend. Ironic.*

"I hear you and Susan are engaged."

"Yeah, that's right."

Mia read the panic in his eyes. He was waiting for a bad reaction. "Good, that's good." She wasn't confident she was being genuine. A lot of familiar feelings were surfacing. The smell of his leather jacket and aftershave permeated the room, and thoughts of snuggling up on his sofa came flooding back. Such special memories.

"Now, I'm sure you two could do with a brew." Mia's mother breezed into the room and plonked a tray with mugs of tea and a plate of biscuits on the coffee table between them.

Both Mia and Vince were relieved by the interruption. The mood was getting too intense.

"Thanks, Mrs Barone."

Saved by the tea, thought Mia. They then launched into some meaningless chatter about people they both knew. Mia thought she gave a good impression of someone who still enjoyed catching up on the gossip. It caused Esme to give her a quizzical look. Mia was glad when Vince said he had to go.

"All the best, Mia," he said. She knew Vince was genuinely sad as she let him out of the front door. It almost made her falter because she felt the same.

"You too, Vince, and I mean that." She pecked him on the cheek, then closed the door and leant against it. Her life was moving on despite her love for Vince. She would have fought to win him back before. But not now. Not that it would be possible. Vince was different somehow. He had committed to Susan, something he never even mentioned to Mia. It felt strange — Susan, his future wife. Mia felt a sudden sense of loss and grief for her former life. It sometimes threatened to overwhelm her. She likened it to when a child discovered Father Christmas wasn't real. You can't go back to believing. Your time as an innocent believer was gone. And so it was with her previous life — gone.

"Mia?" Esme called from the kitchen.

Mia ignored her and ran upstairs to her bedroom, threw herself on the bed, and cried.

Esme arrived outside Mia's door a few minutes later to say food was ready. However, after standing and listening, she walked away. Food was the last thing on Mia's mind, she thought sadly.

"Enough crying. It is what it is," Mia reprimanded herself. "Suck it up, girl."

She was due to see Lisa tomorrow night. She felt like her older, wiser big sister rather than her best mate these days. It was still sad to think like that, but like everything else, her relationship with Lisa had changed too. They were going to the cinema and a tavern after. Old favourites of them both. It would be a good night, despite the distance they felt between them. She would make a big effort and make Lisa feel good about it; Lisa would do no less; she was sure of that.

CHAPTER 19

Oscar walked into the sitting room, balancing an armful of maps. He found Mia with her laptop open.

"Dad, there's no point in looking at paper maps when we've got the Internet."

"Now that's where you're wrong, Mia. These are original European maps I borrowed from Alma. They show the boundaries as they were back in the war. Isn't that what you're after? Some villages that existed back then have been amalgamated with bigger towns nearby. Like most places, the landscape has invariably altered too, with new roads, bigger farms and industrial developments."

Oscar dumped the pile of maps on the coffee table. Some were brown around the edges; others were falling apart, as they had been folded many times.

"Is Alma interested in this too, Dad?"

"Yes, she's done a lot of research, actually."

"What, in the same location we're looking at?"

"Yes, she is not as dotty as you think," said Oscar. "Quite a sharp mind."

"Hmm, who would have known?" said Mia. "You oldies are a surprise sometimes. But I bet we would have eventually tracked the place down on the Internet."

"Thank you. Less of the old, if you don't mind."

Mia smirked, then pushed the laptop aside and spread one map out.

Esme handed her a large magnifying glass she used for embroidery.

"I don't want to see those places, Oscar, so I'll go to bed and read."

Oscar leapt up, concerned. "Esme, love, I'm sorry. I'll bring you up a mug of cocoa, and I'll be up soon. I just need to show Mia some landmarks."

"That's fine, love. You stay and help Mia. Come up a bit later. I feel like a long, hot bath and an indulgent read."

Mia already had her head down, scanning the areas where she believed the concentration camp must have been located. She found a map of the same area on the Internet. But her dad was right. The names of many small villages no longer appeared on the Internet map. She suspected a part of the reason would be that the locals wanted to forget about the horror enacted on their doorstep and in their names. A natural development of an area would also be a factor. If they were correct in their assumptions about the location, everything pointed to that part of the map. She decided to trust their research, the information from her dreams and her instincts.

"I know we're near a river."

Oscar noticed Mia used the present tense and 'we' rather than 'they', but he said nothing. He looked at Mia and felt a rush of love and pity. Leaving all the anguish her dreams caused Mia aside, Oscar found it remarkable. Given what she had been through, Mia showed just how tough she was to continue her pursuit of the truth. The change in her was unmistakable. She was more mature, that was certain. But they had concerns too.

The way she talked sometimes made them feel she was so deeply affected by her dreams that she was slipping out of her own body and into Rachel's. And if he was right, their fear for her physical and mental state was more than justified.

His dreams had been similar many years ago, but they were *about* the concentration camp. He didn't feel the reality of being there. Even then, his dreams were dreadful enough. Considering what Mia told them, the horrors she had witnessed would undoubtedly have an enormous impact on her, even when her dreaming ended. That's if it ever did. He glanced at her nails, bitten short but painted with a clear polish. It gave him a sliver of hope that a little of the old Mia was still in there somewhere. He liked this new Mia; she was less frivolous and obsessed with her appearance. She was kinder, too; no disparaging comments these days about her friends or the company he and Esme kept. Her dreams were responsible, but he didn't want her to be too serious or obsessed with what was happening in that other world. The new sensible young woman would benefit from a dash of the pre-dream Mia. He could only hope it would happen eventually.

"It could be any of these villages along the river here, Dad. One guard said he had a billet in the town just here. It would make sense that it was around here somewhere."

"Yes, that's logical."

"The Nazis were known for keeping excellent records, Dad. I wonder where I can get hold of them? All their camps must be documented somewhere." Mia hesitated, bringing a memory to the fore. "Maybe not this one, though, as I remember them burning a lot of paperwork when the Allies were advancing on the camp."

"Did the Allies ever arrive?"

"That, I don't know. Rachel and Sarid were shot before that happened."

"If they got to the camp, surely they'd have recorded its existence."

"You'd have thought so, Dad. But we can't find anything. Records show the other death camps.

Mia caught Oscar gazing at her, smiling.

"What, Dad?"

"I'm so proud of you — we both are."

Mia smiled, and once again, her plight tugged at Oscar's heart. He wished she didn't have to do this, but knew there was no going back. She would find peace and hopefully be dream-free only when she discovered the truth and, of course, whatever Rachel was trying to tell her.

"Are you still happy to call us Mum and Dad?"

"Yes, of course. You already asked me that. You *are* Mum & Dad. But I'm glad I know about my birth mother. I love the photos you and Mum gave me. I feel sad she's gone. Of course I do."

Oscar pinched Mia's cheek with affection.

"Ruth is another reason I must find out why Rachel is trying to send messages. They are of such importance that she targeted me when she didn't succeed with my mother. I was furious with Rachel when I found out about my mother. She was part of the reason my mother took her own life."

"As we told you, there was more to it."

"Yes, I know her partner left after abusing her."

"We tried so hard to get her to come home to Perth, but I think she would have followed him anywhere. She was deeply in love with him."

"Well, I want nothing to do with him. Even if he is my father, which is in doubt given the entry on my birth certificate. He can stay in the UK for all I care. Anyway, he hasn't ever tried to make contact as far as I know."

"No, he hasn't. I often wished he'd get in touch for your sake, but we wanted nothing to do with him personally. We might have felt differently if he had not abused Ruth.

"Shall we get back to the maps, Dad?"

"Let's do that. Shall I investigate the Internet further while you look at the paper maps?"

"That would be great, Dad." Mia threw him one of her sweetest smiles. She enjoyed working with her dad on a project. It reminded her of when she was in her teens, and he helped her with her homework. He always insisted she did the work herself, but he made sure she understood the subject more thoroughly.

Mia wasn't sure what she would do with the information about the camp when she found it. But it didn't lessen her burning desire to track the place down. Locating the camp on a map would give her a mental reference point. It would add credence to her dreams, which were a significant and all-encompassing part of her life. So much so that they had changed the rest of her life and her with it. Not to mention how they dominated her grandparents' lives now. It was as though nothing else mattered to them or existed outside of the dreams and their consequences.

Mia knew now that Rachel and Sarid didn't survive. She suspected that was the case, but she still felt miserable when it was confirmed by her relatives. In that case, she wondered why Rachel was showing her the last days of their lives. Did she need to witness their deaths?

The women sat silently in the gloom on the bottom of two bunk beds, shoulders hunched. Two little boys played with a handful of rocks on the floor. Their presence was the focus of the women's attention. Apart from each boy taking their turn rolling the rocks on a piece of sacking to deaden the noise, neither boy made any noise. A head nod and a pointed finger acknowledged the outcome of each throw.

One of the women spoke. "They put us all at risk. I don't wish them any harm — how could I? They're just children. We know how much you want to see them. Most of us have children or grandchildren somewhere. You're lucky enough to have them in Hut 66. We don't know the fate of our children."

Several women cried.

"It's no good," the woman continued. "We need to weigh up the risks. We all want to see our children again, don't we?" She stopped and studied her hands, her voice lost to a mind in turmoil. She was a tall, angular woman with grey-streaked black hair. Mia knew Rachel believed she was a good person, but one who became agitated sooner than most. The woman had told Rachel that she had three children, who were now in their teens. They had become separated in the trains, and she hadn't seen them since, either in a holding camp or here.

No one answered the question. There was just lots of nodding and mumbling, which was no surprise. Any mother would want to see her children; words were redundant.

The boys abandoned their game and stood by their mothers' sides, sensing the significance of the moment.

"I can see why you're concerned in one way," said Mia. "We're breaking the rules by allowing them to come here. But I'm certain you'd try to see them if your children were in Hut 66."

More mumbling and head-nodding accompanied by sniffing and nose-blowing from tearful women. There were always tears. The women had lost everything that mattered to them. Their grief was ever present. Several women left the group and shuffled back to their own bunks and thoughts.

"Look, Rachel, you and Rebekah are so blessed to be able to see your boys. We all envy you that and don't begrudge it either. We all want to see our children when we get out of this hell-hole," said another woman, "and by breaking the rules, you could be jeopardising any chances of it happening. You *must* see that."

"Yes," said Shoshana, "stop being so selfish."

While many women agreed with the sentiment, they scowled at Shoshana's attitude.

"What?" Shoshana looked at her companions. "I'm merely saying what we're all thinking." Getting no positive feedback, she huffed in annoyance and stood to leave the group. Then turned back.

"The Germans won't go near Hut 66. You know that," exclaimed Shoshana. "It's too close to the hospital wing for them. They're frightened of catching something. They know about the medical experiments with deadly diseases, like on that group of children who were deliberately infected with tuberculosis recently." She looked around the group, aware of the impact she was having. So she kept going. "They are watching to find out how long they live without medication."

"All rumours. And do you have to frighten the boys?" said Rebekah, pulling her son, Dieter, close to her and placing her hand over his exposed ear.

"It's the truth and you know it. Anyway, the wardens in the hut keep the kids under their care separate from the medical wing," Shoshana added aggressively. "Your kids are safe there. So, stop putting us all at risk bringing them here." She walked away in a temper.

"Providing we can supply a few dead bodies for the wardens to burn, it continues to feed their fear. So, I agree with Shoshana," another woman said. She, too, stood and left the group.

The two boys knew what was being said, but looked on passively. Mia knew Rachel didn't trust Shoshana. There were several reasons, not least, that she had enquired about being a helper in the crematorium. Helpers were a group of Jewish workers, selected for their strength, who held their posts for around three to four months before being gassed themselves as replacements took their jobs. There were perks like extra rations and medical care — only for minor issues. A serious injury or illness resulted in joining the next intake for the 'showers'. Shoshana's motive did not differ from theirs: to survive. Every day was a triumph over adversity, but it was a risk. Shoshana said she would prove she was an excellent worker and she would survive the deadline. That aside, Mia couldn't believe anyone would want to be a part of the actual killing process. It showed a nasty side to the woman.

Rachel and Rebekah embraced their sons and then rushed at each other, pulling their reluctant boys with them to embrace as a group. They knew the weight of opinion was against them. Their boys wouldn't be visiting again. As they held their sons close, they talked to them quietly, hugging them tighter from time to time. There was very little response from either boy. They were hardened to camp life and therefore inured to the drama of the situation. Starvation, abuse and deprivation were their everyday life experiences now. This was yet another blow, just from a different quarter. The Jewish men who ran Hut 66 were strict but kind. However, they never felt totally safe. They knew the Nazis could swoop and march them all out to be shot or gassed on a whim.

Their captors also had ulterior motives for keeping some children alive, as they were used to satisfy the deviant appetites of some officers. The children confided in and supported each other as best they could, their scars deepening with each terrible

experience. Sarid had avoided being selected for 'special duties'
by hiding, but his friend Dieter wasn't as lucky. The first time, he
told Sarid, the man rubbed his private parts all over him and
then asked Dieter to lick them.

"Oh, that's disgusting," said Sarid.

Mia understood with a shock that she was now no longer
Rachel, but entirely immersed in Sarid's perspective in her
dream.

"Yes, it was," said Dieter. "Especially when the hot stuff
squirted all over my face."

Sarid decided he would keep hiding whenever the guards
came near their area.

"Then he struck me across my face and told me to get out."

Dieter went on to say that a different guard, Herman, was
very kind on another occasion.

"He told me I could have a bath. Then watched me and even
helped me use the soap, which Herman got very excited about."

"Did he hit you?" asked Sarid.

"No, he dried me, rubbed oil all over me, and then gave me
chocolate." Dieter didn't mind if he didn't see his mother for a
while, especially if it meant he could see that nice guard,
Herman, again, and have a warm bath and some chocolate.

Sarid said he was glad it wasn't him — but he liked the sound
of the chocolate. He loved chocolate.

As children do in any environment, Sarid and the others in
Hut 66 explored their surroundings despite the risks. The adults
used their natural sense of adventure to send them out to find
supplies. Food was their primary target. They often crept

beneath the mess hut to the waste food bin. Some of these scraps were used for the prisoners' soup, but much of it was left to rot. The bin stank in the hot weather, but the wardens in Hut 66 would boil it long and hard to kill any bacteria. It was all food, and so it was precious. They also collected food from villagers who threw it over the fence near Hut 66.

Then there was the need to steal drugs from the medical wing. The older boys and girls carried out these missions. They were no longer easily shocked or frightened by what they saw. Nutritionally deprived, they were all small for their ages. Another advantage. Sarid was sent on one such mission because the boy destined to go was killed when he dared to pass out after being brutalised sexually by a soldier.

Sarid was a keen recruit, as it seemed like an adventure. He also looked and acted older than his years and could remain calm under pressure. He followed the other boy, Simon, who knew the route very well after taking it many times. They slipped through a loose board on the floor, which was quickly closed and covered behind them. Once outside, Sarid and Simon artfully dodged the searchlights. The visits to his mother's hut meant Sarid was well practised in this activity. Crawling on their bellies, they reached the medical wing, but noticed two guards standing near the spot where the boys usually entered the hut. They sat and waited for the guards to move, but they continued to talk and smoke. Sarid whispered to his companion that they could try a window. The medical wing didn't have bars on the windows, so it was possible. They moved to the furthest point away from the chatting guards. Simon slid out from under the hut and up the side like a snake. His legs dangled for a short while and then disappeared. Sarid was unsure about following, so he sat and waited. After a long delay, two packets dropped to the ground — then two more. Sarid scooped them towards him under the hut in a matter of seconds.

Simon reappeared within a few minutes and scrambled to join Sarid under the hut. He was clasping his chest in pain. Sarid signalled for him to rest awhile. Simon showed Sarid a strap underneath his shirt, made from rough canvas material. It was filled with medicine bottles, one of which was broken. Simon winced as Sarid removed a tiny sliver of glass that had become embedded in his side. Simon then demonstrated how to cover their tracks by running his hand across the dirt. After a thumbs-up that the coast was clear, the boys retraced their route back to Hut 66 with their valuable acquisitions.

CHAPTER 20

Mia was first up and busied herself making tea for her parents and milky coffee for her. On the table she laid a tray with a teapot, their favourite cups, and a few biscuits. Leaving the tray by their bedroom door, she shouted to let them know it was outside. Then she ran back downstairs to her maps and online research. Sitting on the sofa, she sipped her coffee and mulled over her dream.

She wondered how it was possible that she witnessed the goings-on inside Hut 66. She had never seen the camp as a spectator, always as Rachel. Was it conceivable that Sarid or Dieter were now talking to her through the dreams? They were only young boys. Or maybe another adult was coming through. Some details were tough to take in for Mia. She felt desperately sad for the children.

"You're up early, love," said Esme, tightening her dressing gown belt. "The tea was lovely. Thanks. Your dad is still ensconced in bed, enjoying his second cup and polishing off the last of the biscuits."

"That's good, Mum. It's been a bit of a one-way street with you and Dad helping me. I'm trying to give back a little. It's not much, a cup of tea, but it's something anyway."

Mia suddenly felt very low. She was determined not to let her dreams affect her during her waking hours, but some details from last night's dream proved too challenging to forget. She tried to shake off the memories by forcing herself to be positive about the task she had set herself. It was an effort, but she was becoming well-practised at mind games. Sometimes it worked; at other times, not so much. She had busied herself making tea for her parents and concentrating on how much she was enjoying her mug of coffee. However, despite her best efforts, her forced cheery demeanour was rapidly wearing off.

"Mum, can I talk to you about my dream last night? I'm finding it impossible to forget it. I never wanted to ask this again, but I'm sure talking will help."

Esme didn't hesitate. "Of course, my darling! Whenever you like. Your dad has been there for you so many times. I want to help too."

By the time Oscar arrived downstairs, showered and looking fresh and happy, Mia had told Esme about her dream. When it came to the abuse of the children, she had felt some hesitation, but Mia had to get it out of her head where it was churning around incessantly. Two miserable faces looked at Oscar.

"What's going on with you two lovely ladies?" he said as he walked over to the kettle and flicked it on. "Anyone for more tea?"

"We're just discussing something, love," said Esme. "Mia, let's go for a little walk and mull it all over. Grab your jacket, love. We can walk straight over to the park, get a coffee and sit amongst the beauty and peace. This is our real life, and it's wonderful. I'm sure it'll help to ground you a little."

Oscar guessed what they were talking about and felt pushed out. Silly, he chided himself, but he desperately wanted to help Mia. Watching them leave the house and walk away from him seemed wrong somehow. "Shall I do something?" he said, attempting to be involved. Mia smiled at her dad and then went over to hug him.

"We're doing lots of hugging in this house, Dad." Mia pecked him on the cheek. "Pass me those ginger biscuits if you can bear to part with them. We can have them with our coffee in the park, Mum."

Oscar handed them to Mia and winked. "It's difficult. They *are my* favourites. But seeing as it's you——"

"Thanks, Dad. We won't eat them all."

"I get the message. Just mum and daughter time. I'll start in the bedrooms, love. Keep me busy while you two desert the old man."

Mia and Esme strolled along without talking for a while as they enjoyed the early morning sunshine. The park was busy with cyclists, joggers and other walkers. A yoga session was already in full swing on a grassed area, and another group was doing Tai Chi. The birds provided a sweet musical backdrop to the darker thoughts of both mother and daughter.

"This is reality, Mia, your reality," said Esme. She swept her arm out to take in the parkland that stretched as far as they could see. "You belong here, love, not in those dreadful dreams. But, before you object, let me finish. I know you're convinced Rachel wants you to know something. I accept that, but don't allow your dream world to change your reality. You need to live your life when this is done."

"Everything ends," said Mia, remembering Ariella's words during her recent dream.

"Yes, exactly. Everything does," agreed Esme.

"I assume that'll be when Rachel dies."

"Sadly, I think you're right, Mia. But remember, you're viewing an old movie with either dead or very old actors who no longer live the life depicted in your dreams."

"Yes, I hate the reference to movies, but it's true in that respect."

Esme was determined to say her piece. "So, if you're so involved living that non-existent life rather than your real one, then when it ends, you'll be at a loss."

"I'll just have to build my life up again. But it'll be different after this."

"And Mia, I don't want this to put you off talking to your dad or me about your dreams. We'll support you where we can. But please heed my warning. You need to live in the here and now when this is all done."

Mia admired Esme for speaking out; she just admired Esme, full stop. Her dreams seemed to have magnetic power, though. Trying to think of anything else was difficult. She felt totally absorbed — even possessed, some would say. Aware that her 'real' world was falling away, she was trying to keep her balance. But the dreams, and everything associated with them, were all-encompassing.

"Thanks, Mum. I really value your input. I'm going out with Lisa tonight for a meal and a chat. I won't find it easy. We each have our own idea of what a chat is, and I find them very different these days. She feels the same way, I suppose."

"Yes, it must be hard for her too, Mia."

Esme linked arms with Mia. "Seeing the yoga session over there reminded me I'm going to my weekly yoga tonight. Haven't been in weeks. You should think about joining me. It's a great way to relax."

"Not sure yoga's for me, Mum. But I'm really pleased you're going again. These bloody dreams have upended all our lives."

"We choose to be involved, Mia. You'll not face this alone."

"Thanks, Mum. You and Dad are the best. I will work very hard to make my life more meaningful after this. I know it was pretty shallow before. Tell you what, though, I'll be incredibly grateful for what I have. Well, I already am."

"It's as though you're living through the war, Mia. You sound the way people did after it actually happened."

"I suppose I am, really."

"Often, people need crises or hardship to appreciate what they've got. I'm not reprimanding you, love. It's an observation of life. How does the song go — you don't know what you've got till it's gone? Or something like that."

Mia smiled. "Yes, that's it, and it's true."

After buying their coffee from the park café, they sat and drank it in silence, enjoying the magnificent display of flowers and shrubs. The early morning sunshine made it quite magical, as it had set the park aglow with a golden light. Mia opened the biscuits, and they munched their way through half a packet before they realised it.

"Bang goes my size-eight figure, Mother!"

Esme smiled. "Right, we came to talk more about your dream."

"Shall we walk and talk, Mum?"

Esme agreed the dream differed from previous nights because Rachel was clearly not the narrator. The thought of other dead people reaching out to Mia from the camp made Esme shudder. It was as though she was some sort of transmission channel for anyone in the camp to use.

"It would seem you needed to know about other aspects of camp life," said Esme. "Maybe Sarid came through, or perhaps one of the other children?" Believing it was Sarid making contact made it better in one way for Esme. But it also confirmed that he went through some pretty awful experiences, and that saddened her.

Mia saw it as logical but questioned why she needed to know such graphic details about the abuse of the children.

"Perhaps you need to appreciate just how bad it was."

"It's all grim. The violence, the sexual predators, then last night added a layer of nastiness and depravity when it involved the youngest and most vulnerable in the camp."

"One thing I wanted to ask you is what will you do when you get Rachel's message? Surely you must report it to someone; otherwise, what's the point of this?"

"But, who? Should I go to the newspapers, the television, or social media?"

"I think perhaps you should go to as many outlets as possible. But I suppose it depends on what Rachel is trying to tell you."

"It must be important, Mum. She has tried for so long to get her message through to us."

"I think you're right. Something has prevented Rachel from resting in peace. She's a restless spirit, Mia. And I think she'll stay that way until you understand her message."

"I'm doing my best, Mum."

"I know, my darling girl."

"I'm determined to see it through."

"Remember how Danny mentioned you look like her? Well, you do, as did your mother. It shakes me occasionally," said Esme. "Rachel chose Ruth, and now you, to be her voice. It's a privilege but a poison chalice, too, given what happened to Ruth. And what you've experienced in that god-awful camp. Dreadful."

"I know you've many regrets about my mother. It must have been really tough for her. She was abused and cheated on, and then he deserted us both. She was on her own in Sydney. Maybe she wasn't as tough as me. She should have come home to Perth like you and Dad suggested. But stop blaming yourselves. She had choices. She made the wrong ones."

"Yes, I think that's true, but it still hurts terribly, Mia. When your child becomes an adult, there's only so much insisting you can do. Now all we want is to make sure you have the support you need. So, don't worry about us giving up others things for now. This is more important."

"Thanks, Mum. I really appreciate all you do for me. Now more than ever."

Esme rested her hand on Mia's arm and smiled.

"So, perhaps I need to write things down," Mia said, "as evidence?"

Esme agreed. "Yes, I think you should. Also, as you're trying to locate the camp, try to note where you are next time. Then those maps will make more sense."

Mia sighed, sat on a bench, and closed her eyes. She was drained. Dream-filled sleep was exhausting. "That makes loads of sense, Mum," she said without opening her eyes.

"I've got a notebook you can use, Mia. I'll put it beside your bed with a pen and pencil."

Esme's true feelings were that she wanted it all to stop, and the sooner the better. But she knew now that the only way out was through it.

Oscar and Mia spent the next few hours poring over the old maps again, making copious notes as they went along. Esme served them lunch while they worked.

Mia was so preoccupied that she forgot her arrangements with Lisa. She rushed to get ready, but her mind was still full of maps and plans. It would be hard to switch off, but she knew she must. A quick glance in the mirror and she decided she looked presentable, if a little gaunt. Lisa would arrive soon to pick her up, and she was determined to make the evening a success. She owed her friend that much.

CHAPTER 21

Mia was now on long-term sick leave from TopTravel. Her attempts to return to work were disastrous. Sherri, her ex-boss, had been shipped off back to Sydney, where her aggressive sales techniques were more appreciated. The six-month sales figures at the Perth city branch had plummeted since Sherri arrived, and Mia's departure hadn't helped. She had heard that Lucas was standing in as branch manager and doing a good job. However, Mia wasn't sure whether reporting to Lucas as her manager would work for her. He was keen to get her back, calling in at the house a few times to ask after her and enquire about the possibility of her returning to work. Her parents were polite but firm; they informed him she still needed to take things easy and would return if or when she felt ready.

Mia's days were spent systematically recording details of everything she could remember from her past dreams and those still happening. She had taken Esme's advice and was proactive during her dreams to see where the camp was located. She had limited success. The scope of each dream was determined by Rachel, at least until more recently, when others in the camp came through to her. Even so, Mia made a point of looking beyond the fence when she was working nearby, and she could make out several buildings. The only distinctive feature about them was a large weathercock on the front of the most prominent building — the processing centre.

She was tied to a bed and alone in a hut. A large female guard entered, undid the straps, and ordered her to take a bath.

"Can I ask?——"

The guard slapped her across her face. "No, bitch, you can't ask. Put this on after you wash your muck off." A white nightdress was thrown on the bed. "They like their bitches to be clean and angelic-looking. We can't wash the Jew out of you, but at least you will be a washed Jew." She shoved Mia towards a small room off the bedroom.

Mia was terrified. She knew what was going to happen. But she couldn't believe Rachel would want her to experience this. "No, please, no. Rachel," she whispered. "Please release me."

She sat in a shallow, tepid bath, silently begging Rachel to spare her. The female guard stood by the door and leered at her. "Wash that filthy hair and the essential places. I can always help you. I'd enjoy that. Maybe get you warmed up a little," she laughed, showing yellowing teeth. "You're a lucky bitch; you get the top man today. He can be a little rough, but you'll get the hang of it. The last bitch cried. He doesn't like tears. She won't be crying again," she sniggered and walked towards the bath. The outer door opened. A guard shouted a warning that the commandant had arrived.

"Be quick, Jew. He's here."

Mia dried herself on a small, thin towel hanging on a rail and held it against her, attempting to cover her naked body as she walked back into the room. A German officer was standing at the foot of the bed. He smiled at her. A let-me-see-what-we-have-here sort of smile. The female guard licked her lips. Mia froze.

"I suggest you do as you're told, bitch, if you know what's good for you." The female guard stepped forward, ready to snatch the towel.

"No, Hilda, I like her being shy. I have to conquer her and make her bend to my will. Perfect choice. You may leave now." Hilda hesitated. "Get out of here, you salivating whore; she's mine."

Mia closed her eyes and tried to wake up. "Please, I need to leave here right now. Please, God, not this."

A firm hand grabbed her wrist and forced her to her knees. "If you wish to leave, please pray to me. I'm your lord and master in this room, and you will be my little pet." He pressed Mia's face to his crotch and let out a sigh of pleasure. She could feel him harden as she begged to be released. He was revelling in his power over her.

"That's right, plead, beg. Oh, I love it. Now release my manhood. He's eager to meet you."

Mia obeyed, and he thrust his penis into her mouth. He withdrew and grabbed her as she gagged, dragging her to her feet. "Oh no, not yet, my little flower. Fun and games first. Lots of fun and games. Get on the bed. Now!"

Mia laid face down, willing it to be over. He stroked her, then slapped her hard, laughing as she squealed in pain. She curled into a ball. He wrapped himself around her body and pressed himself into her back. He licked her neck, then suddenly pushed her over and suckled her breasts. His eyes were wild and greedy as he looked at her. She could smell him, sweat, cigarettes and alcohol. She was clean; he wasn't. After exploring her whole body, he giggled.

"Let's play doggies, shall we?" he laughed again. It was a silly, effeminate laugh reminding her of a madman she had seen in a movie.

Whatever you do, don't cry, she told herself. The last girl died because she cried. She went limp and thought of her son, her dear Sarid. She would be strong for him.

Finally, he left her alone. She crawled off the bed and went to bathe. She needed to clean him off her. The water was still in the bath, so she stepped in quickly before Hilda returned. It was short-lived. Laughing, Hilda dragged her out and held her close.

"Oh, you feel good," she breathed in Mia's face as she put her hands on Mia's breast and squeezed her nipple. "Shame I have to rush you." Her hands slid down to Mia's genitals.

Mia recoiled and gasped at the intimacy.

"I'd have liked a little extra fun myself. But the room is booked for another important visitor, and he doesn't like to be kept waiting."

"Another?" Mia whispered.

Hilda pushed her away.

"No, bitch. He's not here for you. You'll be no good to him. He likes little boys. We've one lined up outside." She roared with laughter. "A little Jewish lamb to the slaughter."

Mia rushed to the hut window. She was ashamed to feel utter relief, as it was not her Sarid. It was another poor little mite.

"Get out, bitch. You can put your rags on outside. Give the other guards a little thrill." The guard slapped her backside, laughing again.

Mia stumbled towards the door and fell. A hand grabbed her.

"I'm going. Please. I'm going."

Arms encircled her, and she realised Esme was holding her close as she crouched on her bathroom floor.

"You must have fallen, love, as you stepped out of the shower. Are you okay? You're shivering. You've got some nasty bruises. Let me get another towel." Then she added, "You look as though you've been in the wars." It was a stupid thing to say, and Esme knew it immediately.

But it was too late to take it back, and it cut through Mia's willpower and her resolve not to cry. She collapsed forward until her forehead touched the floor, and she howled. The animal quality of the noise shocked and startled Esme. She ran back to Mia's bedroom door, shouting. "Oscar, for God's sake, Oscar. Come now. Mia has collapsed. She's collapsed. Something awful has happened."

Oscar ran into the room and stared down at Mia.

"Oh my God, Esme. What can we do?"

"Get the sedatives. Quickly."

"Doesn't she need a doctor, Esme? Look at her arms; she's hurt."

A low groan came from Mia. "No, not the doctor. No doctor. Please, I need a bath and sleep," said Mia as she tried to get up.

Esme helped her to her feet. "But you've just had a shower, love."

"I must wash him off me."

"Oscar and Esme exchanged a worried look."

After a long hot bath, during which Mia couldn't stop sobbing, Esme helped her into a clean nightie and gave her a sedative. Esme saw more injuries on Mia's legs, particularly at the top and her abdomen. Esme was close to tears but knew she must hold it together. "Can I put some witch hazel on those, Mia? It'll reduce the bruising.

"Mia nodded, unable to speak or stop shaking.

"I was raped, Mum. Brutally raped."

"No. Who? Who has done this to you?"

"It was in the concentration camp. I tried to wake up. Tried to come back here. Pleaded with Rachel and God to get me out. But she didn't, and he didn't."

Mia was hysterical. "How can I be raped in a dream and be left bruised and battered? It can't happen, surely?" She looked at Esme, searching for an answer. Esme just shook her head.

Mia knew she was raving, but she was so scared. If this could happen, the possibilities were terrifying because she couldn't control these events. She wanted to run away, but where? And would the dreams still find her? Was there a portal in this house? In this room? Would she be dragged back to that place of horror wherever she was? The dreams had found her at work and at the paintball site. She wasn't safe anywhere.

Mia grabbed her hair with both hands and pulled, screaming and crying. "I can't do it. I can't do it. Save me, Mum. They'll kill me when they kill Rachel. She dies in that place; we know she dies. What if I'm there when it happens? I'll die too. Oh, God. Oh, God. Am I Rachel and not Mia? Do I need to die for Rachel again?"

Esme gave Mia another tranquilliser and held her tight. She didn't know what else to do. If she could just think of something to protect Mia. They had to think of something — or Mia could be raped again, or worse, killed. Esme's mind was working at full speed. Was it possible that Mia was Rachel reincarnated? She shivered. Ruth intended to call her Rachel when she was born, but Esme convinced her otherwise. Esme suggested Mia — as it meant beloved — and thankfully, Ruth agreed. Get a grip, Esme, she reproached herself. She's Mia, *not* Rachel.

"Shh, love. Come on. Come on. You're stronger than this, Mia. We'll stop this somehow. We will. Someone will help us. Hold on. Please hold on."

"No one can stop it from this side, Mum. Not this side. But Rachel could. She's pulling me back there. Rachel can stop it, can't she?" Mia paused, leaving the question hanging in the air and looking for the answers in her mother's eyes. She found as much confusion there as was in her own head.

"Mia, please."

Mia shook her head from side to side. Nooo! I can't do it. The tears kept coming, and her hysteria rose to another level. "Rachel *must* have the power to stop what she's started. I *didn't* die in a Nazi concentration camp," Mia screeched. "I *didn't* get raped there either. Rachel did. I've been raped like Rachel, so I'll probably die like Rachel. How, Mum . . . How? This is my time. I live in this time, not the 1940s."

Esme slipped under the covers as the sedatives took effect and put her arms around a shaking Mia, letting her sob against her chest. She cried silently, too. She was helpless to stop the madness gripping her family.

Oscar found them like that an hour later, both sound asleep, wrapped in each other's arms. He crept out of the room, sat on the stairs, put his head in his hands and cried. He felt he should be able to protect her. But he hadn't. He couldn't. The feeling of utter hopelessness overwhelmed him.

CHAPTER 22

Alma sat, head lowered, lacing and unlacing her fingers. Esme busied herself in the kitchen making tea, and Mia was lying on the sofa, covered in a warm blanket. She looked asleep — she was so still — but Alma couldn't be sure, as she was wearing an eye mask. Mia made her nervous. She had known Mia since she was born, but something about her deeply disturbed Alma. When Ruth brought her home from the hospital and looked at her cradled in Esme's loving arms, Mia's eyes flickered open for just a moment. Alma was shaken by a strange recognition. She said nothing. What could she say? "Mia looked at me with eyes I've seen before — she knew me." They would have thought she was crazy. Then, when Esme and Oscar had charge of Mia after their daughter died, she would give Alma that look from time to time. It was as though she was looking at her from somewhere else, with someone else's eyes.

It all made sense to Alma now, since Oscar explained what was happening with Mia's dreams. Those eyes were Rachel's eyes. Her Aunt Ariella's dear friend Rachel, who, along with Rachel and her son, perished in a Nazi concentration camp. Still, she said nothing to Esme and Oscar. How would it help the situation? She was now convinced Rachel's spirit possessed Mia, but Mia didn't have Rachel's beautiful mind. The girl was spoilt, which turned her into a vain and self-centred person. Rachel had never been like that, and she had known her since she was a little girl in their home village. She smiled at the thought of those happy times as a child playing with Sarid, Rachel's son, and

Naomi. Rachel was a different type of person altogether from Mia. Still, Rachel had chosen to communicate through Mia, her great-niece. Alma felt there must be a reason for that choice.

Because of her Aunt Ariella, Alma knew more about what was happening to Mia than she admitted. She had spoken to Esme some time ago, but she kept certain things to herself even then. She didn't want to get any more involved than she already was. Her life had been affected by her own dreams, not to mention coping with her personal experiences back in the war — a lifelong burden of memories. Wars may end, but they never end for victims of their violence. Such scars were for life.

"Penny for them, Alma," said Oscar as he came into the room.

"Oh, I'm not sure you'd pay me for them, Oscar. Who listens to a silly old woman?

"Alma," Esme exclaimed as she laid the tea tray on the coffee table. "When have we not listened to you? You've given us wise advice many times. And this is one such occasion. Today we'd like your advice. We really would."

Alma felt panicky. She knew this would be about Mia. It was always about Mia in this house. Now all this terrible dreaming was happening. She felt guilty about being resentful. Esme and Oscar were her dearest friends, and they had always been there for her. Even after all these years, she still thought of them as Naomi and Edan. Their name changes had always felt strange to her.

Mia stirred and sat up. "Hi, Alma. I didn't hear you come in."

"Hello, dear. Don't disturb yourself on my account," said Alma, and hoped Mia would just lie back down and she could make her excuses and leave. Like Lisa, Alma found Mia radically changed. It was hard enough being in her company before, but now it was much worse.

"I've got to get up now. I've been sleeping so much lately. I'm drugged up to the eyeballs by the doctor to keep me calm and hopefully stop me from dreaming. So far, great. Three days without dreaming. But I feel like I'm living a half-life on these things." Mia shuffled her slippers on and wobbled to her feet.

"Here, let me help you, love." Oscar rushed to Mia.

"Thanks, Dad, but I can manage."

Alma watched Mia anxiously. She spent years recovering from her own nightmares from the time she spent in Auschwitz as a child — if she or anyone ever really recovered. You just learned how to cope with it by getting on with life, a life shattered by the loss of your family and by your own horrendous experiences. She had worked hard to replace her nightmarish memories with the beautiful recollections of her family and friends before the terrors of the Holocaust. Then came her nightmares about the same place Mia dreamt of. Even though she was taken back in time to that camp as her Aunt Ariella, Rachel seemed to have a worse time of it than her aunt. She had seen Mia there. Even spoken to her. But she didn't want to divulge that, feeling sure it wouldn't help. The girl was already in a precarious state of mind.

"Shall we go through to the conservatory? It's so bright in there," said Esme. "With only the glass separating us from the outside, it always makes me feel closer to nature, and it's a calming atmosphere." Esme chatted as she carried the tray through to the conservatory. "You may not be able to help, Alma, but we're desperate. We wouldn't ask this of you, but we don't know what to do next," said Oscar. Alma's shoulders were hunched as she reluctantly trailed behind them.

They were drinking their tea when Mia spoke up. "You knew Rachel, didn't you, Alma? You know, before . . . "

Alma spluttered on her tea a little at Mia's direct approach.

Oscar went to intervene when he saw a clear reticence in Alma. Esme put a restraining hand on his arm. Her message was simple — leave it. He looked at his wife, querying her action. They thought Alma could help stop Rachel somehow, block her. They didn't know what they expected Alma to do, though, as long as the dreams stopped and Mia was out of danger. The saying "grasping at straws" came to Oscar's mind. But, maybe unreasonably, both Oscar and Esme thought Alma could be the key.

"I'm petrified, Alma. I really need help."

Silence. Nothing.

"Please, Alma. I don't want to die in the past."

Alma felt cornered. "Look, Mia. I know what's been happening. Your mum and dad have told me," said Alma, annoyed. "You belong here in the present; you were born here only twenty-five years ago. How can you possibly die before you were even born? I don't know why you're worried."

It was entirely logical. You couldn't die before you existed. They were stumped for a moment in the face of an irrefutable fact.

"Alma, but I was raped before I was born, so I could die in the past."

"Were you really raped? Are you sure? Perhaps it was such a realistic dream, and you were thrashing about and bruising yourself," said Alma.

Esme and Oscar looked confused but hopeful. Oscar took a long drink of his tea and nodded his head as though all was clear.

"Mia, maybe that was it. I found you on the floor, my darling," Esme suggested, feeling suddenly optimistic.

"That would be a convenient explanation. I'd love to believe it. Forgive me for being so blunt, but my vagina was sore and bruised inside. I also had semen leaking out of me."

The explicit description made them all uncomfortable. Oscar busied himself topping up his teacup. Alma looked at Esme in astonishment.

"So, you think you could even get pregnant," said Alma, throwing her hands in the air and shaking her head.

"No, this is getting ridiculous," said Oscar.

"Well, of course it is," said Alma. "It's not possible."

"Oh, my God! Not that as well. Please God, no," Esme wailed.

Oscar looked at Mia's distraught face, and all doubt drained away. "Look, this is an unusual and extreme situation," he said. "Mia doesn't mean to alarm us, but she needs to be believed and supported. I admit I hoped that it was self-bruising when it happened, but Mia knows what she's experienced. We're not here to cross-examine her."

"Please help us, if you can, Alma. Rachel was your mother's closest friend." Esme pleaded.

Alma's reluctance held firm.

"Alma, please. I know you've had experiences too. You told me about your dreams a while ago, and doesn't your aunt come through to you too, in your dreams?" said Esme.

"Alma?" queried Mia.

Mia and Oscar looked shocked. Esme had said nothing before.

Alma took a deep breath. "No, not really. A couple of glimpses, that's all. I expect it's because Mia has been stirring things up." The accusation in Alma's voice was unmistakable, and she threw Mia a sullen look.

Esme was annoyed. Alma was lying, and she knew she was. Esme didn't understand why Alma thought she could lie to her. She had told her how Ariella saw Isaac, Rachel, and Sarid being dragged away by the Gestapo. And that she had been taken back to the same concentration camp in her dreams.

Alma dropped her head in embarrassment when Esme looked at her querulously.

"Alma, if you don't want to help us, then say so," said Esme. "But I know you've seen more than that in your dreams. Your aunt was in the same camp as Rachel." Esme warmed to her subject, and her anger grew with it. "Also, you said your aunt was on the same transport as Rachel and Sarid." Esme shook her head when Alma did not respond. "As we've been friends since early childhood, I thought our friendship would mean something to you. I can't think why you wouldn't help. Perhaps you just don't want to. I personally had little hope when we asked you here. Seems I was right . . ." Esme trailed off and shrugged her shoulders in defeat.

The implications of what Esme said sank in while no one spoke.

"Oscar, can I have something stronger, please," asked Alma. "If I'm going to talk about any of this, I need a proper drink."

"Oh, thank you, Alma," said Esme. She felt she could breathe again.

After a slow start, Alma got into a flow. In the following hour, during which Alma gulped down at least three large whiskies, she laid her soul bare, crying from time to time. She cursed the whole German race and even the Jews themselves for not rising up against the barbarities inflicted upon them throughout the war. The similarities to Mia's dreams were stark. Still, Alma seemed to avoid the violence when she was there — unlike Mia. The whisky was helping. Oscar topped up her glass whenever it got low.

"Can I get you something to eat, Alma? Just to line your stomach," Esme offered after a while.

Mia turned to Esme and shook her head. The last thing they needed was for Alma to lose her nerve again. However, Alma accepted, and Esme left the room.

"Can you carry on, Alma?" Mia suggested.

"I think we should wait for your mother." Alma was decisive. She took a large gulp of whisky and put her head back on the sofa.

Mia followed her mother out of the room. "Mum, she will go off the boil or go to sleep. Why did you suggest food? She's nearly asleep with all that whisky, and we only just got started on her dreams. Don't start rustling up one of your big lunches, for goodness' sake. I'll grab a bag of tacos, and we can have dips," said Mia as she threw packets and dips on the kitchen counter.

"I've made us all a sandwich, too. Sorry, love. I believed it was the correct thing to do. She *is* helping us. And to soak up the alcohol. Okay, I'm sorry. Let's get back in there."

Mia crashed and bashed around as she put the food on the coffee table. Alma looked as though she was asleep. Mia gave Esme a look of reprimand.

"Here, Alma, a sandwich." Mia shoved a plate into her lap, making Alma jump. Esme and Oscar reacted with disapproval. They knew Alma. She didn't take kindly to anything like this. She already felt pushed around by the situation.

Mia needed to get Alma back on the subject, and fast. She was old, and her concentration would be even less now with all the alcohol inside her. "So, Alma, do you experience life in the concentration camp as I do? Have you returned here to find dirt on your hands or any other physical evidence that you've been there? Have you felt anything, like being sore from abuse from the guards or exhaustion from working long hours?"

Alma stared at Mia. If the girl didn't look so much like Rachel, she wouldn't be doing this. She found Mia far too pushy.

Then Alma saw a look in Mia's eyes, just like when she was born. Rachel was looking at her through Mia's eyes — pleading and sad eyes. Alma gasped.

Oscar rushed to her side. "If it's all too painful, Alma, we can leave it there for today."

"No, no. Rachel is here with us, and she wants me to help."

Esme looked around, half expecting to see Rachel. She shivered involuntarily.

"Okay, dear, if you're sure," said Oscar.

Mia breathed out with relief.

Alma was experiencing very similar things to Mia. Despite everything Esme and Oscar had heard from Mia about the camp, the telling of such horrors in a familiar setting on a sunny afternoon was still shocking. It almost defied belief.

As she had told Esme previously, Alma frequently inhabited the body and the life of her Aunt Ariella in the same camp as Mia in her dreams. She was there when Mia was working in the camp sheds as Rachel. Alma knew it was Mia because Rachel looked confused and disorientated. She even tried to help with Mia's tasks on one occasion so the guards wouldn't notice how slow Rachel was.

Mia cast her mind back to the dream in question and remembered the incident. But how was this going to help her now? Alma was being dragged back there, too. Mia felt distraught. *How can I stop it from happening to me?* She slumped back in her chair, hope slipping away. There wouldn't be any sort of rescue from anyone. What were her parents thinking? Alma was just another victim. How could another victim help her? Although, she had to admit one thing: it comforted her knowing Alma was in the camp.

"Do you recall that, Mia?" asked Alma.

"I do," said Mia. "And when you smiled at me in the sorting shed and gave me that speech between the huts about being brave."

"Did you really, Alma?" said Oscar, grinning.

"Well, if I hadn't stopped you, Mia, you'd have been in trouble. I mean, if Aunt Ariella hadn't stopped you."

"Thank you, Alma. We're so grateful," said Oscar.

Esme nodded in agreement, slightly awestruck by Alma's bravery.

"You're like my guardian angel, Alma," said Mia, smiling with affection at Alma.

Alma was touched by the family's appreciation.

"How many other time travellers are in the camp? Do you know, Alma? You recognised me. So, are there others?"

"I have to admit, I've seen others I suspected were there from the future. They looked like you did — confused and lost."

"But why us, Alma? Could it be because we're neighbours? After all, we're not blood relatives. Is it this land we're on? . . . because no one in the extended family is affected . . . or are they all hiding the truth?"

"The land?" said Oscar.

"Yes, you know, Dad? You see stuff like that in films where people move into a house, and then the haunting starts."

"But that's just fiction, Mia," Esme insisted. "You told the therapist it wasn't a re-run of a movie. *Now* what are you saying?"

"No, Mum. I'm saying it could be like an opening through time in a particular place — that's all."

The discussion led to more questions, and Mia's comments set Oscar's mind racing. He thought about the houses they lived in. First, Jarrahdale, where Ruth was born, then when she left home to be with her partner in Sydney with baby Mia, they moved to the city. He didn't want to move out of the city, as he found Perth to be vibrant and lively. He would walk into town most days and meet friends. But when Ruth died, and they took charge of Mia, they moved out here and bought a house with a garden on a new development. Alma and her husband immediately bought next door.

It was all so rushed when he thought back. They were not impulsive by nature. They acted out of character by pushing so single-mindedly for this house; no other would do. It was this house in particular. It was not a complete surprise that Alma and her husband followed them, except that they had been happy in their old house, and that *was* strange when he thought about it. He was itching to research the area. He remembered old buildings on the land, which were cleared for the development. What were those buildings? Were they relevant? Would knowing help? He intended to check as soon as possible.

"Perhaps it's because of friendship," said Alma. "Aunt Ariella and Rachel were close friends before the war. And Esme, Sarid and I were inseparable as children."

"Yes, we were always playing together," said Esme, looking fondly at Alma.

"Oh, yes, you told me how you and Alma were friends as children," said Mia."

Alma and Mia were now sitting on the sofa together, holding hands. It was touching, as they had never got on, each critical of the other. This was a real turnaround. They were murmuring. And every so often, one of them would touch the other on the arm or smile encouragingly. Alma cried a little, and Mia soothed her — Alma did the same for Mia. Esme and Oscar felt redundant, so Esme took the plates to the kitchen. Oscar went to the lounge and sat in front of his computer. He glanced through the conservatory door from time to time and marvelled at how a shared experience could cause such different individuals to bond. It would have been unlikely in any other circumstances. He hoped the outcome would be positive for both of them concerning the dreams, but he didn't see how.

Mia threw the shoes onto the different piles as instructed. She took Alma's advice about being smelly and objectionable to avoid attracting the attention of any guards on the prowl for attractive women — even going as far as having a snotty nose, with encrustations and dirt in her ears. She hadn't seen Sarid for a while, but she received word that he was safe and being a good boy in Hut 66. Mia worked diligently and made sure she was seen doing so. Good workers were less likely to be gassed or shot.

She was feeling particularly pleased with herself, having been involved (along with a group of other women) in getting five little ones into Hut 66 in the past month. They also smuggled a newborn out of the camp. The tiny scrap of humanity, born in the filth that was their living quarters, was passed through a hole in the fence and into the arms of a rescuer, who was regularly involved with saving babies and young children from the camp. The mother was distraught, but neither would have survived once the guards found them. It was a wonder she had succeeded in hiding her pregnancy. The baby was undersized and sickly; only a small miracle would enable it to survive while being hidden from the local authorities in the outside community. Saving babies and young children was an ongoing activity. Often newly arrived mothers wouldn't part with their children; they could not bear to give them up to what they saw as an unknown fate. Sadly, they, along with their children, paid with their lives. If a woman looked strong and healthy but had a young child clinging to her, she couldn't work. So, the child would be taken away and disposed of. Many beautiful women were earmarked to serve the sexual needs of the soldiers. Their children were summarily executed. Often this happened right in front of their hysterical mothers.

Losing your possessions was part of the dehumanisation process on arrival at the camp, regardless of whether you were sent directly to your death or were "lucky" enough to become a working inmate. The worst fate was reserved for the deformed, mentally handicapped or those with any condition of medical interest. They were immediately sent to the doctors who worked in the research area of the medical wing. According to other prisoners, death was a better option.

Guards escorted the men, women, and children selected for death to the gas chambers. The soldiers acted solicitously and assured the prisoners that they were just going for a shower to freshen up before they entered the camp. This was a deliberate ploy to keep the prisoners from panicking and made the processing of large numbers easier. Those too infirm to walk were loaded on trucks for transportation. On arrival, they were asked to undress. Their captors' civility calmed most new arrivals, who were then willing to walk into the showers, aka the gas chamber. Those who objected or made a fuss were quickly separated and shot elsewhere. After they were gassed, Jewish helpers dragged their corpses out of the gas chambers and removed long hair, jewellery and teeth. Gold teeth were particularly prized. The helpers transferred everything they collected to the sorting sheds. The bodies were burned.

As Mia worked, she tried not to react when the footwear told her stories. A heel worn on one side showed her the image of a person with an uneven gait. When a pair of shoes had a repair, it reminded her of Oscar and, in particular, one pair of shoes he loved so much that he had them repaired multiple times. Then, there were the dress shoes. She imagined the special events and how the wearer must have delighted in how they added the finishing touch to a smart outfit. Or a pair that would fit a pretty teenager. These would tug hard at her heart. She thought about the dreams the girl had about her future before it was snatched away. But the shoes of a child or baby affected her the most. The poor innocents had hardly started their lives before their little shoes had been taken from their feet in readiness for their brutal and agonising murder by gassing. Not for the first time, she wondered where the outside world was during this mass slaughter.

She snapped out of her thoughts and concentrated on the job at hand. It was all about surviving for her son now. She was sure her husband was dead. They dragged him out to the street and savagely beat him because he shouted out how much he loved her and Sarid. When they finally flung him into a waiting truck, he wasn't moving. She had hoped against all reason he had lived somehow, and they would see him again, but she knew he was gone.

"Isaac, I miss you so much," she whispered.

She put a pair of smarter, less worn shoes on a separate pile to be refurbished by Jewish cobblers and sent out of the camp for German feet. She wondered if the new owner gave a passing thought to the origins of their shoes and the unwilling donor who had worn them first.

The guards would wander through the workshop, selecting shoes for their families and friends. Prisoners would switch their shoes for a better pair when no one was watching. Those that were past their best were stacked in another pile. The recycling workshop would collect these in wheelbarrows. The components — leather, soles, buckles and laces — were separated and sent out of the camp for various uses by German factories.

Their work on these sad remnants of murdered prisoners meant they lived another day themselves. While they were of use in contributing to the German war effort, they were comparatively safe. Of course, their ultimate contribution would be their own hair, teeth and shoes. The longer they avoided that, the better. However, they weren't under any illusions. They knew they were on borrowed time. While they were still lucky enough to be breathing, they worked hard, stayed quiet, and survived.

The atrocious living conditions, weather, and disease took their toll on inmates. Food was scarce. They received a cup of watery soup with a trace of vegetables and a chunk of stale bread each day — sometimes not even that. If they survived the hard work and abuse, many would simply lose the will to live or freeze to death in the winter — usually overnight.

Anything that gave them hope they clung to, and recently a glimmer of optimism shone on their lives of violence, drudgery and hopelessness. Rumours were circulating about an Allied advance in the area, which would mean a German retreat. It made their days fractionally brighter. But they knew they mustn't act any differently. The Germans were already nervous and jumpy. People were shot or clubbed to death for petty reasons or for nothing. Mia looked around the dismal shed with beaten-down workers surrounded by the pitiful belongings of hundreds of dead prisoners. She reminded herself not to react. She must lie low and survive.

CHAPTER 23

Oscar was ebullient as he wandered into the kitchen, having spent hours on his computer.

"Now I've something here. It may mean nothing, or it could explain a lot. Where is Mia, Esme?"

"Next door with Alma again. She seems to have gained a great deal of strength from knowing Alma has had similar dreams about her Aunt Ariella. And that she's often with Alma when she's Rachel in that camp. It's all quite surreal," said Esme. "And Mia mentioned there were rumours that the Allied forces were about to descend on the camp. If we didn't know how this all ends, it would be a cause for joy. But we know they perished, so it means that horror is nearer for Mia and Alma if they continue to visit the camp."

Oscar could see the stress on his wife's face. Not that it was new. They were both permanently stressed since this whole thing started with Mia.

With the imminent death of Rachel, Ariella and Sarid, the risks Mia and Alma were taking in the camp had stepped up to another level.

"Sorry, love. What have you discovered on the Internet? I didn't want to dampen your enthusiasm."

Oscar was unsure if he should tell Esme first or wait until Mia was back. He decided on the former. "We lived in Jarrahdale, right? Before we moved to Perth, into the city. And then, wasn't it when we took charge of Mia as a baby that we came here to Menora?"

"Well, yes, the Perth apartment wasn't suitable for a young child."

"Yes, yes, that's not the point," said Oscar impatiently, annoyed at Esme's interruption.

"Oscar?"

"Look, this is important, Esme. Can you follow my line of thought to get this out of my head?"

"Okay, carry on," she said as she peeled and chopped carrots.

Oscar shuffled his papers and then launched into the history of Jarrahdale and how their small housing estate was near a prisoner-of-war camp that held Italians.

"What are you saying?" Esme was all attention now.

"Let me finish, Esme. I need to get everything out. Then you can give me your opinion."

Esme put her knife down, removed her apron, and sat beside Oscar on the other bar stool. He held her hand.

"That's the link. A portal if you like. That's when it all started. We were so determined to move there before Ruth was born. It was beyond our usual enthusiasm for anything."

Esme squeezed her husband's hand. Hairs stood up on the back of her neck, and she shivered. "So, are you saying that some outside force attracted us to Jarrahdale?"

"Yes."

"This is getting very bizarre, Oscar. Do you think you're jumping to hasty and convenient conclusions?"

Oscar ignored his wife's doubt and ploughed on. "Alma mentioned she saw Rachel looking back at her when she looked into Mia's eyes as a baby. So, when we lost Ruth because of those wretched dreams, Rachel needed to channel through Mia. We'd left Jarrahdale, but we moved here to Menora where there were also Italians interred during the war. That's where she was waiting for Mia."

"So, she possessed them," whispered Esme, wide-eyed. "The dreams you had were meant for Ruth and Mia, Oscar. That's why you could deal with them."

Esme became animated, her enthusiasm overflowing. "And then, when Ruth suggested Rachel's name for Mia, we talked her out of it. We wanted to protect them from … well, from Rachel," she gasped. "We must have sensed the danger somehow."

"You're way ahead of me, Esme, and I think you're being dramatic if I'm honest."

Esme was indignant. "Well, what do you think, then? As if what you're saying isn't dramatic enough."

Oscar hadn't completed his research, but thought Esme might have a point. They found Australia open and friendly in many respects and not as judgemental of religious diversity as back in Europe. So why had they tried to protect Ruth and Mia by cutting them off from their extended family? Had they subconsciously been aware of this threat?

"We delivered our girls into the hands of these ghosts from the past, Oscar. Mia doesn't need to live here or in Jarrahdale now. The dreams have followed her wherever she is — even the campsite in Lancelin! So much for a relaxing weekend."

"So, what does that tell us, Esme? I wonder if Alma dreams wherever she is, too?"

"Hang on, Oscar. Remember when Alma came to stay with us in Jarrahdale? She had bad dreams. Don't you remember? She said she had never had such unpleasant dreams before. After that, she was always reluctant to stay over, if I remember rightly. So maybe once the dreams got hold of her in Jarrahdale, they followed her back here, too."

Oscar looked thoughtful for a moment. "You're right, Esme. You're right." He could not contain his excitement. "Where is Mia? She can't still be round there talking, can she?"

"So, shall we move into our apartment in the city for a while? It may break the hold on Mia." Esme was one step ahead of Oscar again.

"It's what I was thinking, Esme. Although it may take time, it could work. Anyway, I prefer to talk to Mia first. I'd also feel bad about leaving Alma here at the moment, too. We've pulled her into this now."

"She was *in* it already, Oscar, but hid it from us. Anyway, the apartment is big enough for all of us if she wants to join us."

"I have my doubts, Esme. What's stopping the dreams from following Mia to the apartment?"

"I don't know. But Jarrahdale has a strong connection to the war, as has Menora. And a large Jewish community — both may be relevant."

"Maybe it's about time, Esme. Mia spends most of her time here, so her dreams are centred here. She's only at work during the day, so they can follow her. The connection isn't lost. Maybe a long stay at the apartment would work."

"The way you talk about it makes it sound like science fiction. You're forgetting Ruth. She went to Sydney. She was there for six months before . . . you know . . . "

"There are several old prisoners of war camps there too, Esme."

"Hmm. Not sure about all this."

"Well, what do you suggest? This is my best shot. We can at least try it."

They could hear Alma and Mia coming through the back door. Esme and Oscar sat up expectantly and waited for their arrival. Before Oscar could relay his findings, Mia spoke.

"We've got a plan, and we think it may just work. We'll look out for one another. If either of us is in danger, we'll shake the other. You know, force each other to wake up."

Alma and Mia looked from Esme to Oscar, waiting for their response.

"After all the talking, you came up with that?" Esme's tone was derisory. "You really believe that shaking will bring you back, Mia? You've been beaten, slapped, injured, and even raped. It didn't wake you. How can shaking do any better?"

Mia flinched at the word rape. "It's different. I've always tried to get myself back here. But, with both of us trying — saying our real names and reasoning with each other——"

"Listen to what your dad has discovered and see if we can stop either of you from going back there again," said Esme. "We think we can break the connection."

Oscar was amused at Esme's sudden enthusiasm about his findings, which only moments before she had doubted.

Once again, they made their way through to the lounge. Alma was coping with what she knew now, and she had formed a new relationship with Mia. She realised the fear of her own experiences had made her project fear and dislike onto Mia, which wasn't fair. But what was going to unfold now? She was unsure how much more she could take. Maybe she was being too judgemental again.

CHAPTER 24

Having met her new family, Mia wanted to meet up with some of her younger relatives. She had a lot of time to catch up on, and she needed a night out, so it would achieve both. She made a call.

"Hi Rach, this is Mia. Remember we met at the family reunion at our house?"

"Yes, yes, I do."

"How are you now? Did the get-together help at all?"

"It was mixed, Rach. It was a bit mind-boggling with revelations coming at me from all directions, but overall, it was helpful. It's great to have such a big family after thinking there were just us three."

"Oh, that's good to hear, Mia. Everyone was glad to be in touch with you and your family."

"Thanks. Look, now I've found you all, I don't want to lose touch. Can we organise something for the younger family members, the young adults anyway? Maybe a night out in Northbridge?" Mia wanted to avoid offending the older members of her new family. But she was hoping to relax and enjoy the new friendship of her cousins. They seemed interesting people. The older relatives would want to talk about her dreams and Rachel. She didn't want that right now. Mia was amused by her own thoughts. When had she ever cared whether people were interesting?

After a few suggestions, they settled on a live music venue followed by a Chinese. Rach offered to set it all up, and Mia came off the phone feeling more normal than she had done in a long while. She knew somehow her cousin would think of something they would all enjoy. Mia felt guilty about Lisa, though. They seemed to have run out of things to talk about. What they had in common and their interests were wildly different now. Lisa hadn't changed; it was her. The dreams and meeting her relatives affected her profoundly. Her previous circle of friends seemed like a memory of another life. She had some fond memories, but she knew she must move on. She decided in an instant to send Lisa an email, thanking her for being her friend and asking her to forgive her for any offence she may have caused. Rather than signing off as her friend, as that would upset Lisa, she would suggest another night out but leave Lisa to contact her about it. That way, Lisa could choose to progress it — or not.

There was a heightened sense of fear in the camp. The rumours of the advancing Allies were on everyone's lips. The excitement of possibly being freed was tempered by the escalation of violence against them. Mia dared not look the guards in the eye — they were agitated and lashed out randomly. The camp had a rhythm they had all become accustomed to. Routines and adherence to rules gave some measure of normalcy in a place that was as far removed from normal as anyone could imagine.

A sudden change was something to fear. Unusual and frenetic activities were happening. It all meant trouble, and it caused disquiet and unrest.

After a lot of shouting and inmates running around, several bonfires were built. Paperwork from the office block was destroyed, with several boxes brought from the medical wing. A worker who wasn't moving fast enough was shot, and his fellow workers were instructed to feed his body to the fire. When they ran low on fuel, prisoners were told to break up some of their bunk beds and put them on the fires.

'You won't need them much longer,' one guard was heard to say.

Morning roll call was suspended in favour of extended working hours. Roll call was pointless, as they could no longer keep track of prisoner numbers. The killing had become random and unrecorded. The commandant became notably violent, summarily executing prisoners for the slightest misdemeanour or for nothing at all. He strutted up and down the lines of workers, swinging his pistol. He would then press it against someone's head and make them beg for their life. Sometimes he shot them; sometimes, he didn't. There was no logic to any of it, just a sudden outburst, and yet more innocents lost their lives. One woman writhed on the ground after being shot. The commandant stepped over her like she was a piece of trash. Then a subordinate soldier stilled her with the butt of his rifle.

The unpredictability of the violence terrified everyone on parade, but their own lives depended on not reacting. A woman next to Mia fainted, but they closed the gap a little, and she was hidden from view. A few kicks finally roused her, and she stood slowly and re-took her place again. She was lucky — very lucky.

One morning, when the commandant's tirade was in full swing, two inmates were pistol-whipped. As he beat his victims, he looked up with a ruddy, angry face and threatened to destroy them.

"None of you will leave this camp alive. None of you."

Then he told them to return to work, berating his subordinates for being too soft. His anger and criticism left the senior officers in a bad temper with the junior soldiers. They, in turn, vented their frustration on the prisoners. There was never a genuine reason for violence. It seemed to Mia that the soldiers, particularly those in charge, were chosen for their role because they were natural bullies. Hence, they enjoyed brutalising vulnerable and defenceless prisoners. As everyone scurried away, fists flew, rifle butts punched any part of anyone's body they could contact. When the parade ground cleared most mornings, there were always bodies lying on the ground — either dead or close to it. Orders were barked at retreating inmates to collect them and dump them on the piles of dead people ready for burning. The piles had increased so much recently that the furnaces could not keep up with the disposal. There was also a higher frequency of sudden death from "natural" causes. Bunk huts needed to be cleared of the dead every morning. Some died of disease, others of starvation, and some simply gave up the fight for life. They had probably hung on by a thread, and then the step-up in violence and random killing made them lose what little hope they had.

The commandant's threat was becoming a reality, as it became clear that they *were* all destined to die soon. There would be no rescue unless the Allies arrived within the next few days. The mass killings began — systematic and rapid. Some were marched to be gassed, and others lined up and shot. They selected the weakest and oldest first, so the remaining inmates could 'clear-up' the dead bodies. The commandant's sadistic nature was on show again when he ordered a large group of prisoners to assemble in the centre of the parade ground. Most came from the medical wing, but the guards also chose a group of weaker inmates to make up his stated number.

Once assembled, he ordered them to strip. Already shaking with the cold and huddled together, they saw him watch and laugh as they were hosed down. When the night set in and the temperature plummeted, they were herded outside the gates and into a field near to the camp. There they were forced into a large, freshly dug pit. Those too weak to walk were shot, and prisoners were ordered to drag them to the pit. Again, they were hosed down; their pitiful cries could be heard inside the huts. Guards were posted around the top of the pit. The night was punctuated with the crack rifle fire as the guards shot those who tried to climb out of their graves. Long before dawn, they had all frozen to death. Once the guards were confident that there was no more movement, they left their posts and returned to their heated quarters.

Mia sought out Sarid and warned him to hide — anywhere, but just to hide. Hut 66 would no longer be safe. After searching, Mia eventually found Alma in the corner of a hut, rocking back and forth, begging to be released from her dream. Mia held her, and they wept together for themselves and all those dying around them.

"We'll both die here," Alma suddenly shrieked. "Everyone will be killed, and that includes us, Mia. We must get back. Rachel and Ariella died, not us. We must go."

"But Sarid. I can't leave him now, can I?"

"Mia, you're not his mother. Rachel will take care of him."

"He's only little, I can't——"

"Mia, Mia . . . please!"

Alma shook Mia and then hit her. The dream released them.

Mia and Alma were locked together in a desperate embrace in Alma's sitting room. They were both sobbing and found it hard to speak.

"So, now they're gone," Mia heaved.

"Yes, they're dead. But in the past, Mia. You can only die once."

"How did they die? We didn't see. It may have been important."

"Mia, we were witnessing history. But given what happened to you when you were raped, you must know we were not just spectators. We would have died too if we hadn't woken up."

"What happens now, Alma? What's all this about? Why have we gone through this?"

"I just don't know, Mia. Maybe it'll all start again, like some continuous loop movie, until we know why it's happening."

"I can't take any more, Alma. I'm done."

###

When the time came for her evening out with Rach and the other extended family members, Mia had lost all enthusiasm for a night out on the town.

"Try to enjoy it, love," Oscar pleaded. "It's been two weeks now. You should be happy that you aren't going back there."

Mia did not respond.

"There's no point in moping around the house or Alma's. It's over," said Oscar. "You've witnessed everything Rachel wanted you to see."

Esme cleared the lunch plates, but stopped to give Mia a long, warm embrace.

"Have a long soak in our bath, love. I have lavender oil on the side. Run a deep hot one and put a few drops in. You'll feel wonderful after. I always do."

Without comment, Mia left the room. She laid out her clothes in her bedroom and then went through to her parents' ensuite. She preferred to shower, but felt a long, hot soak was what she needed right now.

She laid back in a deep bath, and the beautiful aroma of lavender and hot water soothed her more than she dared hope. Her mother's relaxation candles flickered on the side of the bath. It created a soothing and relaxed atmosphere. Her mum was right.

Suddenly, the candles guttered wildly and went out. A scene from Mia's dreams was right there in front of her, projected on her parents' bathroom wall. Rachel held Sarid by the hand, and Ariella was by their side. They were all naked in a line, and moving slowly towards the pit. She knew what was about to happen. Rachel lifted Sarid into her arms.

Mia screamed and thrashed about in the bath, desperate to get out and away from the vision. She didn't want to witness their death.

"Mia, Mia. It's okay. You're at home. You're safe," said Esme as she rushed into the room.

Mia fell into Esme's arms, dripping wet and hysterical. "She hasn't finished with me. She wants me to witness her death. I can't do that, Mum."

Esme was at a loss. It hadn't finished at all. The dreams still had a hold over Mia and Alma, even though they had already witnessed the mass killings. They were still at the mercy of the dreamworld, which could take them back to the camp at will. Esme knew Rachel as a gentle and loving woman in life. Why was she doing this to her granddaughter? Was it deliberate, or was being a restless spirit an uncontrollable state, driven only by the need to rectify wrongdoings when people were alive? Esme wrapped a warm bath towel around Mia and helped her back to her own room.

"Mum, I'm going to bed. I can't face anyone right now. Would you mind calling Rach?"

"Of course, love. Here, your sedative. Get yourself off to bed."

Mia left all the lights on in her bedroom and lay in bed waiting for the sedative to take effect.

"Hi, Rach. I'm sorry, but Mia can't make it tonight. Difficult to explain, but she's too upset."

"Her dreams again?"

"Yes, unfortunately."

"Look, Auntie Esme, it was a tough call for some of us tonight. If she can make it next Saturday, it would be better, anyway. I'll ring round. Tell her not to worry."

PART THREE

Almost 70 years after the end of the Second World War, a ground breaking forensic archaeological study by the University of Birmingham has unearthed evidence of hidden burial sites at a former death camp where more than 800,000 Jews perished during the Holocaust University of Birmingham Online News, 2012.

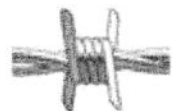

Many rescuers acted out of a sense of altruism. Some heroism was based upon religious beliefs or moral codes; others acted on the spur of the moment, offering to help a stranger in need. Yet others acted out of loyalty to people with whom they had developed close personal ties. If caught by the Nazis, they were sent to prisons, concentration camps, or immediately executed. Rescue put both the immediate family and sometimes even the entire community in peril. Some rescuers survived with their charges until the end of the war, only to be murdered by their neighbours for having had the audacity to help Jews. Elie Wiesel

CHAPTER 25

Her bags were packed. After seeing what was about to happen to Rachel, Ariella, and Sarid, Mia decided to visit the place where they had died. It was something that she had been mulling over, but the bathroom vision made her mind up. When Mia saw them in the line, moving towards their inevitable death, Rachel's eyes locked with hers across the years. It was a fleeting glance, but it said so much. Mia couldn't translate it into words, except that it was a look of desperation. It left Mia with a burning desire to know more, and the only way she could do that now was to go to where the camp was located during the war. Alma was coming with her. Like Mia, Alma had not seen the last moments of her aunt's life, but knew she had died with Rachel and Sarid. There were no survivors from the camp besides the rescued children and prisoners transferred to other camps.

Most of the notorious Nazi extermination camps were accounted for, and their activities were recorded for posterity, but not the camp where Rachel, Sarid and Ariella had been held. Oscar and Mia had searched extensively, but it was as though it had never existed. It was a formidable task, as it was known that 44,000 camps existed of varying sizes and for different purposes. Despite their careful record-keeping at the camp initially, Mia had witnessed the Nazis destroying much of the documentation and physical evidence.

Nonetheless, Mia's concerted efforts to confirm her whereabouts during her dreams gave her a strong, if rough, sense of its location. She and Oscar confirmed it during their research.

Comments made by guards, and inmates also helped narrow down the area. She knew, for example, that the camp was near a factory because it had been requisitioned by the Nazis as a processing centre for new arrivals.

The camp had also housed a gas chamber. It would be another landmark if it still existed. Mia accepted it was improbable.

Mia had witnessed Rachel and Sarid's arrival at the camp, so she observed where the trains stopped to offload the prisoners. Another landmark. She also heard a reference to the last 500-metre walk of freedom from several inmates and how they wished they had tried to escape at that point. It would have been their last chance.

It was all extremely helpful information if nothing much had changed over the intervening years.

None of their research gave Mia much hope. Time had moved on, as had — Mia was sure — the physical landscape where the camp had been located. It would be foolish to think otherwise. It posed the question: what possibility did Mia and Alma have of finding a place that looked as though it had disappeared? All evidence had surely been destroyed and wiped off existing maps. They only had a few clues and an approximate location.

Despite Alma's advancing years, she was delighted that Mia asked her to accompany her. She wanted to go if it was the last thing she did; was how she had put it to Mia. Esme and Oscar thought it was their place and felt offended that Mia was going with Alma. But Mia remained firm. She knew this was right; she and Alma would finish this together. She wasn't sure what "finishing it" would entail. But she was driven by that look from Rachel to pursue this until it was over, and, right now, it wasn't.

The uncertainties aside, the research Mia had undertaken with Oscar she considered invaluable. They had found what they were fairly convinced was the camp's location. It was just outside a village called Hübsches Dorf, which means 'pretty village'. An ironic name for a place where they might soon uncover an ugly truth. The location was the key to everything. Now that they had found a place worth exploring, they could investigate further when they arrived.

Mia booked into a local hotel via the Internet. She picked one that had existed when the concentration camp was in the area. It had changed little, that's if the pictures were any indication. They decided on a twin room, feeling they may need each other's company and support.

When they arrived, they were not disappointed with their choice. The hotel was old-fashioned and cosy, and the staff were friendly. The food was delicious too. After their long journey from Australia, they both slept well. But the effects of jetlag had them waking too early. They filled the time making tea and watching television. The TV was still playing when they fell back into a deep sleep.

Before leaving Perth, they had arranged to meet a local journalist on arrival in the new town of Hübsches Dorf. Someone called Abigail was interested in meeting them after Mia emailed a local newspaper with a few pertinent questions in readiness for their arrival.

They stepped outside after a hearty breakfast and were greeted with a fresh autumn morning and a bustling German town that had grown considerably since the war. The hotel looked ancient amongst its neighbouring shops and houses. They walked arm in arm along the road towards the town centre.

After an hour of sightseeing, with Alma reluctantly enjoying herself, much to Mia's amusement, they made their way to the coffeehouse in the town square to meet Abigail as agreed. They sat in an alcove by the window and noted that Abigail had chosen what tourists would describe as a traditional old-German cafe. It had a dark wood interior and was highly ornate, with beamed ceilings. The staff even wore traditional German clothing, like dirndls and lederhosen.

"I feel uncomfortable in here, Mia."

"Yes, I do too. I wonder why?"

"At a guess, I'd say it's because the murdering bastards probably frequented this place, and their stench is still in the air."

Mia was taken aback by the ferocity and suddenness of Alma's aggressive response. She covered her companion's hand and smiled reassuringly.

"Maybe, Alma, but let's not risk making enemies at this stage. We need information, and calling people murdering bastards won't help. So far, you've done really well today."

Alma nodded miserably.

Mia reflected for a moment. She wouldn't have bothered with Alma in her past life. Wouldn't have even given her the time of day. Mia, the Puma and ace saleswoman, was far too sophisticated for that — or so she had thought. How she had changed! And, she reckoned, for the better. Now she was here in Germany, tracking down a lost concentration camp and being mature enough to comfort Alma. How strange it was to think of her past life. Because that's what it felt like to her. She was a different person, and she liked what she had become. She wondered what Lisa or Vince would make of the new Mia. Would they be impressed or find her even crazier than they thought she was before she left Australia?

Mia saw a young woman walk through the door. She was a perfect fit for the photo Abigail had emailed. Mia raised her hand.

"Oh, give me strength," Alma whispered. "Oh God, give me strength!"

Mia squeezed her hand again and waved and smiled at Abigail.

After two coffees and a large puffy cake, devoured by Abigail, they got down to discussing the reason for their visit.

"To be honest, you're lucky we're here and talking about this," Abigail advised them. "You sent your email to the news desk, and by chance, I saw it and forwarded it to my inbox before our Chief deleted it. His father fought in the war. He was someone senior, I believe. He could have been sensitive about such an enquiry."

"I bet he would," said Alma viciously.

"Sorry, Abigail. Alma is a little uptight about this whole thing. She had a relative who died in the war." Mia hoped this would suffice in taking the look of surprise and enquiry from Abigail's face. It didn't.

"So, let me get this straight, and I understand feelings can run high about this subject. I can remember my grandparents talking," said Abigail.

Mia gave Alma a warning look as she appeared to be on the point of making another controversial remark.

"You're looking for the site of a concentration camp you believe was in this area. You don't know exactly where it is, but in this general area. Have I got that right?"

"Yes, that's right", Mia answered quickly.

Abigail made notes on her electronic notepad. "Well, I don't want to disappoint you so soon after your arrival, but I did some research, and I think maybe you're wrong." She looked from one woman to the other and saw disappointment on their faces.

"Did you ask anyone," said Alma. "Or just look on the Internet? Because Mia has already done that. She found nothing, either. Perhaps ask that Chief of yours. That's if he lived in this area back then with his family. His father was a soldier, you said."

Mia was impressed. For someone who must feel she was consorting with an old enemy, Alma had spoken without malice or aggression.

Abigail nodded slowly. "Ah, okay, so the Internet has been fully investigated. I'm not being funny, ladies, but if you didn't find it on the Internet, how do you know there was ever such a camp?" Abigail spoke English with an accent they couldn't place.

Both Mia and Alma were momentarily stumped. They had no intention of telling anyone here about their dreams and 'visits' to the camp. But how could they progress this further with Abigail if they didn't? Abigail could see they were struggling with her question.

"Look, I'm being a bit 'German' — blunt. I'm Polish by birth, but my grandmother was German, and I think it comes through sometimes."

"Slept with the enemy," Alma whispered.

"Sorry, what?" said Abigail.

Mia glared at Alma. "Forgive Alma, Abigail. She's tired from the journey." Mia hoped she wouldn't have to excuse Alma again. Or they stood a chance of not getting anywhere with their investigations.

Abigail gave Alma a look of mistrust and then continued, but turned slightly to face Mia. "You must have your sources, or you wouldn't be here. I find this all intriguing, so I'd like to help. Very little happens in this town, so a bit of investigative journalism would be great. Being serious for a moment, I need to show my boss something if I do this. He will want stuff for the paper."

They had been in the coffee shop for three hours, and now it was lunchtime. They ordered a light lunch and chatted about the differences between English, Italian, Polish and German cuisine. Neither Mia nor Alma had agreed to the idea of Abigail showing her boss anything. They let the comment slide. Abigail's boss sounded suspect, as he had deleted their email. He also had a direct connection to the war. Mia and Alma knew they needed to stop Abigail from talking to her boss. Both were unsure how to do it. As they enjoyed their lunch, Mia and Alma tried to think of a way of putting it to Abigail tactfully. It was Alma who addressed the prickly issue.

"Abigail, we really appreciate your help with this. But for now, could you avoid mentioning any of this to your boss?"

Her request was met with silence. We've blown it, thought Mia.

"Okay," said Abigail slowly.

Another silence.

"I have to give him something, though, ladies . . . I have an idea. Can I say that you're cartographers studying old maps in Europe? Well, that's what you're doing, isn't it? Your other interest in Hübsche Dorf's war years can remain between us. After all, you're an unusual couple with an interesting project that's perfect for our local rag. We struggle every week to find anything exciting to report. I'll hype it up a little, too."

Alma and Mia thought it was an ingenious way of legitimising their interest in the area. And it would be acceptable for them to ask questions as they looked around. Mia and Alma were relieved to have a cover story. It would also keep Abigail's boss at bay. Mia had packed copies of the old maps for reference, and now they could carry them at all times. It might help trigger memories if they stopped and spoke to local people. It was always good to have a reason to strike up a conversation.

Alma apologised to Abigail for any offence she may have caused. The apology was accepted with grace. Then Mia and Alma returned to their hotel, satisfied with their first day in the town. After eating dinner in the overly ornate dining room, they retired to a big comfy lounge. Like the coffee house interior, it was old German in style, with the addition of big chairs of studded red leather, all neatly arranged around a roaring log fire. Mia emailed her parents to give them the daily update, as she had promised faithfully before leaving.

"How do you feel about this place, Alma? It's very similar in age and style to the coffee house in town."

"Strangely enough, I like it here. Well, so far anyway."

"Me too, Alma. I wonder why?"

Both women relaxed, transfixed by the fire. A man appeared from nowhere, stoked the embers, threw on more logs, and checked if his only two guests in the lounge wanted a nightcap. They ordered a small whisky each and thanked him for his attention. He bid them goodnight and advised them he was now off duty, but the night manager at reception would assist them should they need anything further. They relaxed back into their chairs, each absorbed in her own thoughts.

"It's because it's nowhere near that hellish place." Alma's voice was low and aggressive, and it sent a rush of fear through Mia. Alma frightened Mia sometimes. She noticed her take on a faraway look, as though dragging something from the recesses of her mind, and when she spoke, it didn't seem to come from her. "What, Alma?" Mia responded, worried by the possible shock Alma was about to give her.

"We feel comfortable here because it's not as near to the camp as the coffee house," Alma whispered, sitting forward and looking into Mia's eyes. "That's it. I'm sure it is."

Mia looked around to check no other guests or staff had entered the room. She could hear voices out in reception, and the ancient lift was carrying some late arrivals up to their room, creaking as it ascended. The relevance of Alma's comment sank in. It was a distinct possibility, she thought.

They had talked about their intuition on the long journey from Australia and realised they both had what people called a sixth sense. However, neither of them had verbalised it before. Alma's ability seemed more developed than Mia's. Perhaps it had grown stronger over the years, Mia thought. If she was right, it was a clue regarding the camp's location. Logically, it would be on the other side of the town, and the area beyond the street where the coffee house was situated was more rural.

"That place was called a *Konditorei*." Alma hesitated and then said dramatically. "It means to die!"

"What?"

Yes, a rather appropriate name for that coffee house, don't you think?"

Mia felt shivers run down her spine and desperately wanted to change the subject. She was sure the name meant the cakes were to die for. Even so, it was a horrible coincidence. "Alma, what if the site of the camp has been built on? You know, completely gone and hidden beneath a housing development or something? I've always imagined it how it was in my dreams." Mia looked around again. She was unsure why she was nervous about anyone overhearing. Sixth sense again, she wondered.

"No, it'll be a deserted place or agricultural land. I know it."

"How can you be so sure?"

Alma had a faraway look in her eyes again. "I just know."

CHAPTER 26

Jet lag hit them more forcefully on the second day. Alma in particular. So, they took it easy. A late breakfast was followed by another coffee in the hotel lounge. They also read the American and British newspapers, the only ones available in English, but that was fine — the distraction helped with relaxation. The rest of the day was spent meandering around the local area for Mia while Alma took a nap.

Refreshed and full of purpose the next day, Mia and Alma strode out of the hotel wrapped up against the chill with small day bags on their backs. They were pleased with the decision to buy walking boots on their first day. Now, they felt they looked the part. As they chose lightweight boots, breaking them in wouldn't be necessary. If they were right about the camp's location, there would be some walking and maybe a little cross-country trekking. Mia's old maps and the one purchased locally showed the hotel's distance from the centre of the former village to be at least eight kilometres. Mia felt they were on the right track as the town gave way to open countryside. But Mia was concerned that Alma may be unable to walk the expected distance. Alma insisted she was okay if they took it slowly. However, when they spotted a bus coming their way, Mia flagged it down. They were not at any visible stop, but the driver brought the bus to a halt alongside them and greeted them warmly. Being careful to use the current map, Mia showed him where they wanted to go.

"Ah, ja, ich kenne das alte Dorf, kein problem. Steigen Sie ein. Ich werde Sie bei der alten Fabrik absetzen. Es ist eine gute Stelle. Sie müssen dort warten, wenn Sie mit diesem Bus zurückkommen möchten. Passt das? (Ah, yes, I know the old village, no problem. Come on board. I'll drop you off at the old factory. It's a good landmark. Wait there if you want to come back on this bus. Okay?)"

Alma could speak Italian because, of course, she was an Italian Jew. But both women also understood and could speak German, too. Neither of them had taken any lessons. Alma had learned a lot as a child in Auschwitz, and it was reinforced each time she visited the concentration camp in her dreams more recently. But in Mia's case, the only German language she had heard was in the camp. Despite this, they preferred to speak English. But using German today seemed necessary.

Mia replied confidently, then waited for the driver to look confused. He didn't.

"Yes, yes. All okay," he said in heavily accented English. "Please sit. I'll take you. Come, come. You're English ladies."

"No, said Alma firmly, we're Australian — from Perth.

"Australian sind Sie? Sehr gut. (Australian, are you? Very good.)"

Mia paid. Alma, satisfied she had made it clear they were not English, marched onto the bus and nodded cheerfully to the other occupants. She believed the locals would like them better if they were Australians. Given all the responses she received, Mia thought perhaps she was right. Alma was throwing out the *'Guten tags'* like confetti. No doubt because she was tense, thought Mia, who followed her down the bus. She, too, nodded and smiled back at those who acknowledged her. What would Rachel think of them being friendly to people who may be descendants of the Germans who killed her and Sarid? She put the thoughts to the back of her mind. They would achieve nothing if they didn't behave in a friendly manner.

"Warum musst du in das alte Dorf gehen wollen, da ist nichts," barked an old man sitting across the aisle from them. *"Nur ein paar Häuser verstreut und eine geschlossene Fabrik. Da ist nichts.* (Why do you want to go to the old village? There is nothing there? Only a few scattered houses and a closed factory. Nothing there.)" And he shook his head.

"Es tut mir leid, ich spreche nur wenig Deutsch," said Mia. (I'm sorry, I only speak a little German.)"

The man continued to stare unpleasantly. *"Sie haben keine Antwort.* (You have no answer.)"

"Kein Deutsch," said Alma, staring back and matching his aggressive tone.

Mia grabbed her hand in warning. This wasn't what they wanted.

"He said, why are you going to the old village as there's nothing to see?" said another woman in perfect English.

"We're cartographers," said Mia quickly. "We study original maps and visit areas that have changed significantly."

"It's a long way to come to visit one insignificant little village." The woman screwed her face and scoffed in disbelief.

"Oh," said Mia with phoney confidence, "we're visiting many places in Europe." Her heart was beating wildly. What if the woman asked where else they were going? She was still gripping

Alma's hand, and Alma squeezed back encouragingly while feigning interest in the passing scenery. She pointed something out to Mia, enabling her to turn back around to face the front without seeming rude. They heard a few other exchanges in German — all referring to them.

They arrived at their stop, and Mia saw the 'Fabrik'. It was only just distinguishable through thick undergrowth. But what she could see of the building made it unmistakable — it had the weathercock she had seen from the camp. Her heart was in her mouth as she descended the steps and stood facing what she knew as the prisoner's processing centre. Waving casually to the driver, she then helped Alma down the last step. An elderly woman followed, giving Mia a brief smile before rushing off toward a small bungalow on the other side of the road.

Glancing back at the bus windows, Alma noticed the none too friendly stare of the man who had spoken to them so unpleasantly. The bus drove off, and Mia consulted her map unnecessarily. She needed to still her racing heart and let the bus get out of sight. Alma searched around in her backpack and pulled out a bottle of lavender oil. She tipped a little on her hand and dabbed some on her forehead and wrists. Then she did the same to Mia.

"A little bit of calm," she said.

"That's what Mum does. Thanks, Alma." Mia smiled with genuine affection at Alma.

A special bond was building between them, and Alma and Mia liked it. For Mia, Alma was no longer that batty old bird next door, but rather an intelligent and interesting companion.

For Alma, Mia no longer upset or annoyed her with her superficial behaviour and silly friends. Mia had matured before her eyes, and she was enjoying spending time with her. To Alma, Mia not only looked like Rachel and Ruth, but had now also shown that she had some of their best qualities.

The two women watched as the bus made another stop further down the road, and a group of people alighted. The aggressive man was amongst them. He took the time to look back at Alma and Mia. The other passengers dispersed, but he stayed at the bus stop, staring back down the road.

"Come on, Alma, let's walk down the road a little first, away from the factory."

They crossed the road and took a side path into a wooded area. Mia glanced back to see if the man had gone. He had. They waited a couple of minutes and then doubled back to the factory. Only when they returned did Alma really look at the building in front of them. She went pale. Seeing her reaction, Mia held her arm to give her support and encouragement.

"Come on, Alma. You can do this."

More of the building came into view as they pushed through shrubs and high grass. It was fenced off with barbed wire running around the top. The wintry day and the sheer size of the building reinforced their feelings of dread. They walked around the perimeter, grateful for their sturdy shoes and long trousers. Eventually, they found a gap in the fence big enough to squeeze through.

"Must have been kids," said Mia.

"Over many years, I should think," said Alma.

Mia and Alma held on to each other for strength as they walked toward the building. It would have been a building that held so much fear for thousands of people who came here hoping the lies they had been told may be true. They had undoubtedly hoped they could work as the propaganda led them to believe, and they would be treated fairly. However, it was hard to understand such trust, given what they must have witnessed before arriving at the camp.

Once inside, the silence was all-pervading. Mia and Alma felt unable to move. Then Mia spotted something in a corner piled with dust and rubble.

"Oh, Alma, a shoe. Such a small shoe."

Both women stood and gazed at the tiny baby's shoe. Mia's mind fled back to the dream of sorting the shoes of murdered prisoners.

"And over here, clothes, Mia."

"How can there be anything here after all these years?" said Mia, astonished by their finds.

"If it's been closed up since the war, why wouldn't there be signs of what it was used for?" said Alma.

"Clothes rot."

"Yes, if they're exposed to the elements. Mia, I've got clothes my mother wore in my wardrobe. They'll be at least fifty years old. It's dry in here."

"I suppose it's possible."

The two women found more clothing. Most of it was covered with debris, or plants grew through or around them.

Some had indeed rotted and were in tatters. But other items were well preserved.

"How can this place have remained like this?" said Mia. "After all these years."

Standing in the place of their nightmares was shocking. Both women were lost in their own thoughts — their minds back in the war. They were walking on a floor trodden on by the camp's inmates and very few people since. It was a strange sensation. They moved from room to room, almost reverently, taking photos. Their mood was low and sad.

"Hey, what are you doing in there? Come out now."

The suddenness of an aggressive male voice made the women start. With minds already filled with thoughts of the horrors that would have taken place around them, the voices became a part of their memories. Fear rose in their throats.

"Oh no, a guard," said Mia without thinking.

"Close, Mia. But no. It's the police," said Alma as she peeked through a window. "That man from the bus must have reported us. Quick, take a few more photos while I distract them. Then hide your phone." Alma whispered.

Mia took as many photos as possible, then joined Alma at a smashed window with the phone in her bag on silent.

"Da ist der andere. Raus da, ihr beide. (There's the other one. Get out of there, both of you.)" one officer shouted from the gap in the fence.

"Too fat to get through," said Mia, whispering.

They heard a second officer behind him speaking into his phone as they neared the fence.

"Ja, wir haben sie, Sir: zwei englische Frauen. (Yes, we have them, sir: two English women.)"

Alma and Mia squeezed back through the gap in the fence.

"This is private property," said one officer. "It is serious to trespass in Germany."

"We were trying to find the owner," said Alma, a little out of breath.

"In here? Who would live in a building so old and deserted?"

Mia held onto Alma, and they made their way slowly towards the road. Alma was finding the going tough through the undergrowth.

"What's an old woman doing going into this derelict old place? You will hurt yourself."

"Don't worry about me, young man. I'm tougher than you think." Alma stood up a little straighter and looked the officer defiantly in the eye.

"Do you know who the owner is, sir?" Mia asked.

The two police officers looked at each other, sharing a knowing look. Their brusque manner, uniforms and pistols strapped to their sides made Mia nervous. Police in Perth carried guns, but on the German police, it seemed more threatening.

"He won't give permission. People have asked before. Anyway, who are you, and why do you want to visit this old factory?"

"We're Australian researchers — cartographers — we're updating the maps for this area," said Alma.

Mia was impressed by Alma's quick and convincing response.

"It doesn't match current maps," Alma continued.

"Well, we know nothing about that. All we know is you're trespassing. Now, come, ladies. We will take you to your hotel."

"And, ladies," the other policeman warned, "please do not come back here, or the consequences may be serious next time."

CHAPTER 27

Mia and Alma sat in the hotel's lobby and went over what they knew about the camp. They also looked at Mia's photos of the factory. They tucked themselves away in the corner, well away from anyone to ensure they were not overheard.

"Factory, my foot," said Mia. "That was the camp. I'm sure of it. I know those police officers were only doing their job, but I wonder what those guarded glances they gave each other meant? Who did they call, and what do they know?"

"More than they'd ever tell us," said Alma.

"That's for sure."

"Did you email all the photos back home, Mia?"

"I did it the moment we returned. I was tempted to send them when we were in the police car, as they may have confiscated my phone."

"Look, Mia, I'm concerned. How do you know we can trust Abigail?"

"You know when you get a gut feeling about someone? Well, I get that with Abigail. I think we can trust her. I also think she may be Jewish.

"Well, that's interesting." Alma smiled and then settled back in her chair. "That would be a stroke of luck. But maybe a bit too convenient, Mia."

Mia looked up to see Abigail waving at them from the hotel entrance.

"Hello, nice to see you again."

Mia and Alma rose to greet the young woman, who Mia guessed was in her thirties.

"Hi, Abigail," said Mia and shook her hand.

"Call me Abi."

After a bit of chitchat about the weather and traffic, Mia switched quickly to the purpose of their meeting.

"You found the place?" said Abigail with enthusiasm and surprise.

"Yes, and we attracted some unwelcome attention, too."

Alma explained what they had found and about the police turning up.

"How did they know you were there?"

"I'm pretty sure a vindictive old man from the bus reported us," said Mia.

Abigail nodded knowingly. "Many of the older village residents seem to be sensitive about the topic," said Abigail.

"That doesn't surprise me, considering what happened in their own backyard," said Alma.

Abi advised that she had some information too, but very little. "No one wants to discuss the place at the newspaper. I either get evasive answers or blank looks. Even when I said it was for your work on maps — nothing. I stopped asking pretty quickly. There seemed to be a conspiracy of silence about it. Older staff members met some of my questions with open aggression. I did some digging on my own — mainly after hours."

"That's very kind of you," said Alma.

"Oh, not at all — it's actually something I've been looking into since I got here."

That came as a surprise to Alma and Mia.

Abi suggested they go to their bedroom for privacy, as she had something to show them. Mia was both excited and uneasy. This conflict of emotions had been with her since they arrived in Germany. The nearer they got to finding answers to their questions, the stronger the feelings got. Once inside the room, Abi laid a thin folder on the table.

"Sorry, it's not much. It was hard to find — even this. But the good news is: there definitely *was* a prisoner of war camp on the site you visited."

Shivers ran up Mia's spine, and Alma gasped.

"So, it's true," said Alma.

"According to these papers, it was hardly used. A small camp, from what I've discovered," said Abi. "So, I suspect it's not the site you're looking for."

Alma and Mia's hopes plummeted.

"Really? That's all you found?" said Mia, after scanning the paperwork and passing it to Alma.

"Yes, that's it." Abi saw Mia look at Alma, who was shaking her head. "You're sceptical, I take it?"

Neither Mia nor Alma believed the report.

"It's false," said Alma. "We know it is."

"You know? I actually got this from a reliable source," insisted Abi.

No one spoke as Mia flicked through the paperwork again. Then she threw the folder on the table, sat down, and sighed.

"Would you do us a favour?" Alma asked.

Mia wondered what she was about to say.

"Would you drive us out to the site we found?"

Abi looked from Alma to Mia. She was clearly uncomfortable about the idea, given the reception they had already received. She didn't want a run-in with the law. But she also knew it was a potential scoop if they were correct.

"I'm nervous about going out there, to be honest. There must be a cover-up if you're right about the camp's operations. It would have to involve powerful people. And from the reaction I'm getting at the newspaper, their influence is far-reaching."

The three women were quiet.

"I'll lose my job if I upset anyone important. It's a small town."

"We understand, don't we, Alma?"

Alma walked over to the window. Then suddenly swung around.

"Are you Jewish, Abi?"

Abi looked sheepish.

"That's why you offered to help us, isn't it?" Alma continued.

"No one knows that here, and I'd rather they didn't. There's still an underlying mistrust of Jews in Germany."

Abigail's fear of being known as a Jew reminded Mia of her own parents' concerns about admitting they were Jewish.

"Mia guessed as much," said Alma.

Abigail looked at Mia with concern. "Look, I'll be honest," said Abi, lowering her voice as though someone may overhear.

"I applied for work experience here because I know of a woman who has been having nightmares, horrible nightmares about a Nazi concentration camp. She was convinced it was in this area, but it seems she's wrong. Well, not on the scale she has seen in her dreams, anyway."

Mia looked at Alma and shook her head in warning. She wasn't ready to discuss her nightmares. They didn't really know Abi or if she was genuine. They were taking a lot on trust. But, of course, she was curious about the woman Abi mentioned.

Abi continued. "What made you come all the way from Australia? Not exactly a quick trip." She looked at Alma. But Alma wasn't prepared to say anything if Mia was uncomfortable.

"Abi, can you tell us more about the woman having nightmares?" asked Mia.

"Yes, sure. It's a second cousin of mine. Most of her parents' relatives died during the Holocaust. Her parents were both taken in by neighbours, so they escaped the deportation to the camps."

Alma suspected there were more time-travellers in the camp. "And, Abi, are her nightmares about a camp that should exist just outside this town?"

"Yes, well, I thought so initially. Then I decided she must be mistaken when I couldn't find anything," said Abi.

"How is she coping?" said Mia.

"They're the most terrible nightmares. And they're getting worse. Her family is desperately trying to help her."

Just like me, thought Mia. It feels like the whole thing is building to a climax.

"Did you think coming here would help?" Mia asked.

Abi didn't answer straight away. Alma rested her hand on her arm. "You've nothing to fear from us. Quite the opposite, my dear."

"I was impressed when you found the camp almost immediately," said Abi.

"We did a lot of groundwork before leaving Perth," said Mia.

Abi looked at both women and then told them everything she knew about her cousin's nightmares. She thought perhaps they could help each other. Despite being in the area for a while, she had made no progress.

The telling of Abi's story was painful for all three women. The similarities of her cousin's dreams to Mia's were shocking and drew gasps and tears from Mia and Alma. Halfway through the telling, Mia stopped Abi and shared a little of her own experiences. Then Alma did the same. Time passed in a blur of shared sorrow. The room darkened as the night drew in, but they hardly noticed.

Mia had been free of dreams since arriving in the town. She found this strange, as she was physically closer to where Rachel and Sarid were imprisoned and died. She heard what she thought was the sound of many voices wailing in the factory, but there was a strong wind, and she could have imagined it.

"We can't go back there today. It's a little late now."

"Does that mean you'll take us?" asked Alma.

"Yes, but we should leave early in the morning. Is there somewhere I can pull my car off the road so it won't be seen?"

"There's a small layby before you reach the camp and a few tracks that lead into a nearby wooded area. I'm sure you could park out of sight. But we'll need to walk back to the site after we park. Maybe we could drop Alma off first."

"If you don't mind. I'd appreciate that. I realise now that my trekking days are long gone."

CHAPTER 28

The birds made more noise than the three women as they made their way through thick undergrowth to the Hübsches Dorf Fabrik. They skirted around the main building this time and found another broken section of fencing. Abi and Mia pulled it back, and Alma got through with some help. She shrieked.

"Shh, Alma."

"Sorry, Mia. I saw train tracks and an old freight wagon. Just gave me a shock."

Abi and Mia clambered through the gap in the fence, went over to Alma and stood looking at the wagon that had surprised her.

"Nature has all but covered it, but it's still obvious what it is," said Mia as she climbed inside.

"Careful, Mia. The wood will be rotten," Abi warned.

As Mia cautiously inched her way into the wagon, the memories of one of her earliest dreams hit her with full force. She stared into a dark corner where Rachel would have crouched down and cuddled Sarid in a wagon just like this. Tears sprung to her eyes. "I'm here, Rachel. Tell me what I need to do," she whispered.

"Are you okay?" Alma called through the door.

Minutes later, Mia appeared at the opening and climbed out of the wagon. Abi pointed at a sign near a dilapidated gate with *'Linie hier für Duschen'* burnt into the metal. It was barely legible, as it was severely corroded.

"The showers," breathed Mia.

The women walked towards the gate. It was wedged open with bushes and rocks. Like the rest of the area, the once heavily trodden route to the gas chamber was overgrown. Mia picked up a stick and slashed at the weeds and shrubs. They pushed through until they were in front of another large, derelict building. The entrance door was locked, with a rusty padlock hanging from the bolt. Alma pushed the door. The bolt held firm, but she noted the wood around the lock had rotted in places. Mia picked up a rock and threw it at the lock. She raised it again as Abi appeared from around the side of the building.

"There's a door hanging off around here."

They entered a small room. Mia went to an inner door of metal with a wheel locking mechanism. Open, but it wasn't wide enough for them to get through. Abi and Mia pulled the door together. It grated on the concrete floor, making a loud, screeching noise, but it opened just enough for them to squeeze through. The moment Mia stepped into the room, an onslaught of noise hit her. She fell to the floor, clutching her head. Abi dragged her to the door, and Alma helped pull her through from the other side. Mia crawled into a corner, gasping for breath.

"Mia, what happened?"

Alma saw the terror written on Mia's face. She went into her bag and pulled out her bottle of lavender oil, dripped the oil onto a tissue, and held it under Mia's nose.

"Come on, Mia. You'll be okay. Take a few deep breaths."

Abi crouched down beside Mia. "Did you see something?"

"No, I heard screaming, shouting, and wailing. Men, women, children . . . and little babies. Little babies. . . "

"Oh, God," said Alma.

"Alma, can you feel anything?" asked Mia.

"Just a continuous feeling of dread and fear." Alma flopped down on an old metal chair. "I'm praying all the time, Mia. Maybe it blocks everything."

Abi rubbed a small, dirty window that overlooked the room they had entered. She could see water outlets at intervals on the ceiling and a centrally located trapdoor. There was another entrance with a metal door at the end of the room. It made sense that the other door would be where the prisoners must have entered.

"This was the control room," Abi said. "The Germans administered the gas through a trapdoor and stood and watched from here as the people died in agony."

"Heartless bastards," Alma growled.

Abi climbed a small ladder. "There's a walkway up here."

"It's where they dropped the poisonous pellets on the prisoners through that trapdoor in the middle of the room," said Alma, shaking her head.

Exhausted emotionally and physically, Alma regretted accompanying them on the trip. It was like a visit to hell. When she was Ariella in the camp back in the war, she was younger and better able to cope. But here, now . . .

After taking more photos, the threesome left the building in contemplative silence.

Once outside, Alma became more agitated. "Mia. Can we come back tomorrow? I can't take much more."

"Why not sit on that log in the sunshine? I feel I must just look a little further. We may be prevented from returning."

Alma sat with her water bottle and watched Mia and Abi disappear out of sight as the undergrowth closed in around them. She felt nervous. What if the dream world manifested itself? She hummed to distract herself and wished that Mia and Abi would hurry back.

The two younger women found debris that looked like remnants of the prisoners' sleeping huts. There was very little else to see apart from cattle lazily chewing grass a little way off.

Abi stopped. "Look over there. The ground dips down where it's been cleared for grazing."

A memory surfaced from her dreams as Mia looked at where Abi was pointing. With it came a recognition that she had seen the area before. But in her dreams, she was looking through the camp's gates. As they walked toward the cattle, a flood of emotions threatened to overwhelm Mia, but she held it together. She busied herself searching for remnants of the gates and the outer perimeter fence as they passed the spot where she was sure they must have stood. Nothing. Then Mia mentally paced it out until they arrived at what she was convinced was the edge of the pit where Rachel and many others were murdered. It was extensive enough, she decided, and definitely lower than the surrounding area. The cattle continued to graze, glancing at the two women out of curiosity.

"We're being watched, Mia."

"Yes, but I don't suppose they'll report us. I think they're more interested in the grass."

"No, over by the trees. There's a woman by the woods on the opposite side of this indented area," Abi said, pointing.

The woman hid as Mia looked at her.

Mia scrambled to her feet, ran towards the woman, and saw her enter a small house. Mia returned to Abigail.

"It was a woman from the bus. She seems very interested in this place," said Mia.

"No doubt she's reporting back to someone," said Abi.

"Sorry, Abi. I don't want to get you into trouble."

"No, it's okay. I'd looked so hard for this camp and came up with nothing, so I gave up. Thanks to you two, I've something solid to work with."

"We should take a few more photos and then leave. We've enough, I think."

"I'm going to visit the old woman, Abi. Not today, though, but I want to know why she's watching us. It might prove useful."

"I think we'd better collect Alma and go," said Mia. "Before the police turn up again."

That night Alma talked in her sleep. Then screamed.

"Alma, wake up. You'll wake the whole hotel."

Alma awoke choking and coughing. Her mouth hung open as though she couldn't get any air, yet her chest heaved up and down.

"Here, Alma. Drink some water."

"Can't breathe. My lungs are burning. Help me," she gasped, heaving lungfuls of air.

Mia panicked. Perhaps she should call a doctor. Alma had over-exerted herself at the camp. She reached for the phone, but Alma grabbed her hand.

"No, don't." She wheezed and fell back onto her pillows. "I'll be fi … fine. Give me a minute."

"But, Alma, you may need a doctor."

"Dream," was all she said as she struggled for breath.

Mia made them a hot drink and then sat by Alma's bed. "The camp?"

Alma nodded.

"I'm sorry to put you through that, Alma."

Alma recovered sufficiently to sit up to sip her drink.

"A little brandy or whisky would help," said Alma, smiling.

"I think I'll join you."

"I chose to visit the camp, Mia. You don't need to apologise."

Mia took two miniatures from the fridge. They sat and sipped their drinks for a while in silence.

"Would it help to tell me about your dream?"

Alma didn't hesitate. "I was in the gas chamber. They threw pellets through the trapdoor above us. We were all crying out. It was agonising. The babies and children succumbed first. Small mercy. I can still see their little faces twisted in agony and clawing at their parents as they took their final tortuous breaths."

Mia held Alma while she wept.

"That must have been awful, Alma. Just awful."

"That's the worst nightmare I've had about that camp."

"But you lived!"

"As the pellets fell, I screamed. It released me before I breathed in much of the poison. I had a small piece of sacking over my mouth and nose. It must have been just enough."

"Oh, Alma!"

"I can't go back there, Mia."

"No, and you don't need to."

"But we've come all this way."

"Abi is happy to come with me again. Well, not happy, but she said she'd come."

"Thank God for Abi."

"Your aunt didn't die in the gas chamber, Alma. So, someone else was channelling through you."

"Of course Mia. You're right.".

Mia went to the fridge and held up another two small bottles. "There's another whisky and brandy?"

"No, Mia. They cost too much from the mini-bar."

"I think we deserve it."

"Look, I'll go to the library and see what I can find when you and Abi return to the camp."

"Right, excellent." Mia hesitated. "Yes, just one last visit."

Mia told Alma about what they thought might be a mass grave at the camp. She also mentioned the woman they saw in the trees.

"I expect she reported you. We may have the police calling here in the morning."

"Hopefully not, because I think we're finally getting somewhere, going by the vision I had at the camp and now your dream."

"It's hardly evidence that can be used in court, Mia."

"No, it isn't. And that's why we need to go back. We need to find something conclusive that proves it was a big camp and killing centre."

"And it was used for medical experiments, too. Don't forget that, Mia."

Mia thought about her dreams that featured the medical wing. Scenes that were seared on her memory.

"From what we could see, most of the infrastructure has been destroyed. And time and nature have buried much of what was left."

"I'm surprised it hasn't been developed," said Alma. "Or that those two remaining buildings are still standing."

"Some of it has, but they needed to hide a mass grave. Any further development would have been unwise," said Mia. "Maybe the buildings are subject to a preservation order."

"That's possible," said Alma. "And that's what I'll research at the library. Development and building projects over the years."

Mia was now very animated. "It stands to reason the mass burial site will be within the area that hasn't been developed."

Verbalising the reality of the situation cast a sombre atmosphere in the room. Neither relished the idea of actually finding a mass grave. With Alma refusing to go back to the camp, Mia knew the discovery would now be hers and Abi's.

Mia checked that Alma had recovered from her nightmare and then slipped back into her own bed. As she found it difficult to sleep, she pulled out her iPad and wrote a long email to her mum and dad, updating them on developments. Then she played online solitaire for a while. Alma was asleep and snoring gently. Finally, Mia's eyes grew heavy, and she too drifted off into a deep sleep, her iPad slipping from her hands.

After putting a call into Abi, Mia and Alma had breakfast in their room while planning their day ahead. They left early, not wanting to risk the possibility of the police turning up to question them about their return visit to the camp the previous day. Evidence needed to be gathered. It might be their last chance. They'd deal with any outfall later. Mia and Abi dropped Alma off in the town centre — she didn't want to face the police by herself.

Alma decided to visit a small café that appealed to her after seeing it on a previous walk. It was just off the village square opposite the library. She thought she would treat herself to one of the delicious cakes she had seen in a window display. The waitress sat her in a window seat that gave the best view of the square.

She gazed out, lost in her own thoughts, when she saw them. They were marching across the town square, boots hammering the cobblestones in unison. Alma sat terrified as they were coming straight towards the café. Soldiers. She looked behind her. No one else was reacting to their impending arrival. There was no escape. They had seen her. She must at least try to hide. She pushed her chair back so hard it crashed to the floor, and then she made for the back door. The café's front door opened, and a rush of air, loud voices, and laughter spilt into the café. Too late. Someone grabbed her arm.

"Bist du in Ordnung?"

Alma swung around to face her attacker. Be strong, she instructed herself, and she stood tall and looked right at him. Kind eyes looked back at her.

"Kann ich Ihnen helfen, zu Ihrem Platz zurückzukehren? Oder möchten Sie die Toilette benützen? (Can I help you get back to your seat? Or do you need the toilets?)"

"Oh, yes . . . *ja, die Toiletten bitte.*"

As she made her way to the toilets, Alma glanced at the people who had just entered. A sizeable group of boisterous walkers were now removing their boots at the entrance.

The other patrons were looking at her, some with sympathy, others fearful of the crazy old woman. She rushed into the toilets and into a cubicle, sat down, and tried to regulate her breathing. Feeling foolish, she was loath to return to the café. "Calm yourself, Alma," she chastised herself. The pull of the dreams was strengthening. She'd be ready when it happened again and wouldn't panic, or would try not to. The visions were realistic and incredibly frightening. Her thoughts went to Mia and what she had endured with her nightmares. Alma hoped she was coping at the camp. Mia had impressed her repeatedly on the trip with her strength and determination. But they had clearly disturbed the dead with their last visit to the camp. Alma suspected their spirits would not rest in peace now, not until the truth was uncovered. She feared for Mia and Abigail.

CHAPTER 29

Abi and Mia made straight for the area they had seen before. It was a large piece of land that looked different from its surroundings. They could see it was a rough circle from their elevated position.

Mia walked towards it with growing trepidation. The voices had returned with hysterical screams, weeping and shouting, which became louder the nearer she got. She swung around, expecting to see something or someone. Nothing.

"Are you okay, Mia?"

"They're calling out from beyond the grave. So many voices."

Abi was not familiar with Mia's experiences of the dead talking to her, so she found her behaviour extremely worrying. She felt an urgent need to leave.

"Rachel is near, Abi. I can feel her. This is where she died with Sarid. They shot them."

Mia fell to her knees and cried out. "What is it, Rachel? What are you trying to tell me?"

Abigail looked about her, dread rising in her throat, fear stiffening her spine. "I think we'd better go now, Mia."

Mia stayed on her knees. "Please, Rachel, I'm here. I know you died here with Sarid. Tell me what I need to know." Mia wept.

"The woman is back again. See there in the trees?" said Abigail, trying to distract Mia.

Mia looked up, tears blurring her vision, but she could see the old woman watching her. "I wonder why she's watching us?"

"I dread to think. Probably one of the old-guard who lives around here," said Abi.

Mia got to her feet. "Do you think it'll get back to your boss?"

"Possibly."

"But, your job."

"I was ready to go home, anyway. It's Dullsville here. At least, I'll go out on a high. If my boss causes problems, I'll send the story to another paper that I know will cover it."

"Well, what's the story, do you think?"

"Mia, it's obvious. Rachel, Alma's aunt, and all the others coming through in your dreams want you to tell the world they died here," said Abi. "No one knows about this place. So, no one knows they died here. The locals have covered up its existence. And they have done a good job until now."

"Oh God, you're right. It was right there in front of us all this time . . . so much so that we missed it. Why didn't I realise that? But we've got so little evidence."

"We should take a few more photos and then leave," said Abi. "Maybe try to grab that sign for the showers. It's hanging off, anyway."

They snapped more photos and took the sign.

Abigail was relieved to be leaving.

When Mia got back to the hotel, she found Alma asleep. She woke her gently and relayed some of what Abigail had said.

Alma didn't answer at first. "A Nazi killing centre that doesn't exist as far as history and records show. And we found it. It's quite something, Mia."

"Yes, but I certainly don't feel like celebrating. We've discovered something terrible, not a treasure. But it will be a relief for many people who couldn't trace their relatives."

"And a damning indictment for those who have concealed its whereabouts," said Alma. "It's horrendous enough that these people died the way they did. But not being able to trace or mourn them at their burial site is desperately sad for those they left behind," said Alma.

"Despite everything we know, I still feel the picture is incomplete somehow, Alma. Don't you?"

"Well, we know where they died and how they died."

"But we didn't see them die, Alma. They were shot, but we didn't see it."

"I don't want to see the moment of death. What we saw was close enough for me. There was no escape from that, Mia."

"I think we needed to witness it, Alma."

"Well, what we saw is enough for me," Alma repeated.

Alma got off the bed and poured them both a drink.

"Alma, it's like reading a book to the end and finding the last page missing."

"I suppose. But this is a very realistic and violent book."

"I feel I need to see it through to the end," said Mia. "Anyway, what did you discover at the library?"

"Nothing we didn't know already, but it confirmed a few things."

Mia told Alma about the old woman and suggested visiting her together. "She may be harmless enough. She certainly looks it. But I suppose you'd say that about any war criminal when they are old and frail."

They agreed to visit the old woman the next day. The worst that could happen was that she would ask them to leave. It would be a small price to pay if there was any chance she could give them more information about the camp. They weren't in any doubt that it was the concentration camp they had been looking for. But the more information and evidence they had, the better.

Sarid, Rachel, and Ariella crouched down behind a hut. Rebekah joined them moments later with her son, Dieter. The camp was in chaos. The approach of the Allied troops was on the lips of everyone — prisoners and Germans alike. Hundreds of inmates were marched out of the camp. They left on foot with an armed guard and hadn't returned. The remaining prisoners were rounded up in batches. They were being marched towards an enormous pit dug by prisoners outside the perimeter of the camp. The little group of women and children could hear volleys of gunfire, screaming, and shouting.

"Oh, my beautiful boy, how can I save you from this?"

Sarid responded by hugging his mother.

"Rachel, quick, let's hide in the rubbish tip behind the kitchens," Rebekah shouted. "It stinks. They won't look there."

As they ran, Shoshana came towards them, pointing. "Schau, da sind sie. Sogar ein Kind. (Look, there they are. Even a child.)"

"*Du rsheim* (You wicked woman)", Alma cried out in Yiddish as the soldiers surrounded them. "*Narish froy. Keyner blaybt nisht.* (Stupid Woman. No one survives)." The soldiers grabbed Shoshana and pushed her towards the group.

"*Kein schmutziger Jüdisch* (No filthy Jewish)" one soldier shouted at Alma.

"But I told you where they were," Shoshana cried out as she stumbled towards Alma and Mia. "Surely that counts for something."

A soldier smashed Shoshana in the face with the butt of his rifle, and she collapsed, her arms and legs thrown out to the side.

"Just shoot her now, and we can throw her into the pit later. She's a troublemaker." The soldier did just that and shot Shoshana just as she was coming round.

Sarid clung to his mother, terrified.

"Mia, wake up. For God's sake, wake up," Alma hissed.

"No, I won't desert my son."

The soldiers pushed them out of the camp gates towards the pit. Alma continually tugged at Mia's arm, trying to wake her without attracting the guards' attention. They lined up with others, and, when instructed, they stripped and joined the line that snaked around to the pit's edge. Rachel shielded Sarid's view from the killing as each row of prisoners, some clutching children, were shot and pushed or fell forward into the pit.

"Mia, please. We don't have to die."

"Just stay close to mummy," said Mia. Then she lifted Sarid into her arms as they reach the front of the line, raining kisses on his head and holding him very close.

"Mia, you're not Rachel. You didn't die. Rachel died with her son. Now wake up, shouted Alma. Esme and Oscar are waiting for you." At that, Alma hit Mia as hard as she could.

At the same time, a soldier grabbed Mia and pushed her to her knees. She pulled Sarid close and wrapped her arms around his head.

The soldier leant down and tried to disentangle them. Mia punched out at him and grabbed Sarid again, just as another soldier took aim and fired.

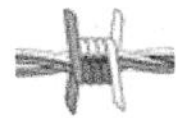

"Ow, that hurt, Mia."

Mia was lying on the floor of the hotel bedroom sobbing.

"They were shot and thrown in the pit. I saw them. Oh God, Alma. That was horrific."

"Yes, beyond words. My Aunt Ariella was there, right by Rachel's side. They died together with that poor little innocent, Sarid and so many others."

Mia remained on the floor, and Alma fell back on the bed, exhausted.

"We nearly died too, Mia. You just wouldn't come back, whatever I did. We were so very close to being a part of that horror.

A knock on the hotel bedroom door shook them back to reality. "*Ist da drin alles in Ordnung?* (Is everything in there in order?)"

"Ja, es tut meir leid, es war nur ein sehr schlimmer Albtraum," Alma replied. "(Yes, I'm sorry, just a terrible nightmare.)"

"Kann ich Ihnen etwas bringen? (Can I get you something?)"

"Ja, ja bitte. Zwei Whisky und Limonaden. (Yes, yes, please. Two whiskies and sodas.)"

The man moved away from the door.

"Bloody, fucking Germans. I don't want their whisky or anything else from them. Killers, fucking killers," said Mia. She got up from the floor and sat on her bed with her head bowed, sobbing.

"Look, Mia. We need to stay civil while we're here. *You* keep reminding *me* of that."

Mia went into the bathroom. Alma heard the shower running. When Mia returned to the bedroom, the drinks had been delivered. Alma was relieved Mia was in the shower when they arrived; she was sure Mia would have abused the porter.

"Now we know exactly how and where they died," said Mia.

"They want the world to know," said Alma.

"It makes sense. Abi was right," said Mia.

They talked as they sipped their drinks, working out how they would make it happen with Abigail's help.

"A memorial on the site. That must happen too. But Mia, I don't think the bodies should be disturbed," said Alma.

"I'm not able to think about the details, Alma. But what I need right now is to sleep without dreaming. I'm shattered."

"Okay, let's plan it all tomorrow."

CHAPTER 30

Alma and Mia walked toward the old woman's house with a measure of caution. They saw the curtains flutter on their approach. They were being observed. Before they could knock, the door opened.

"Kommen Sie bitte herein," she said, smiling as she held her arm out, welcoming them to step inside.

Alma and Mia stepped inside, surprised at the warm welcome. Mia asked her whether she knew the purpose of their visit.

"Wissen Sie, warum wir hier sind? (Do you know why we are here?)"

"Ja, ich glaube, ich weiß es. Ich sah dich dort drüben weinen. (Yes, I think I know. I saw you crying over there.)"

"She saw you cry in the camp, Mia?"

"Yes. But I was outside the actual camp itself, by that awful pit. I got a little overwrought when I realised that we were standing so close to where they died.

"Sprechen Sie Englisch?" Alma asked.

"Nein, aber mein Sohn. Er kommt, gleich. (No, but my son does. He's coming.)" She showed them into a sitting room.

"So, her son is on his way. This should be interesting. He's probably going to see us off," Alma whispered.

The woman left the room smiling. She returned minutes later with a box from which she pulled out a pile of photos. She spread them in front of Mia and Alma on a table. They were pictures of young children and babies. As she moved them around, she watched Alma and Mia's faces. She saw a reaction from Mia and moved two or three photos nearer to her. Mia touched one photo in awe.

"Sarid. It's Sarid."

The woman smiled and then found more photos of Sarid.

Alma looked at the photo, astonished. "Yes, it is." How can this woman have photos of Sarid?

"Woher kennst du Sarid? (How do you know Sarid?)"

"Das ist mein Sari. Und sie sind meine Hilda und Frederick," she replied, pointing to the pictures of the other children — all old and browning. ("This is my Sari. And they are my Hilda and Frederick.")

They didn't know what to say. It was too much to take in.

"Your Sari?" Mia queried after a moment.

"Ja, mein Sari."

Before they could ask any further questions, a boy ran into the room and went directly to the old woman.

"Oh, it's Sarid. It's Sarid," Mia cried out.

"Oh, yes, it is!" said Alma.

"No, I'm Sarid," a tall man with grey hair said as he walked into the room.

Mia felt faint. "You died. I saw you die."

Sarid kissed the old woman. *"Hallo Mutter. Geht es Ihnen gut?* (Hello Mother. Are you well?)"

She pinched his face and beamed. *"Umso besser, dich zu sehen, mein Sohn.* (Better for seeing you, my son.)"

The little boy climbed on her lap and stared at Mia and Alma. They stared back: they couldn't get over how much he looked like Rachel's little boy, Sarid.

"But I don't understand," said Mia.

"Mutter saved me, along with others. She was part of a local group. They called themselves *Kinderrettungstrupp* — Child Rescue Group. Very brave people."

Mia and Alma still couldn't take it in.

They were right there when Rachel, Ariella and Sarid got shot. They missed the bullets themselves by mere seconds.

"Mutter, tut mir leid, dass ich für unsere Gäste Englisch sprechen muss. (Mother, I'm sorry I have to speak English for our guests.)"

"We can speak German, but I still think in English, so I'd appreciate it if we could continue in English," said Mia, smiling at the old lady.

"Es ist in Ordnung. Bitte hilf ihnen es zu verstehen. Die Frau war so verzweifelt im Lager. (It's fine. Please help them understand. The woman was so desperate in the camp.)"

"My mutter says you were very distressed in the camp. It's the only reason she trusts you. That and the fact that you're English."

"Yes, I understood what she said," Mia confirmed.

"Australian," Alma corrected him.

Mia gave Alma a reproachful glance. It wasn't the time to be petty.

Sarid, the old woman, and the little boy sat and waited for Mia and Alma to speak.

"I can't take this in, Sarid," said Mia. "It's like you've returned from the dead. My family has mourned your death since the war. Well, it's your family, too."

"Really? I have a family in Australia?" He looked astonished.

"You certainly have."

Once Mia gathered her wits, she explained why they were at the camp. She also advised Sarid how she was related to him and his mother, Rachel.

"Mutter said you looked like my mother when she called me. That's why she got out the photos to see if you recognised me. And you *do* look *just* like her." Sarid's voice became thick with emotion. The shock of Mia and Alma's visit and the revelations they brought with them threatened to overwhelm him, preventing him from continuing further.

Instead, he got to his feet and drew Mia into a firm embrace.

"Dieter, geh und spiele draußen, bitte," said Mutter. ("Dieter, go and play outside, please.")

The little boy left, and the old lady followed him out of the room.

"So, you remember your mother?"

"Yes, and I've always carried a photo of her. Even when they forced us to strip, I held onto it."

Alma shook her head slowly from side to side and dabbed her eyes. The imagery was too much.

No one spoke for a while.

"So, your mother is my Aunt Naomi?" Sarid asked.

"No. She's my grandmother. My mother died. My grandparents raised me, so I always thought they were my parents until recently."

"Oh, I'm sorry."

"I had a wonderful childhood. But it made me so sad when I learned how and why my mother died. But please, we're not here to talk about that."

"I want to know everything about you and your family," said Sarid. "I also find it hard to take in."

"It's so incredible to find you alive, Sarid. The family in Australia will echo that sentiment when they find out," said Mia. "But it puzzles me is that you were only small when you were in the camp, yet you remember my grandmother," said Mia.

"Yes, Naomi and I were close in age, more like cousins, or even brother and sister."

"My grandmother said as much to me," said Mia.

"Do you remember me, Sarid?" Alma asked.

"Alma, of course, and your Aunt Ariella. We played together as children — you, me and Naomi — at your aunt's house."

Alma swiped the tears from her eyes and stepped forward to embrace Sarid. "How wonderful it is to see you, Sarid. I thought perhaps you didn't recognise me." Alma then sat by his side, and they held hands. Two small children reunited after so long. It was a touching sight.

Mia wiped tears from her cheeks and felt so much gratitude that she had witnessed this reunion.

"My grandmother will be eager to see you, too," said Mia. "I can't wait to see the three of you together again."

"And I, her, Mia," Sarid replied.

"Can we Skype tonight? Does Mutter have the Internet? I'm not sure that it would be wise to make the call from the hotel."

"We all like to keep in touch with Mutter, so I got her connected. Do you think Naomi will recognise me?

"I'm positive she will recognise you instantly," said Mia. "Of course you look much older, but I can still see it's you. And I wasn't around when you were children."

"Even though you mistook my grandson for me." Sarid laughed good-naturedly.

"He's your double," said Alma. "Seeing him took me right back to when I played in your garden as a child."

Sarid and Alma exchanged fond memories, lost in the past, as they continued to hold hands.

"I apologise if I seem reticent" said Sarid. "After so many years of keeping secrets and trying to live a normal life, it's hard to open up about what happened back then."

"Given how much we witnessed in that camp, we can understand that, can't we, Alma?"

"Oh, yes. I still find it hard, Sarid."

Sarid looked confused. "Forgive me if I sound rude, but how could you witness what went on in that camp?"

"Through dreams, Sarid. Rachel, Ariella and others have been coming to us in our dreams to give us messages," said Mia. "And now we know what they've been trying to tell us."

"Dreams?" said Sarid.

"Well, they were so awful that really . . . they're better described as nightmares," said Alma. "Especially Mia's. We actually become Rachel and Ariella. It sounds extraordinary, but that's the way it happens."

"Happens? It still happens?"

"Yes, Sarid, it does," said Mia.

Unfortunately, I also have my own experience of a Nazi concentration camp, as I was in Auschwitz," said Alma. "So, being taken back into another concentration camp as my aunt is particularly hard for me."

"Oh, Alma," said Sarid. "That is terrible indeed. We must put time aside to talk about our experiences. It may help us both."

"Thank you," said Alma. "I would like that, Sarid."

Mutter returned and asked if they would like a hot drink. After they all agreed to have coffee, Mutter returned to the kitchen, leaving them to continue their conversation. "Is this distressing Mutter?" Mia asked.

"Mutter witnessed some awful things at that camp, so any discussion about it does distress her somewhat."

"Why didn't she move away?" asked Alma.

"She was only a young woman during the war and had only recently moved to this bungalow," said Sarid. "Her husband died early in the war before they had children of their own. I think it left her longing for a child, which may have driven her to help other children. She is also a great believer in justice and fair play. The terrible injustice being metered out so close to her house was too much for her. So, she joined the *Kinderrettungstrupp*. Her parents and siblings were against it, as they felt the risks were too great. A few times, she and others nearly got caught, but it didn't deter them. Even now, she won't move away from here because she feels her job is not done."

"An amazing woman," said Mia.

"Sadly, some children she rescued died soon after and were buried in her garden," said Sarid. "She kept a record of them all and still waits for their families to claim them, even if it's only to visit their graves."

"Many owe her so much," said Alma.

"She wasn't alone, Alma. Being part of the group, she had plenty of support. Such brave people," said Sarid.

Sarid told them more details about the work Mutter and others did. Mia and Alma were full of admiration.

"They were all in constant danger," Sarid added.

"Such self-sacrifice is the ultimate expression of love, Sarid," said Alma. "Mutter poured all her love into her rescue work and the children she saved. You are all truly her children, and your loyalty to her is a credit to you, and so well-deserved."

"Thank you, Alma. I agree with you about Mutter and others like her who risked their own lives to save us. After the war, I learnt about many such groups. They couldn't accept what was going on, so they did what they could to help. Some paid with their lives. Mutter was lucky."

"It gives you hope for humanity," said Alma.

"I am a little confused, though, Sarid," said Mia. "In my last dream, I saw you and your mother walk to your deaths."

Sarid took a deep breath and shook his head. He had never spoken about that moment. Mutter tried to talk about it, as she believed it would help him heal. But he could never bring himself to say aloud what he held in his heart and mind for so many years. He felt he could do it now. It was time.

"We were both shot and fell into the pit."

Mia and Alma gasped.

"But my mother held me so close and covered my head, which was the soldiers' preferred target. So, the shot went into my shoulder."

"How did you escape?"

"My time in the camp taught me how and when to stay quiet and still. So, I stayed under my mother's body without moving until I heard the soldiers go back into the camp."

No one spoke as this horror was absorbed.

"I could see sideways. Anyone who moved was shot again from above. But I just closed my eyes and tried to think of something beautiful, the way my mother and I would when we were frightened."

Mia and Alma's tears flowed unabated. Sarid continued.

"I crawled from beneath my mother when I couldn't hear any more noise. It wasn't easy, as she weighed heavily on me. When I was finally free, I kissed her and said goodbye." He heaved, and his voice became high-pitched. "What a terrible way for a little boy to say farewell to his mother."

"Don't go on, Sarid. This is too much for you," said Alma, weeping.

"I'll be okay in a minute."

They sat without speaking for a while.

"I then crawled to the edge of the pit. Another boy, Dieter, was doing the same. We instinctively went in a direction that took us as far from the camp perimeter fence as possible and towards the woods where we knew we could hide. Dieter and I were in Hut 66 together. He was a friend. We often talked about escaping and living in the woods. So, I suppose that was on both our minds."

Sarid paused to wipe his eyes.

"We didn't speak as we tried to crawl over hundreds of bodies. Many of the people we knew. Some were very cold; others were still a little warm." Sarid stopped and put his head in his hands. His body shook as he wept.

Mia and Alma moved to either side of him and put their arms around him. They wept together.

"Men, women, and even children." His body shook with emotion.

Eventually, Sarid's crying eased. He wiped his face and nose. "The older I get, the more sensitive I am. Take no notice."

Mia tightened her grip on his shoulders. "You and Dieter were so brave, Sarid. Faced with such a horrific situation, you both had the presence of mind to escape, even as little boys."

"Dieter was badly wounded, but he kept up with me. When we got to the pit's edge, we started to climb out. There were plenty of roots and buried branches to grab onto. We were halfway up the side when a voice above us urged us to go faster."

"Who was it?"

"Mutter, of course."

"Oh, so I understand a little better now," said Alma.

"She climbed down when Dieter couldn't continue. She pushed him up in front of her until they were nearly at the top, and then I helped pull him out."

Mia thought of the frail little woman in the kitchen. Such athleticism was hard to believe of her.

"Mutter had brought a wheelbarrow because she never knew who she would need to rescue. Sometimes it would be adults. She lifted Dieter into the wheelbarrow, and we ran to the nearby trees. We only just got to the woods when we heard the Germans returning."

Mia pictured the woods where she had seen the old woman twice. Still keeping her vigil, it would seem.

"Mutter knew they'd return to spread more quicklime on the recently murdered prisoners. Do you know we could hear them talking and laughing as though they were just doing an ordinary job?"

"And you came back here?" said Alma gently.

"Yes. Mutter nursed us and fed us nourishing food."

"And Dieter? Is he alive and well?" asked Mia.

"Sadly, the severity of his gunshot wound and extensive burning from the quicklime he was unlucky to land in meant he only lasted a few days. He's one of several buried in this garden: the ones already sick or too severely wounded when they were shot or from the fall into the pit."

"Oh, how sad," said Mia.

"How many did Mutter rescue?" Alma asked.

"I don't know the exact number, but there are a few of us. The group was involved in smuggling babies and children out of the camp during its entire operation. Dieter and I were the last ones she rescued. Some went to other homes, but Mutter kept a record of them all. The babies, of course, cannot be identified other than through DNA testing. But Mutter, along with other brave individuals, gave them their lives."

The old lady returned with coffee and cakes, assisted by Sarid's grandson, Dieter.

"He's named after my eldest son, who I named Dieter in honour of my friend. My son and his son carried it on," said Sarid. "A small tribute to a brave little boy lost to the cruelty of ethnic cleansing. So many innocent lives were taken during that war, many of them near where we sit."

Mia and Alma shook their heads while mopping their eyes.

"I would like you to meet my family. I have three children, six grandchildren and one great grandson — little Dieter who you have met already. Sadly, my wife passed away several years ago. She would have been thrilled about your visit."

"Hast du ihnen alles erzählt? (Have you told them everything?)"

"Nein, Mutter, aber das meiste. Mehr will ich vor Dieter nicht sagen. (No, mother, most of it, but that's all I want to say in front of Dieter.)"

Mia and Alma helped themselves to coffee, and Dieter offered them cakes. Mia gave the little boy a hug as he passed her.

"Such a sweet boy," said Alma.

The old lady pushed a footstool towards Alma and insisted that she used it. *"Wir sind nicht mehr jung. Wir brauchen unseren Komfort.* (We are no longer young. We need our comfort.)"

Alma admitted she was tired, but Mia saw the look of surprise at the special attention. She knew Alma liked to hold her own, despite her advancing years.

After they chatted a little more, Mia and Alma left, promising to return later for the Skype call. Sarid dropped them back at their hotel, and embraced them both before he departed.

"He's a fine young man, considering all he has been through," said Alma.

"Maybe it's partly *because* of what he has been through, Alma. And he's hardly a young man."

"Well, he's younger than me."

That made Mia laugh. "Most people I know are younger than you, Alma. But you're incredible for your age."

Alma smiled at that. But she was so exhausted she felt ancient right at that moment.

Mutter had insisted they come back for their evening meal before the call to Australia. She was so excited Sarid had found his family that she couldn't stop hugging and kissing Mia and Alma before they left.

Mia found it hard not to call and tell her parents about Sarid ahead of the Skype call. She didn't want Esme to be too shocked when she saw Sarid. Alma suggested Mia email beforehand explaining how Sarid survived but leaving out the grisly details. Mia did so, and also attached a photo she had taken on her phone of Mutter, Sarid, and Dieter, explaining the relationship. The news and the photo would be shocking enough. She visualised them both: Esme crying and Oscar only just holding it together. She hoped they would be more composed by the time they made the call. Alma and Mia rested in readiness for what would be a momentous event for all concerned.

CHAPTER 31

More of Sarid's family had shown up when they arrived back at the cottage. As introductions were made, emotions ran high. Hugs and kisses were passed around as tears flowed with the joy of reunion and sadness of the circumstances. They all planned to be present at the big reveal on Skype. As the time drew closer, the excitement grew. Sarid, Alma, and Mia went for a walk together to pass some time.

"I tried to trace my family when I got older," said Sarid. "I knew we were Italian, and I could remember a certain amount about my hometown. But I found no one. It was like they all vanished."

"Of course, many changed their identity and fled Europe, including my grandparents. I thought their names were Esme and Oscar. I only found out recently that their real names are Naomi and Edan."

"Are they ashamed of being Jewish?"

"No, but they wanted to give my mother and then me a new start without the risk of prejudice. There's still anti-Semitism, but very little in Australia. Well, not that I know of. But they were not to know that. They'd suffered so much prejudice in Europe — I'm sure that affected them."

"Did you ever suspect?" said Sarid.

"I hate to admit it, Sarid, but I was too self-centred and busy with my own life. I simply accepted my life for what it was."

"It's not unusual. I think most kids do that," said Sarid. "Your life is normal to you. Why would you think anything else?"

"I'm quite ashamed of the way I was. Selfish, judgemental and self-absorbed doesn't cover it."

Alma put her arm around Mia's shoulders. "You've come a long way as a person, Mia. It's been a tough road for you. I doubt anyone would choose it. But don't regret things. Life's too short."

"Thanks, Alma. That means a lot."

On returning from their walk, they found Mutter had made more tea and a fresh batch of biscuits. They sat and chatted for a while.

"Do you stay nearby for Mutter?" Alma asked.

"Yes, I'd never leave here while Mutter lives. I owe her my life, and she has been wonderful to all of us survivors. She kept us hidden for over a year after the war was over until she was sure we would be safe. Then she took us to school as though we were her own children. There were a few raised eyebrows, but nothing else. It was post-war, and no one wanted to make a fuss. It helped that she shortened my name to Sari. Ironically, it's an Arab boy's name." Sarid smiled. "But you know, it's hard to have any prejudice against anyone after the Holocaust."

"And are you practising Jews, Sarid?"

"Not very. Most of my family observes some customs. We aren't ashamed of our ancestry, but we're not orthodox. Mutter encouraged us to learn about our faith, but not openly, as she thought it was safer that way immediately after the war. Now we're in the habit of keeping things low key regarding religious observance."

"You must come to Australia and see your extended family. You'd all be welcome."

"Very Jewish," Sarid laughed.

Mia couldn't stop marvelling at finding Sarid alive after her horrendous nightmares. It all felt so surreal.

"Mia, we must let Abigail know about all of this," said Alma. "She'll need it for her report."

"Report?" Sarid queried.

"Yes, we contacted a reporter here, and she's taking the story to the media."

"That won't be appreciated in many quarters around here. The secrecy surrounding the camp has prevailed for a long time. If it weren't for Mutter, I'd have done something about it. But she made me promise not to. She believes evil people have always controlled information about the camp and its activities. It has been a constant fear of hers that we would be attacked if we said anything. I tried to reason with her a few times, as did some of the other kids she rescued, but she was adamant."

"So, the secret was kept by intimidation and fear," said Mia. "The Nazis continued to punish the prisoners and their families even after the war was over."

"It sounds awful when you put it like that, Mia," said Sarid.

"Sorry, I wasn't criticising you, Mutter, or anyone. I was just reflecting on how evil can be all-pervasive."

"There was a time — a long time ago — when we thought it would be exposed," said Sarid. "There was a big hunt in this area for Nazis that may be hiding. Sadly, it came to nothing. They are too clever and well-practised at hiding."

"You must have been tempted to speak out," said Mia.

"Yes, we all were. But we respected the wishes of our adopted families. They were all fearful for us if we were outed as Jews."

Sarid stood. "Come, let's go into the garden. It's a beautiful place of calm. Mutter is a keen gardener."

They walked and talked and admired the garden. Alma noticed Mutter had a thick screen of bushes and shrubs facing what would have been a view of the concentration camp. Below the shady canopy of a tree were several large pots of flowers with name plaques hanging on the side of each. Sarid touched every pot briefly and offered up a silent prayer as he walked from one to the other. Mia and Alma sat on a nearby bench to allow him some privacy.

"Gone, but not forgotten," whispered Alma.

Sarid joined them on the bench.

"How can you bear to be so near that awful place, Sarid?" asked Alma.

"As you probably noticed, the view has been obscured by Mutter's plants. What the eye doesn't see . . ." His words trailed off. Then he seemed to spring back to life. "But of course, I am aware of it. Over the years, I'd sit at the edge of the woods and gaze at where my mother died. First, I cried a lot and then I'd sit there and try to feel close to her. I never did, strangely enough. I only stay here for Mutter.

"Does she always observe the goings on at the camp?"

"Only if she hears people in there. She feels compelled to check for relatives coming to find loved ones. After all these years, you're the only ones to come here."

"Given that no one knows about the camp," said Alma, "it's not surprising."

"There'll be many making the journey here when they do. Will Mutter mind?" said Mia.

"No," Sarid laughed. "She will probably set up a viewing gallery of all her 'babies' so people can find their lost children. Then feed them all cake."

Despite the reality behind the remark, they laughed, enjoying the warmth and humour in his image.

But then Sarid grew serious again. "Also, she stays to bear witness to what happened here," he said. "She'll want your journalist to interview her so she can tell her what she witnessed during the camp's operation. She and others did more than rescue babies and children. The group also passed food and medicine to the prisoners. Many good people tried to mitigate the evil that was perpetrated here."

"She'll be an extremely valuable witness. However, we wouldn't want to endanger her."

"I'll film the interview," said Sarid. "Then take Mutter away for a holiday, if she'll let me, until the initial fuss dies down. But she'll want to come back. It's her life's work to watch and wait."

"Did she ever feel it was too dangerous?" Mia asked.

"It was always dangerous, and the consequences would have been dire if any of the group had been caught," said Sarid. "But they looked out for one another."

"So, there are more people around here who could be witnesses?" asked Alma.

"Not so many now," said Sarid. "Many have passed away or have moved out of the area. Mutter knows them all, so she could contact those that are still alive."

A thought struck Alma. "Mutter can unveil the monument along with all the other heroes. Because that's what they are, Sarid — real-life heroes."

"What monument?" queried Mia.

"The one we'll have erected right in the middle of the camp. We must make sure it's a fitting tribute to commemorate the lives of the people who died there."

"Excellent idea, Alma," said Mia.

The distinctive sound of the Skype calling tone interrupted conversations. Mia swung her laptop around, so it faced into the room.

"Hello, hello."

They could hear Esme's voice from the blank screen.

"Mum, turn the video on. We can't see you."

"Esme, let me do it. I told you that was just the voice," said Oscar.

Esme and Oscar suddenly appeared on the screen. Other family members from Perth had gathered behind them, peering quizzically at the screen. Mia made sure Sarid was front and centre of the group. Mia saw the shock on Esme's face.

"Iz dos take ir, shrid?"

"Mum, speak English. I suspect Sarid cannot understand Yiddish — neither can anyone else here."

Esme reached forward and touched the screen. "Is that really you, Sarid?"

Sarid cried out in anguish. "Yes, it's me, Naomi. My dearest, how I've longed to see my family. I've looked for you all for so long. It's so wonderful to have Mia and Alma here."

Sarid's family gathered around him, placing gentle hands on his shoulders. He wept. They wept. Alma and Mia wept. Those who had gathered in Australia to make this momentous call wept. Some beat their chests and thanked God.

"*O, danken got. Loybn got. (Oh, thank God. Praise God.)*"

Mutter stepped forward, and with her arm around Sarid, she spoke to the screen. "*Mein Herz geht zu dir. Sari war ein wunderbarer Sohn für mich, aber ich betete, dass er seine Familie finden würde.*"

Mia could see Sarid was far too emotional to translate. She stepped in.

"Mutter said her heart goes out to you. That Sarid has been a wonderful son to her, but she always prayed he'd find his real family."

Esme shook her head and wiped her eyes. "It's a dream come true, Mutter."

"*Sie sagte, dass es ein Traum ist, der wahr wird, Mutter,*" said Mia, translating.

Mutter touched her hand over her heart and smiled at Esme. Sarid scooped his bewildered grandson onto his lap.

Esme gasped at the likeness of little Dieter to Sarid. "Oh, my goodness!"

Sarid hugged his grandson. *"Das ist deine Urgroßtante Naomi und dein Urgroßonkel . . .* (That's your great, great aunt Naomi and great, great uncle …)"

"I'm Oscar."

"Großer, großer Onkel, Oscar (Great, great Uncle, Oscar)," Sarid finished, smiling.

Each member of the extended family was introduced from each side. Esme thanked Mutter many times over for saving Sarid. Plans were made to visit Australia. Esme and Oscar promised to visit when things settled down after the media got hold of the story. The call was ended with a chorus of well wishes and promises to speak again soon.

"Mutter insists you both stay tonight. She has made up your beds."

"Is Mutter okay with all this, Sarid? You and others are her children. Doesn't she fear losing you?"

"She won't lose us. All my family — children and grandchildren — adore her. She is a treasured member of all our families and all those families who owe their existence to her bravery. While she lives, we will always be here for her. My whole family is settled here now. There is no reason for that to change."

"You'll stay around here when she is gone?"

"No, probably not. I'll move away, though not too far from my extended family. Being so close to the camp when it is a tourist attraction or a mass mourning site holds no appeal for me."

###

By the time they retired, Mia was relieved to climb into bed. Her mind was churning everything over, but she was also exhausted. She knew she must plan their next move regarding the camp. She wondered what Rachel would want as a memorial. As she drifted off to sleep, the far end of her room flickered. She peered into what was now a misty scene and saw the vague outline of two women holding hands walking towards her. Mia sat up, staring hard.

"Rachel? Mum?"

"Thank you, Mia. I saw my boy, my beautiful boy, through your eyes. What a wonderful thing that woman did saving my son," said Rachel.

"I'm pleased you know he survived, Rachel," said Mia, tears springing to her eyes.

"And he has a lovely family, too. I can rest now. You found the camp and my son. Mia. But I'm so sorry for all the upset this has caused you and your family. Please forgive me. I was reaching out to you, but I couldn't control how that expressed itself to you."

The tears now spilled down Mia's cheeks. She smiled. "Of course I forgive you, Rachel. Of course I do."

Now the hazy image of her mother moved towards her.

"Mum?" said Mia.

Ruth's presence came so close that Mia felt her mother all around her. The smell of lavender filled the air; it was the smell of home and comfort to Mia.

"You've been amazing, my darling daughter," said Ruth. "I couldn't be prouder of you. I love you, Mia, and I always will. Never forget that."

A sob of longing and loss caught in Mia's throat. Tears flowed. She felt overwhelmed with joy and sorrow all at once.

Both women swirled around Mia as she wept. Featherlight touches on her face and shoulders filled her with the essence of her visitors until she felt at one with them.

"No more tears, my girl. Be happy now. Tell my parents it wasn't their fault. I was too weak to cope. I'm with Rachel now. Find us in the beauty of your life until we meet again."

The two women were fading.

"Mum, Mum, I love you."

Rachel and Ruth's hands reached for Mia's outstretched hand, their touch cool. Then they disappeared, leaving an echo, and the smell of lavender, in the air where they had been. Mia was bereft. She knew she wouldn't see them again. Lying in darkness, crying at her loss, she heard a gentle knocking at the door and Alma whispering.

"Come in, Alma."

Alma sat on the bed, and Mia relayed her dream between sobs. Hugging Mia tight, Alma said nothing. There was nothing to say. The dreams were finished for Mia, and now the reality of what they had done needed to play out. She wondered momentarily if her Aunt Ariella would visit again in her dreams to say farewell, but she sensed that it was over for her, too.

Coming down for breakfast in the morning, they found Sarid sitting at the breakfast table, relaying to Mutter a dream he had the night before.

"Guten Morgen (Good morning)," said Mutter. *"Ich vertraue darauf, dass du gut geschlafen hast?* ("I trust you slept well"?)

"Danke, sehr gut," Mia and Alma said in unison.

"I was just telling Mutter about my dream," said Sarid. "My mother came to me last night. It was really extraordinary. She told me how she longed to see me and that now she had found a way through. I even felt as though she embraced me." Tears rolled down Sarid's face, and Mutter put her arm around his shoulders.

Alma looked at Mia.

"Sometimes the dead find a conduit and can reach us," said Mia.

Sarid looked up at Mia. "And you're that conduit?"

"Yes, I have been for some time. Alma, too. But when your mother visited me last night, it was to say farewell. I won't see her again," said Mia.

"Well, it was wonderful to see her after all this time," said Sarid. "She looked as she did before she died. Thank you, Mia."

Sarid stood and embraced Mia. "I owe you so much," he whispered in her ear.

"Komm, komm, lass uns frühstücken (Come, come, let's eat breakfast)," said Mutter.

Mia's sadness lifted at Sarid's words. She understood that she had had a role to play, and finding Sarid and bringing him back into the fold of his family was as important as finding the camp.

Now she needed to make sure that the exposure of the camp's whereabouts and its insidious role during the war was brought to the world's attention.

Mia and Alma planned to mail various media outlets with copies of their evidence, then leave Hübsches Dorf. Abigail was doing the same with the various newspapers. Sarid was taking Mutter away until things settled down. He would ensure she provided more testimonies via email, and Mia and Alma would forward the same to the media. If, or when, Mutter identified herself would be a decision left to her. But hers and others' testimonies would be essential.

WORLD MEDIA PRESS RELEASE
The Pretty Village that Hides an Ugly Secret

There is now irrefutable evidence that Hübsches Dorf, a small rural village in Germany, was the site of a Nazi Concentration Camp and a killing centre during WWII. Its existence has been covered up since the end of the war.

Hübsches Dorf, which translates to Pretty Village, has kept its ugly secret hidden with the help of many local people, including the current owner of the land on which the camp was located.

Newly emerged evidence proves the camp was the site of mass killings, medical experimentation and torture. There were very few survivors, as the Nazis hurriedly conducted mass exterminations when the Allied forces were bearing down on the area. But, miraculously, some of those prisoners survived, and their extraordinary stories will be covered in the coming weeks.

The camp photos can only show the way it looks now. They were taken by a relative of a survivor. Until recently, she believed he had died in the camp as a young child alongside his mother. Her joy in finding him alive will be covered in a later interview.

The women who traced the camp and secretly took the photos have now left the village for their own safety. From the moment they arrived, their presence was met with a great deal of hostility. The gas chamber, bunk beds and changing room are still recognisable, as is some of the signage. The site is overgrown and difficult to navigate on foot. Still, these intrepid investigators had a personal interest in finding it and in documenting what they uncovered.

Excavators have now been brought to the site to reveal what is thought to be a mass grave just outside the camp's perimeter. There are mixed feelings about the excavation. Many believe that all those buried at the site should be left to rest in peace. However, the veracity of the claims about the camp needs to be proven. Excavating the burial site and examining remains is the only way this can be achieved.

A key witness to the camp's operations has provided extensive information based on personal experience. As a local resident during the war, she has many stories to tell the world. The identity of this crucial witness will be kept secret to protect her from reprisals.

It is surprising that the camp has remained undiscovered for so long. But it transpires that many locals conspired to keep it that way.

Reporters will be present when the human remains in a mass grave are exhumed.

Many will ask why bother after so long? The perpetrators are probably dead or extremely old. Maybe we should show them mercy. But the response of survivors and relatives was unequivocal. They did not believe time lessened the crimes committed, and if any of the guilty parties were still alive, they should be brought to justice.

If this report has resonated with you, or you can contribute to the information currently held on this camp, we would like to hear from you.
REPORT ENDS

###

Esme could hardly contain herself. She and Oscar were at the airport early. They bought a coffee, and then Esme stood directly opposite the doors in the arrivals' hall, watching each time the sliding doors opened. A continuous stream of new arrivals spilt out into the waiting arms of their families or scurried off to cars or taxis.

"It won't make him appear any sooner, Esme."

"Oscar, I know that, but I want to ensure we're right here when he does. I feel we know him and his family already after so many Skype and WhatsApp calls."

Oscar risked embracing his wife, even though he knew it would momentarily obscure her view of the new arrivals. She surprised him by hugging him back, thus prolonging the obstructed view.

Mia arrived with Alma and several members of the extended family. Esme had organised a welcome party. Mia mentioned they may be too tired on arrival for a party, especially the children, but Esme was adamant. Mia made sure the beds were made so that anyone who needed to rest could do so. Alma also offered to host some guests at her house. It would be a wonderful time for reunion and celebration.

"Oh, there they are. There they are," Esme cried out.

"Where?" Oscar asked.

"I saw a glimpse of them through the doors."

Esme's exclamation brought everyone together. A welcome banner was held aloft by excited children eager to meet long-lost relatives.

Finally, the group emerged. Esme didn't wait. She rushed forward and hugged Sarid before the doors had closed behind him. Both of them wept.

Drawn by kinship and longing, the family rotated around, touching, embracing and repeatedly kissing until each had greeted everyone else. It was as though they needed affirmation that it was all true and they were really there. They shared a history of heartache, loss and separation, and now they had found each other. They were lost in a display of love and affection. Spectators of this outpouring of emotion could only witness it. But they smiled and enjoyed the happiness of a reunion. If only they knew, Mia thought.

A flash of a camera caught Mia's attention. As she looked toward the source, a young man stepped forward in front of the camera, holding a recording device.

"Can you tell me what this reunion means to your family?"

Mia realised the intrusion was because of her recent interviews with the media and her photo appearing in the West Australian newspaper. She wondered how they knew about Sarid and his family's arrival.

"This family reunion results from many months of planning. We're delighted to welcome Sarid and his family to Perth. There'll be many more celebratory events in the coming weeks."

"What made you believe he was still alive?"

"As I mentioned in my previous interviews, we didn't know he was alive until we found him in the village of Hübsches Dorf. It was an amazing moment."

"Can we have a few photos of the family group?"

Mia brought the family together. A crowd gathered, realising this was not just an ordinary homecoming. Just as the photos were complete, TV cameras arrived to film this now high-profile event. Mia said a few words to the camera on their way out to the car park.

For the entire time, Esme did not let go of Sarid. It was as though she thought he would disappear again if she did.

EPILOGUE

The land on which the camp stood in Hübsches Dorf was seized by authorities, and a full investigation was undertaken. Over the following five years, the site was cleared of vegetation and reconstructed with the help of survivors and other witnesses. The pit, containing hundreds of bodies, was designated as a grave after the preliminary inspection of a few remains. It was then backfilled and landscaped with a beautiful array of flowers and shrubs. A plinth featuring a sculpture of a mother holding a young child and a man raising his hand in a wave was erected on what would have been the camp's parade ground. The inscription read: 'Here lies hidden an undisclosed number of unknown men, women and children murdered by the Nazis during World War II. We honour them with this sculpture — a permanent reminder of the cruelty of war and racial bigotry.' Flowers were regularly laid at its base together with teddy bears and other toys. These additions were a touching tribute to murdered babies and children who had lain hidden for many years. Little ones that were deprived of such ordinary pleasures in their brief lives.

Mutter provided photographs of the children she had saved for the museum on the site, hoping their relatives would be found, as did others involved in the rescue operations. Photos were also donated by courageous photographers. Many images showed the deplorable conditions endured by the prisoners, and some were shocking photos of the brutality enacted against them.

Many travelled back to the village on hearing the news about the camp's discovery. Along with others who worked with her during the camp's existence, Mutter was recognised and applauded for saving many children and several adults. She stood proudly alongside other rescuers and over one hundred rescued prisoners, all now in their later years. They expressed their gratitude with gifts and speeches of love and affection. Mia wondered if the smile would ever leave Mutter's face.

Six camp guards were tracked down. Two still lived close to the site. They and others were arrested and tried. One of the accused owned the land on which the camp had stood, and the reaction of his descendants was notably unpleasant. His eldest son shouted 'death to all Jews' outside the court and repeatedly gave the Nazi salute. He was arrested and tried as a public nuisance and engaging in hate speech.

At the official opening of the camp to visitors, Mia, Alma and Abigail, together with Sarid and several members of the families from Perth and Hübsches Dorf, were among the guests of honour. Hundreds who had been affected by the Holocaust joined them from all over the world.

It was an opportunity for the media to revisit the atrocities carried out during World War II and to remind the world of the dangers of racial prejudice and intolerance to those you perceive as different from you. They pointed to other such atrocities as examples. While these comparisons were made, they also clarified that never before or since had a country built a state-sponsored, meticulously organised killing machine expressly to systematically and mercilessly murder one particular group of people defined by their religion (Jews) together with other 'undesirables' as defined by the Nazi dogma.

The German government made a commitment to maintain the camp. It would be a permanent memorial to all those who suffered and died at the hands of the Nazis.

Sarid continued to live close to Mutter until she died some years later. Mia and her family travelled to Germany to see Sarid and his family every year. Sarid and his family did the same, coming to Perth. One of Sarid's grandsons moved to Perth with his wife, much to the delight of Esme and Oscar, who treated them as their own children.

Alma still lives next door to Oscar and Esme. She is not planning any more overseas adventures. When there is a Barone family event, she is always invited and spends time with Sarid when he visits. Sometimes their conversations take a dark turn as memories of the time they were both held by the Nazis come to the fore. But most of the time they just enjoy each other's company along with Esme and Oscar. They reminisce about their blissful childhood in Italy before the war and constantly delight in their reunion.

Mia did not return to her job at TopTravel. After attending university in Perth, she pursued a career in investigative journalism. She now lives with her partner in the vibrant beachside Perth suburb of Scarborough, where her home overlooks the ocean.

Mia and Alma do not dream anymore.

AFTERWORD

Some of my readers may question if or when Northern Italian Jews were sent to German concentration camps. Were they sent directly to Germany or transferred from the many Italian camps set up in 1940 before Italy joined the war?

My source (named in the acknowledgements), who lived in Northern Italy throughout the war, assures me that both scenarios were true. It is hard to doubt a first-hand testament, albeit anecdotal. The following link may also give some clarity.

https://primolevicenter.org/printed-matter/the-fascist-concentration-camps/

Some others may query whether my characters, who are Italian Jews, would speak Yiddish.. As they came from the far north of Italy, where there were communities of Ashkenazi Jews speaking Italian and Yiddish, the answer is in the affirmative. My source also mentioned that her Jewish friends and neighbours spoke Yiddish in her company. The following links give further details:

https://bit.ly/3zOfpLR
https://bit.ly/3PUcfvM
https://bit.ly/3SpGRa7

There are many other questions around the Holocaust. The first of the two following quotations attempts to explain why the prisoners in most of the camps chose resignation over resistance, and the second tells how the work of secret rescuers depended on wearing a mask, for their own sakes as well as for the sake of those they saved.

I shook with helplessness and rage, but also with fear. This was what fighting back earned you. More abuse. More death. Half a dozen Jews would be murdered today because one man refused to die without a fight. To fight back was to die quickly and to take others with you.

This was why prisoners went meekly to their deaths. I had been so resolved to fight back, but I knew then that I wouldn't. To suffer quietly hurt only you. To suffer loudly, violently, angrily — to fight back — was to bring hurt and pain and death to others.

Alan Gratz, *Prisoner B-3087*

If we were stopped and questioned, I always smiled at the officers, and they always smiled back. In my heart, I was seeing them dead. But on my face, I was an open invitation. If you are only a girl, this is how you destroy your enemies.

Irene Gut Opdyke, *In My Hands: Memories of a Holocaust Rescuer*

Probably the biggest question concerns the role of the Holocaust in history and its significance for the future. Genocide has been committed with frightening regularity in different parts of the world at different times over millennia. It shows humanity at its worst and most degraded. But in the modern world, with its illusion of human progressiveness and evolution, the Holocaust remains one of the starkest reminders of the depths to which we can still sink. The third quotation here brings home to us the role of everyday people in that massive crime and its dire consequences for the future of humanity.

It's all too easy to imagine that the Third Reich was a bizarre aberration, a kind of mass insanity instigated by a small group of deranged ideologues who conspired to seize political power and bend a nation to their will. Alternatively, it's tempting to imagine that the Germans were (or are) a uniquely cruel and bloodthirsty people. But these diagnoses are dangerously wrong. What's most disturbing about the Nazi phenomenon is not that the Nazis were madmen or monsters. It's that they were ordinary human beings. David Livingstone Smith, *Less Than Human*

I close with a final quotation of universal appeal. It is from William Faulkner's address, given at his daughter's graduation.

Never be afraid to raise your voice for honesty and truth and compassion, against injustice and lying and greed. If you, not just you in this room tonight, but in all the thousands of other rooms like this one about the world today and tomorrow and next week, will do this, not as a class or classes, but as individuals, men and women, you will change the earth; in one generation all the Napoleons and Hitlers and Caesars and Mussolinis and Stalins and all the other tyrants who want power and aggrandizement, and the simple politicians and time-servers who themselves are merely baffled or ignorant or afraid, who have used, or are using, or hope to use, man's fear and greed for man's enslavement, will have vanished from the face of it. William Faulkner

ACKNOWLEDGEMENTS

My thanks go to:

Giovanna Janes (nee Zaganelli) & Francesco Zaganelli

Giovanna advised the author that she witnessed Jewish families being forcibly removed from her hometown in Northern Italy and taken to Italian and German concentration camps.

As her family disapproved of this and the many antisemitic sanctions implemented by Mussolini as early as 1938, they often took action to support Jewish friends and neighbours. For instance, Giovanna and her mother were involved in hiding Jewish families before raids by Mussolini's Brownshirts and, later, the Gestapo. The scene in which Rachel and her family are seized is based on a raid Giovanna witnessed. Giovanna also joined the resistance and ran messages on her bike. She, like the witness above, smiled her way through German checkpoints while her heart was filled with fear and vengeance.

Giovanna's brother, Francesco, a young Italian student of seventeen years, was taken by the Gestapo when Italy joined the Allies in 1943. Francesco was held in a forced labour camp in Germany, which, in his case, was attached to a concentration camp. His treatment was appalling, but what he witnessed in the adjacent concentration camp was far worse. When his camp was liberated, he walked home to Italy, as the infrastructure in Germany was all but destroyed. It took weeks. He attributed his survival to his age, then just nineteen, and the food, shelter and occasional transport he received along the way. On his journey, he also witnessed the results of what he expressed later as 'indescribable atrocities' carried out by the retreating German troops.

While the author acknowledges that the situations and conversations in the concentration camp are fictitious in her novel, Giovanna and Francesco's recollections provide the basis for much of the content.

Michèle Drouart

My editor, Michèle Drouart, has been invaluable in helping me knock this book into shape. Her editing skills cannot be doubted, and her ability to take a bird's-eye view of structure, content and pace is remarkable. She took what she described as a very good story and assisted in giving it the polish of a novel.

I believe she has aptly identified this work that moves between dream and reality as an unusual hybrid of historical and speculative fiction.

https://au.linkedin.com/in/michele-drouart-b764982a

Frances Payne

Frances designed the excellent cover for this book. Her daughter, the beautiful young actress Millicent Payne, is the face of Mia. I could not have asked for anything more appropriate and professionally executed. The design is dramatic, demands attention, and perfectly embodies the main character's dual life.

https://www.francespayne.com/cv.html
https://www.spotlight.com/2790-1208-8866

Go Ballistic Paintball ®

Go Ballistic® kindly agreed to the use of their name in this novel. They are a genuine paintball operator, but apart from that, most aspects of their portrayal in this novel are fictitious.

QUOTATION SOURCES

Introductory Pages
John Irving, in an interview with Joseph P. Kahn, Boston Globe, 6 September 2011.

Part One – p. 4
Loyd Auerbach, *Psychic Dreaming,* Llewellyn Publications, 2017.
Richard Paul Evans, *The Christmas Box*, Simon & Schuster, 1st edition, 1995.

Part Two – p. 117
Amy Harmon, *Sand and Ash,* Lake Union Publishing, 2016.
Hannah Lewis, Holocaust survivor, Metro News, 2020.

Part Three – p. 229
University of Birmingham Online News, 2012:
https://www.birmingham.ac.uk/news/2012/archaeologis
t-reveals-evidence-of-mass-graves-at-nazi-death-camp
Elie Wiesel, quoted in **Carol Rittner and Sondra Myers,** *The Courage to Care*, NYU Press, first published as an EBOOK in 1986, in paperback in 1989.

Afterword – p. 308
Alan Gratz, *Prisoner B-3087*, Scholastic Inc., 2013.

Irene Gut Opdyke (with Jennifer Armstrong), *In My Hands: Memories of a Holocaust Rescuer*, Random House, 1999.

David Livingstone Smith, *Less than Human: Why We Demean, Enslave, and Exterminate Others*, St. Martin's Griffin, 2012.

William Faulkner, speaking at his daughter's graduation at University High School in Oxford, Mississippi,1951. Documentary film, *William Faulkner*, 1952. https://bit.ly/3vtmSgP

Alice Haro
AliceHaroAuthor@outlook.com

Printed in Great Britain
by Amazon

15320703R00183